Praise for *It Ends At M*

'A blisteringly brilliant read. Harriet Tyce is at the very top of the thriller game.' Sarah Pinborough

'*It Ends At Midnight* has it all – mystery, murder, courtroom drama, revenge and sex, in an explosive mix. I devoured this gripping novel in a couple of sittings, and raced to the shocking end.' Alex Michaelides

'*It Ends At Midnight* takes us into the deepest, most toxic recesses of human behaviour. With the author's signature blend of courtroom suspense and relationships in mortal crisis, this is another delicious treat from Tyce.' Louise Candlish

'Intriguing characters, deceptive twists and a punch-to-the-gut finale. Harriet Tyce always delivers.' John Marrs

'Another compelling read from the utterly brilliant Harriet Tyce.' Lisa Jewell

'Smartly structured and plotted and even darker than *Blood Orange*.' Sarah Vaughan

'Excellent. High on tension and twists.' *My Weekly*

'Full of twists and turns. An unpredictable, unforgettable read.' *Woman's Weekly*

'A cinematic gut-punch of a book that will linger in your memory long after you've finished it.' Mark Edwards

'Harriet Tyce cements her position as Queen of unreliable narrators in *It Ends At Midnight*. A must-read high-stakes thriller.' Fiona Cummins

'Harriet Tyce is so good at writing flawed characters pushed to their absolute limits. This is another top-notch thriller from her: as compelling as it is compulsive.' Kate Riordan

'Harriet has a true skill for peeling back her characters' layers and exposing every dark, twisted thought. Gripping and truly unpredictable.' Jack Jordan

'What a dark, delicious read – with an ending that made me literally gasp.' Charlotte Duckworth

'Fantastic, intricately plotted, skilfully woven and beautifully tricky.' Helen Fields

'Murky, twisty, and twisted – a roiling cauldron of courtroom dramas and toxic friendships, damaged relationships and vengeful spectres of bloody, long-buried secrets.' Ellery Lloyd

'A true page-turner!' Amanda Reynolds

'Intense, clever, important and deeply chilling, *It Ends At Midnight* proves that Harriet Tyce is a writer at the top of her game.' Phoebe Morgan

'Pure drip-fed tension leading to a gob-smackingly good reveal – I devoured this and yet didn't want it to end.' Susi Holliday

'Expertly plotted and executed, it's a deliciously dark and twisty thriller about toxic friendships, secrets and betrayal. It kept me guessing until the last page.' Sarah J. Harris

'I could not put it down! *It Ends At Midnight* is a roller coaster of a ride. I loved it!' Rachael Blok

'It's a spectacular display that you won't want to miss. *It Ends At Midnight* will have you reading into the small hours.' Trevor Wood

'*It Ends At Midnight* is a searing and suspenseful psychological thriller full of tension, toxic friendship and uncomfortable truths.' *Culturefly*

'*It Ends At Midnight* sees Harriet Tyce on top form once more. A masterpiece of plotting.' *Living Magazine*

Praise for *The Lies You Told*:

'A slow-burning mystery, full of intrigue and menace, it creeps up on you until that final explosive twist.' Alex Michaelides

'A breathless read – with a shocker of an ending!' Shari Lapena, bestselling author of *The Couple Next Door*

'I read *The Lies You Told* in two days, barely able to turn the pages fast enough. It's spare and taut, the sense of wrongness building in chilling, skilfully written layers, with a jaw dropping last line twist.' Lisa Jewell, author of *The Family Upstairs*

'Every bit as intriguing, well-written and addictive as its predecessor.' Sara Collins, author of *The Confessions of Frannie Langton*

'Totally addictive – I was gripped.' Sophie Hannah, author of *Haven't They Grown*

'With lots of twists and turns, this thriller is impossible to put down.' *Independent*

'An insightful look at the realities of motherhood and work, and competitive parenting, *The Lies You Told* is gratifyingly sinister.' *Observer*

Praise for *Blood Orange*:

'Harriet Tyce brings a new layer of visceral, addictive dark to domestic noir. At once shocking and riveting, I simply couldn't stop reading. Bravo.' Sarah Pinborough, author of *Behind Her Eyes*

'A classy thriller with complex and compelling characters.' Clare Mackintosh, author of *I See You*

'Fans of *Apple Tree Yard* and *The Girl on the Train* will love the atmosphere of clenched ambiguity Tyce sustains so well.' *Guardian*

'*Blood Orange* is dark and immensely readable. An impressive debut.' *The Times*

By Harriet Tyce and available from Wildfire

BLOOD ORANGE
THE LIES YOU TOLD
IT ENDS AT MIDNIGHT

HARRIET TYCE
A LESSON IN CRUELTY

WILDFIRE

First published in 2024 by
WILDFIRE
an imprint of HEADLINE PUBLISHING GROUP

1

Cataloguing in Publication Data is available from the British Library

Hardback ISBN 978 1 4722 8012 1
Trade paperback ISBN 978 1 4722 8013 8

Typeset in 11/13.75pt Sabon LT Pro by Jouve (UK), Milton Keynes

Printed and bound in Great Britain by Clays Ltd, Elcograf S.p.A.

HEADLINE PUBLISHING GROUP
An Hachette UK Company
Carmelite House
50 Victoria Embankment
London EC4Y 0DZ

www.headline.co.uk
www.hachette.co.uk

To Agnes Frimston

OUTSIDE

This is what I would do to you.

I'd drug you. Don't worry, you wouldn't feel a thing. I'd say go to sleep, go to sleep now, and I'd take a knife – your knife – and I'd cut and cut, all the way up your veins. That's how they do it. I read about it at school.

Then I'd watch you bleed out like the PIG you are.

Sorry, sorry, you're not a pig. Everyone says you're lovely.

But I can't take it anymore. I'm outside waiting, WATCH-ING, but I want to be inside.

God, I want to be inside.

Deep breath now.

Clearing dead wood, that's all it is. A sacrifice – Iphigenia on her altar. A fair wind to take him all the way to Troy. I'm doing him a favour – all that mewling and puking will interrupt his work.

There's nothing more important than his work.

I should have done it sooner. It's not my fault, though. It's YOURS; you kept it hidden from me. Better late than never.

1

When it's over, the cuts made, the veins bled out, that's when my work will be done. He'll be free.
And I'll be inside. Where I belong.

Part 1

1

Just one more night. Then it's done. Anna has packed, a clear plastic bin bag that contains all her worldly goods – tracksuits, a few toiletries. A pile of letters tied with string, pushed into the middle of her clothes. She gave away her mugs, her box of teabags. Travelling light.

Saying goodbye was easier than she'd thought: a rush job in the end, not the drawn-out farewell she'd feared. Anna's done her best not to get close to anyone these last years – such things only bring bad luck. Naomi, her pad mate, got closer than most; persistent. Kind. The long months spent in lockdown during the pandemic forced the intimacy. Give it a week, though, and she'll have put Anna out of her mind.

Anna doesn't deserve to be remembered.

It doesn't feel like it now, but it was only a couple of hours ago that Naomi showed her a bottle of vodka she'd sneaked in. *We should make a night of it.* But Anna didn't have time to say no – without warning, she was moved out of their cell into a spare bunk in the First Nights Unit, her bed needed because of an emergency on B wing. Naomi argued, but Anna didn't bother. *You don't mind, do you,* they said, not really asking. *You might even have the cell to yourself.* Anna

5

nodded, picked up her belongings, followed the guard. It's not like it mattered. She was already halfway out, mind flying slipstream behind the train she sometimes hears rumbling in the middle of the night.

It's good to have this time on her own, adjust to the fact that in a matter of hours, she'll be out. This prison's been her home for more than three years. Should she feel sad to leave? Sad would mean feelings, though, and Anna doesn't do feelings. Not when she can help it. Locks them away with the rest. If she can't see them, they're not there. That's the thing. It doesn't matter that she'll be free soon. She'll never escape, not really. The voice will still be there, asking why she's still walking, breathing, eating, sleeping – all the things she shouldn't be.

So many nights she's woken with a scream, bolt upright in the dark, sweat prickling on her scalp, across her neck. At first, Naomi would jump up, ask what was wrong, but Anna could never find the words – an agonising jolt, the stink of hot metal, smash of glass. A small boy crying out for his mum.

It didn't take long for Naomi to stop asking.

Other nights, Anna's lain awake in the dark, replaying the last moments before it all went bad. There's another Anna out there, one who sleeps in a comfortable bed, wakes to an alarm, not to the sound of her own cries. In that world, thirty-something Anna has hit all the milestones she was meant to. Boyfriend, mortgage, solicitor at a big city law firm.

More than any of that, a family that wants her.

That Anna didn't fuck up. That Anna made a different choice.

A split-second decision that caused all the pain in the world, when everything spiralled out of her control. Now, the ruins of her former life lie behind her, every last item

6

scraped together like the trash it is. At least it won't be much for them to sort out in the end.

Shouts from the cells around her, the sound of banging, a pounding on the walls. The atmosphere's sharper in the First Nights Unit, an expectation of pain to come in the air. She's come full circle on her last night inside, back where it all began. Memories itch under her skin. She still picks at the rash on her hands – sometimes until it bleeds. She remembers the waiting, the shame, the wave of sound as the cell door slammed shut for the very first time.

She rolls over in the bunk, trying to find a comfortable position, her shoulders hunched up. It's the top bunk like the one she was used to, but this feels hostile, unfamiliar, the bedding inadequate, not like the soft duvet and pillow she ordered from a catalogue a year into her sentence. These she left with Naomi. Now it's back to basics. Comfort or not, she wouldn't be able to sleep anyway. Too many thoughts circling her mind, looping back and forth.

Tomorrow. That's the easy part. They'll let her out early. She's got cash, nearly fifty quid in a hard roll stuffed into her bra.

She'll get her bag back, the holdall she packed so carelessly years ago, the night before she was sentenced. Not much more to pack in it now. Then it'll be time to go. She's been told it's a long wait for the bus, but she can't afford a cab. Time was she'd have thought nothing of dropping fifty quid in one go. Even more. But that was before.

Before. She can barely remember that Anna, what she used to think was important. She had everything wrong. Soft, defenceless. Now she's calcified, all weak spots enclosed – nothing but shell.

Bus, then train. She's made the journey so many times in her thoughts, the slow stops through the countryside as the buildings get closer and closer together in the approach to London. A tube across the city, another train.

The last train she'll catch.

She's meant to have an appointment in the afternoon with probation, but she's not going to bother with it. There's no point. Not now.

She rolls over again, trying to dig herself into the thin mattress. Caught between sleep and waking. As she said goodbye to Naomi, it was as if the distance between them was expanding, the woman growing smaller and smaller as Anna pulled away in her mind, even as they hugged. Keep in touch, she said, Anna nodding yes, thinking no. No point in causing any more upset.

There'll be no joy when she takes her first step outside the gate. No reunion for her, no partner waiting with a hug and a smile. Anna hasn't had a single visitor since she's been inside.

It's not like she didn't try. That last letter she sent to her sister. *Please. Just tell me how he is.* She'd posted it with such hope. A few words came back. *Not known here, Return to sender,* letters in black scrawled across the envelope.

The pain hasn't gone anywhere. It still sticks to her, clawing at her chest. Their faces are blurs now.

Breathe in, breathe out. Slowly, slowly, her heart rate lowers again. She's got a plan. The pain will be over soon. One more night, then she puts an end to it. She can see the sea stretching out in front of her, feel the cold water lapping at her feet, her thighs. Her face.

Bus, train, tube. Whatever's left of the fifty, she'll spend on a one-way ticket to the coast, the short shingle beach at St

Leonards where she went as a kid, her sister always close at her heels. The sea again, for one last time.

She won't need a return.

YOU KILLED MY SON
YOU KILLED YOUR MUM
I WANT TO KILL YOU

Round and round the words dance in her head, flashing before her eyes. The notes arrived every now and again through the years. She kept them all, a little pile of loathing, though she knows every word by heart.

Shifting over in her bunk, moving from flat on her front to foetal position, she clutches her arms across her head. The roll of cash digs into her breast again, reminding her of the final gift from Naomi as they hugged goodbye. She digs into her bra, pulls out a twist of toilet paper stashed next to the cash. In the middle of the wad of tissue, a pill that Naomi thrust into her hand. *You could do with a decent sleep on your last night*, she muttered in Anna's ear as she did so. *No nightmares.*

There's only one thing that will stop them, though. This isn't it. She should throw the pill away, flush it down the loo, hide it under the mattress – someone else's escape.

But there's so much to face tomorrow, so much to do. She's so tired . . .

No more thinking. Not for now. Anna puts the pill in her mouth and, with an effort, swallows it down.

2

Shit. It's not working. Her mind's racing now, not quietened. Serves her right, trying to outrun the thoughts that hound her. What was it, anyway? She didn't ask, assuming it was a sleeping pill. Maybe it wasn't.

Anna had always said no when Naomi had offered them in the past. She didn't deserve the peace, fleeting as it might be. Besides, she's found herself out of bed too many times, stuck in a nightmare, hands raw from pounding against the door.

Sedatives can't stop that. They might even make it worse.

One night, she woke to see Naomi pacing the room, folding and refolding her clothes in a pile, until she lay down abruptly on top of them and fell asleep. When Anna asked her what she was doing, she got no response – and Naomi had no memory of it in the morning, either. Anna doesn't take risks like that anymore. She knows what happens when she loses control.

So stupid of her to swallow it down. The voice in her head is chirping at her again – *Let this be a lesson to you.* All she wants is for it to stop, but she can't make it quiet, can't make it go away, louder and louder and louder it grows . . .

Until it's gone, drowned out by waves of calm. Anna's brain is slowing in real time, pulse after long pulse as the

10

sounds disappear behind a wall of water, slower and slower. Sleep is pulling at her, small hands tugging her down. Her eyes close, her breathing deepens . . .

'You're sleeping in here,' a voice says, jerking her awake. She doesn't know how much later it is.

Anna stirs. The background noises in the building around her have merged into a dull roar, but not this. It's immediate, as if someone is in the cell, the door clanging open. She rolls over, opens an eye. It's bright, not dark anymore. Someone *is* in the cell.

'This is your bunk. Not much, but maybe it's better than the streets.'

It's an officer speaking. The shock of the light is harsh and yellow, dazzling Anna. She squints but can't make out the features of the woman who shuffles in past the officer and sits down heavily on the side of the bottom bunk, her hair across her face. She's sobbing quietly, her breath catching with an edge that jags at Anna, hooks into her.

'Get some sleep now,' the officer says, her voice almost kind. 'It'll seem better in the morning.'

'There's someone else in here already.' The woman's voice is soft, emerging through the sobs.

'She's being released first thing. She won't bother you.'

'When will I get my methadone? I need the prescription.'

'In the morning. The doctor will definitely be in then.'

'They should have been there tonight.'

'I know, but there it is,' the officer says.

No reply. The light goes off and the door slams behind the officer, the click of the lock loud, echoing throughout the cell. Silence descends, a moment of calm before the noises of the wing start up again.

Are you all right? What's your name? Were you waiting in reception long before they processed you? The questions Anna could ask rise half-formed in her mind but she can't speak them. She's trapped somewhere under warm waves lulling her to sleep, spinning her in their riptide. She can't offer any help, any comfort to this poor woman. The tranquilliser is working its magic. It doesn't matter what's going on around her now, how much pain there is. Anna is floating off away from it, out of any control.

Another sob; a long, broken breath. The air in the cell calms, less prickly than it was before. It sounds like the woman is unpacking, getting her stuff in order as much as she can in the twilight of the cell.

A long sniff, then, 'Is there a toilet?'

Anna opens her mouth to reply but the words don't come out. She can't make her tongue work, can't form the words. She wants to say, *It's at the end of the cell*, or at least to roll over and point to the metal toilet bolted to the floor. She can't. It'll be obvious soon enough, though, behind its inadequate screen. The reek of bleach and ammonia cuts through even the depths of Anna's torpor.

The woman stands up, the bunk beds shifting with the movement, and for a moment Anna senses her presence beside the top bunk, her eyes burning through the blanket that's covers Anna's head. Then footsteps, slow and heavy, to the back of the cell. There's the sound of the removal of clothes. And something else. A rustling noise.

Water hitting water now, the flush, and the steps shuffle back to the bunk before she subsides on to it heavily. She's not sobbing anymore, but her breathing is laboured, the harsh inhalations reverberating around the cell.

'It's me. I'm on remand. I've been staying at the Jericho hostel but I got nicked in the Westgate Shopping Centre. I guess it was always going to happen.' A hoarse whisper. Her voice is so bleak that it cuts through Anna's haze. Freezing cold water floods through the warm waves.

She's not talking to Anna. She's talking to someone else. The rustling. She must have brought something in, contraband hidden up inside herself that the strip search didn't find.

A phone.

Crying again, smaller sobs, broken as she struggles for breath.

'I know what you said,' the woman says. 'But I can't bear it. I need to know she's OK.' Her voice rises. Anna tries to stay motionless. There's a clicking noise coming from the phone, the distant sound of someone speaking, though Anna can't make out the words.

'Someone in the hostel gave it to me. What does it matter how I got the phone in here? Is everything all right?'

More crying. More clicking.

'What do you mean, never again? You can't do that. It'll break her. She's my mother.'

The clicks rise in volume, sharp staccatos of sound.

'So I can't even contact you? I thought I could trust you.'

A long pause. More indistinct words in reply.

'I won't let you do this.'

Silence. No clicking.

'Leave her alone. I'm begging you. Help me . . . Why won't anyone help me?'

Clicking. A pause. Then a thump, the phone hitting the concrete floor.

13

'I've lost everything now. My poor Louise . . .' Her voice trails into nothing.

Quiet now. Only ragged sobs. Anna can't hold her breath anymore, exhaling as quietly as possible. She's desperate for sleep, to shut everything out. She feels herself caught in the current of this woman's despair. It's unbearable.

The woman keeps crying, quietly now. Not for long though – soon the sobs from the bunk below subside, and the pill begins to work its full magic for Anna, smoothing down the jagged edges.

Sleep.

3

Anna wakes with a start. Her heart's pounding and she's filled with a cold terror. She lies rigid, hands pressed into her sides, eyes tight shut. Petrified.

But there's no one there. It's quiet as the grave, the prison silent in the deep of night. She listens out, waiting to hear the smallest shuffle or sigh. Hardly daring to breathe, she opens her eyes a crack, looks from left to right, her head unmoving. No trace of life, the cell dark other than the silver gleam of moonshine leaking through the window.

Nothing. Nothing at all. Not even stirrings from the bunk below. It must have been another nightmare. Anna releases her breath, only a little, and shifts over on to her side. The dread is passing, some warmth returning to her hands.

But she's not in her bed, she realises. The surface beneath her cheek is concrete. She's on the floor. She must have climbed out of bed, the night terrors driving her into the unknown. She shouldn't have taken the pill.

She opens her eyes fully, sees there's enough light from the moon that she can get herself back into the top bunk without disturbing her pad mate. She slowly shuffles herself to her feet and climbs up.

Lying back down on her side in bed, the money in her bra digs in again. The night terror has lessened, thoughts of the day ahead taking its place. The bus, the train, the tube, the other train. Her final journey to the sea.

Anna closes her eyes, screwing up her face against all of it, everything, willing herself out of existence, waiting for sleep to come.

The next time she wakes, daylight is creeping through the cell from the window. The fear has eased its hold on Anna and she's breathing easier now, the terror of the night before forgotten. She's not dead yet.

The rays of sun are weak, sickly, but totally beautiful. She allows herself a moment to imagine them on her face for real, their warmth. When it happens, it won't be in a bare enclosure, or a garden watched constantly by cameras and prison guards. She'll be free to walk as far as she wants, to hold her hands up to the sky.

A flush of shame takes hold, scorching as it spreads from her gut, moving all over her. This is not her freedom. Hers is a life sentence. She shuts her eyes and turns away from the light. Back to where she was.

She's thought it all through. Thought of nothing else for months. She promised herself one last attempt to contact her sister, to see if any forgiveness was possible. She knew it was futile, but one shred of hope that they might reconcile remained.

Hope died hard. *Return to sender.* That's all she got back.

Everything's gone. Family, friends, home. Her career. Nothing left to live for. No one cares.

It's better to focus on the practicalities. The effects of the pill are gradually wearing off. It's morning, time to get on

16

with it. She's got a mini box of cereal and a quarter pint of milk on the floor for breakfast. She's not hungry, but she'll have to force it down. She needs to keep her strength up, for just a little longer.

A scream in the background, a woman crying, incoherent shouting from somewhere down the wing. A buzzer rings and rings and rings. Morning is breaking. Anna doesn't want to move. She wants to stay cocooned in her blanket, pinned here forever between dark and light, night and day.

But her bladder has other thoughts. She needs to pee.

Her pad mate is silent in the bunk below. Anna shifts herself over the side of the bunk and goes to the toilet at the end of the cell, sitting down with a sigh of relief. It's still early. She can go back to bed, get a bit more rest, shore herself up against the day to come.

She rises to her feet and wipes herself, flushing because the smell is worse than the noise. Anna remembers the stranger's conversation in the middle of the night; the whispered voice, the cry, the plea. Everyone here has something they've lost.

She goes to stand by the window, watching for the lifting of the light, then turns to get back into bed again. She bashes her knee on the edge climbing back up on to the bunk and lies back, swearing loudly. The impact wasn't that hard but it stings, the skin broken, beads of blood breaking through. She wipes them off with the heel of her hand, swearing more loudly. The pain has broken any sense of calm she had – Anna's filling up with panic, a stressed rage building up through her gut. She's past caring if she disturbs anyone now. Gripped by an urge she can't control, out of all proportion to the injury she's suffered, Anna starts shouting at the top of her voice, an inchoate, wordless scream.

Nothing from the bunk below.

'Fuck. Fuck's sake.'

A bang on the pipes, thumps on the wall from the cell next door. Anna has woken someone up. Not her pad mate, though. Still nothing, still quiet.

Why the hell hasn't the woman woken? Wincing at the sting in her knee, Anna jumps down again from her bunk and seizes the lower bunk's blanket by its outside edge, pulling it straight off the bunk. She's losing control now, a scream building up inside her, however unfair it is to disturb the woman like this. Anna needs a witness.

Nothing. No sound. No movement. No scream in reply telling Anna to fuck off. She bangs her head in frustration against the wall before kneeling on the ground to look inside the bunk.

4

The woman is face down in the dark corner of her bed, lying at an awkward angle, her feet dangling over the side.

'Wake up,' Anna says, 'wake up, damn it. Talk to me.' She reaches forward and puts her hand on the woman's shoulder, shaking her, gently at first. Nothing. She shakes her harder, determined now.

No response at all. The frustration in Anna begins to subside, a sense of foreboding rising. She takes a deep breath, aware now of a metallic, sweet tang in the air. Bracing herself against the side of the bunk, she firmly grips the woman's left shoulder, holding it with all the strength she can muster. She pulls up slowly, steadily, and the woman begins to move. She's not heavy, Anna realises, more inert. A dead weight.

Finally, Anna gets enough traction to pull the woman completely over on to her back. But as she does so, there's a sickening thud. The woman's head flops over to the other side of the bunk, beams of sunlight shining straight into the lifeless face. It lolls back at an awkward angle to reveal a gaping wound across the throat, a cut inflicted with absolute intention.

Anna drops her grasp and reels back, a sour taste rising

into the back of her throat. She recoils to the other side of the cell, as far away as she can in that tiny space.

The stranger's face is sheet white, the lips pale. There's blood everywhere around her, soaked into the sheet and the pillow. Anna takes in a deep breath and steels herself, edging closer to try and assess the damage. Curly hair swirls out dark against the stranger's blanched skin, spreading out over and under her neck and shoulders, matted and sticky.

She looks down the woman's body to see the grey track-suit, bloodstained and dirty. A delicate hand protrudes from a blood-soaked cuff, the wrist bird-thin. Compelled by some instinct she can't name, Anna touches the cold hand, picks it up in hers. As she moves it, there's a clink as something metal falls from the dead fingers to the floor – a loose razor blade, its edges stained. Something else the woman must have smuggled in with her.

Anna looks again at the hand in hers; the hand of someone young, the skin soft, uncalloused. The nails are short and bitten. A breath catches in Anna's throat. She turns the hand over to see deep cuts up the wrist, inches long, vertical, each one clearly made with a fixed intention. The sodden sweatshirt sticks to Anna's hand – she places the dead arm back down with as much control as she can muster, fighting the urge to scream.

She steels herself, moving closer still, holding her breath, trying to keep out the stench of blood. She touches the side of the woman's face, pulls her fingers away and brings them up to her own cheek, rubbing along the solid breadth of it, tracing the curve of her brows.

She can't hold her breath anymore. Though she inhales as lightly as possible, the smell hits the back of her throat and she retches again, desperate to spit it out. Iron, sweat.

She thinks back to the conversation she overheard last night, the horror in the woman's voice, the pain. Anna knows about desperation. But to cut her own throat? However dark Anna's feelings have become, however devoid of hope she is, she doubts she could do it. A gentler way, yes, but nothing as brutal as this.

She leans back on her heels, light-headed suddenly. Her hand moves to her cheek, still as cold as if she were lying on that stone floor. She'd woken there in the middle of the night. She didn't remember how she got there. Maybe there's more she doesn't remember.

She stretches her hand out in front of her, the other too, turning them over. *Who would have thought the old man to have so much blood in him?* leaps unbidden into her mind. She's barely touched the woman's body, but her hands are coated, dark red encrusted under her nails and splashed up to her wrists.

Did Anna do it? Did she take that razor blade and slash her up like this? She's walked in her sleep before. The pill . . .

She sits back on her heels, tries to survey the scene dispassionately, gulping down the escalating fear that she might have been responsible. It *could* have been a suicide. But the grimness of it is sinking in, the sheer horror – a diorama of death, a horror movie in real time. The blood spatters, the splashes of it up the grubby wall beside the bunk, the mattress sodden.

Anna leans against the wall opposite the bunk, her eyes closed, fighting for memory. What happened on that call?

But the more she thinks about it, the less sure she is what the woman even said to the person on the other end of the phone. It's misty, murky, the edges blurred, words slipping through her mind like smoke. It might have all been part of her twisted nightmare, the one that drove her out of her bunk. Could it have driven her even further? To kill?

If she walked in now, to see herself sitting covered in blood like this, Anna would have no doubt that she'd done it. The woman is so slight, Anna could easily have overpowered her, slit her throat.

Anna brings her knees up to her chest, bends her head down to meet them. Today was supposed to bring relief, at last. Now it looks as if everything she's gone through these past few years, the immense pain she's inflicted on others, all of this was just a pale rehearsal for what's about to come.

She was going to go to the sea, hear the waves, taste the salt on her lips for one last time. But Anna doesn't deserve that. She doesn't deserve anything, now. An eye for an eye, a tooth for a tooth. She turns to the wall behind her, hits her head against it, wincing at the impact.

Again, and again, and again.

OUTSIDE

Where does it start? Like all the best stories, at the beginning.

I see you, you see me, our eyes meet.

You don't need to speak, you don't need to smile, you don't need to say a thing. I know what you're thinking.

Across the lecture theatre, across the seminar room, in the tutorial. I always know what you're thinking. You're thinking about slipping your fingers up my top, caressing my skin, unbuttoning my shirt, pulling it gently off my shoulders, kissing my neck, your kisses trailing further and further down.

I'm thinking about it too.

Oh professor, you make a girl blush.

5

Anna can't keep it up for long. Fucking hell, she's pathetic. She can't stand even the smallest amount of pain.

It's brought her back to her senses, though.

Nightmare or not, she knows what she heard. The words of the call last night go through her mind. *Why won't anyone help me?* Anna could have helped; she slept instead. But she didn't harm her. She stares down at the bloody mess that was the woman's throat.

Of course it wasn't Anna. She knows well enough what she's capable of – it's not this, not even in her worst state. She can be aggressive when she needs to be, like when she punched a woman who attacked her in the canteen. But Anna doesn't seek out trouble.

Her head's sore where she's been hitting it against the wall, blood trickling down her forehead. She brushes it away, red on the dark dried smears of blood from the dead woman that stick still to her fingers.

The prison's waking up. Shouts from the cells, the banging of doors. Footsteps along the concrete corridors. It won't be long before they come to her cell. *Think.* She's doesn't have long.

She hasn't called for help yet. That may count against her, when they review the evidence. Evidence that all seems to point to her – the sole other occupant of the cell, covered in blood. Means, motive . . .

The means – yes, sure. She's staring straight at the blade, though she knows it's not hers. But motive?

A fugue state. A night terror turned into a living nightmare. She wouldn't need a motive. She turns her hands over again, looking at the blood-encrusted nails, flexing the fingers in and out.

If she'd slit this poor woman's throat, there'd be some mark on her. The woman would have struggled, put up a fight. There's nothing, though. No stiffness, no pain. Her hands are chilled, sticky with dried blood. But they feel completely normal.

Anna's scalp is tingling. She flexes her fingers again, closes them into a fist which pulsates to the beats of her heart, strong and insistent.

Alive. It's too late for this poor woman. But it's not too late for Anna. She looks at the body for a moment more, emblazoning the image into her mind. Another emotion is playing through her, stronger than guilt, stronger than fear, too. It's anger. This is not how anyone should die.

Fragments of the woman's conversation floating round her head. *It'll break her. She's my mother. My poor Louise . . .* Who was the woman talking to? What happened to her mother?

Anna closes her eyes again. She's so tired, so fucking tired. She climbs back on to her bunk, wrapping the blanket around her, over her head, wanting to make it all go away. But she can't settle, thrashing her legs around under the cover and thrusting her hands under the thin pillow. There's something in the way, something small, hard. She takes it, rolling over on to her back. It wasn't there the night before.

Without even looking, she knows exactly what it is, the tiny object encased in a tacky, rubbery cover. She can feel buttons under the surface – a miniature phone, wrapped in a condom, smuggled in inside the woman like so much contraband Anna has seen before.

I'm begging you. Help me. Anna knows how it feels to be helpless. There must be a reason that the phone was left in her bed. It was deliberate, of course. The last act of a woman resolved to die.

However, Anna's got her plan. She's out, she's going to the sea. She's not coming back. She can't help anyone else.

Any minute now they're going to come and open the door for her release. Then all hell will break loose – the phone will be the first item they seize. Without thinking, she rolls out of bed, throws on her clothes, and tucks the phone into the foot of her right trainer, where she curls her toes over it, gripped by an urgency she can't ignore.

Phone safely stowed, Anna turns her attention back to the dead woman. She hasn't done any basic checks – is the woman still breathing, even if only slightly? Is there a heartbeat? She squats next to the corpse, half-wondering if she's hallucinating. But there's the gaping wound across the windpipe – she's dead all right.

A bang on the door. Tears well up in her eyes. She brushes them aside with the back of her hand.

No time for tears.

6

The key grinds in the lock. The door bangs open. Before Anna can even stand up, a prison officer files in. He stands quiet for a moment, taking in the scene. Anna watches the expression change on his face from one of professional calm to sheer panic before he slaps the mask back on again, calling immediately for back-up. Two other officers come in so fast that as she starts to get up, they knock her to the floor. They yell at her to stand back while one of them leans over the body in the bed, putting his fingers to the dead woman's neck.

They all turn and look at Anna. She's scooted to the side of the cell to get out of the way.

'What the fuck's been going on here?' one of them asks.

Before Anna can open her mouth to speak, the other two officers, one woman, one man, have hauled her to her feet so she's face to face with the officer by the bed.

He looks her up and down. It's not even a lack of kindness in his eyes – he doesn't see her as human, his gaze is as cold as that. Anna lowers her head. He reaches out and grabs hold of her right wrist, gripping so hard he could crush the bones with only a little more pressure.

28

'What's this?' he says, forcing her arm upwards so that her hand is in front of her face.

'What's what?' Anna says, though she knows perfectly well what he means.

'This, you stupid bitch.' He waves her hand back and forth. 'What's all over your hands?'

The blood drains out of Anna's face. She feels it happen, a chill from within. She knew what was going to happen to her, she's known all along, but now it's real. Her fingers clench into a fist, loosen again, weak. He pushes her backwards against the wall, so hard that she hits the back of her head and collapses to the ground once more.

'Get the fuck up,' he says.

Anna pushes herself upwards. 'I didn't kill her.' She knows the words are futile even as they leave her mouth.

'I didn't ask,' he says. 'Look at yourself. Dead woman, your hands covered in blood.' A pause. 'I don't need to ask.'

Anna shakes her head. 'She did it to herself,' she says, knowing full well the reception that's going to get.

'I'll be the judge of that.'

Words spring up to Anna's tongue, but she forces them down. All she has now is her gut and it's telling her to be quiet. She remembers the terror of the night before – maybe this is what it was warning her of. The woman dead, Anna blamed for it. She keeps her face impassive.

'Keep searching,' the officer yells at the others, who are rummaging round the bed. They're not trying to administer first aid, nor paying any respect to the woman's body. Any vestige of doubt Anna felt about hiding the phone leaves her, her toes clenching around it even more tightly.

'Get back up,' the officer screams into her face. 'I didn't tell you to sit down.'

Anna had not intended to crouch, but her legs are wobbling under her. She pushes herself up again, wanting to avoid more yelling. The noise is overwhelming, shouting from the officers as they try and ascertain what has happened, yells and bangs from along the corridors as the other residents start to realise that something is up, something more than the normal upheaval.

'Out the way,' the other officer shouts, 'get the fuck out of the way,' and he's pushing her aside to let a paramedic get to the bunk. Anna moves towards the door to clear some space, but officer number one, the shouty one, grabs hold of her arm so hard that she cries out in pain. He drags her right next to him and screams again.

'I didn't tell you to leave the cell – do what you're fucking told.'

Anna stands still. If she stops moving, maybe she'll become invisible, or at least shrink until she's so tiny they won't notice her, and maybe she'll be able to slip out between their fingers and slide under the bunk and lie in peace . . . She glances over at the dead woman. At least she's far away from all this.

Officer number one twists her round and handcuffs her hands behind her back.

'You're coming with me,' he says. 'Move it.'

He pushes her in front of him, out of the cell and along the corridor to a room next to the officers' room. It's bare, containing only a metal table and chairs, all of which are bolted to the floor. Before he thrusts her on to one of the chairs, he rubs her down, front and back, pushing his hands hard against her breasts, her thighs. Between her legs. When he's finished the search, he pulls her arms up painfully tight as he unlocks the cuff on her left hand. Leaving her right hand locked up, he clips the other cuff on to the table leg. She shuffles towards the edge of the seat to lessen some of the tension, but he pushes her back into place.

'Stay exactly where you are,' he says. He's not shouting now, but there's still force in his voice. He flicks at her right hand, catching it with his nail. 'Literally caught red-handed. What the fuck were you thinking?'

Again, Anna stays completely still, and as if bored with her lack of response, the officer backs away. He walks out of the room, muttering something under his breath – she can only catch the words *fucking stupid*.

The minutes tick on. As the blood dries on her hands, it itches. She scratches it as far as she can reach while handcuffed, the eczema rash thick beneath her fingernails. A sharp sting tells her she's broken through – new blood to add to the stains. She remembers when it first started, this patch of itchy flesh, sometimes burning so much it couldn't be sated, however hard she went at it with her nails. She was sitting in a hospital bed, her head aching from the impact of the collision, horror mounting in her as the grim-faced police officers told her what she'd done.

She scratched.

Words she couldn't process, words like *life-threatening injury* and *caution* and *court*. All the time, she scratched, and scratched, and scratched, unable to stop.

She can't stop it now, either. She's spiralling off, unable to get a grip on anything. On top of everything else, the pill hasn't fully worn off yet. Anna wishes she could disappear between the cracks in her own mind.

She knocks her head on the hard table, snapping herself back into now. This isn't the same as last time. There's a tiny chance she's responsible, she can't rule that out, but she finds it impossible to believe.

Murder, though. Someone is dead, and she's going to be charged for it.

Even if they have questions, they won't bother to ask them. They'll want to tick it off as fast as possible. Why would the police even care about the death of one prisoner at the hands of another?

She knows how suspicious it looks. It was Anna the inmate, in the cell, with a razor blade. But deep in her bones, she's sure it wasn't her. She slept right through it, drugged up to the eyeballs. She should never have taken a sedative when she was in a new cell, with the risk of encountering someone she didn't know. Anna's got through these years as much by her wits as by luck – her guard was down, so close to the end, and now look what's happened. She could have put a stop to it, talked to her, maybe saved the woman's life, if only she'd been in control.

A beat. Another. The image of Naomi, her old pad mate, comes back to her, the woman kneeling in the cell, folding clothes and unfolding them over and over again.

Back again to the start. She stares down at her left hand again, transfixed by the bloodstains, staring into the darkness. Thinking about those hours of nothing between sleeping and waking.

Knowing that she's innocent of the attack changes nothing.

If she admits that she took the sedative, it gives them an opening to convict her. If she says that she slept through it all, they'll never believe her. She's fucked, whichever way you look at it.

7

The clamour is building – finally, the noise is loud enough to break through Anna's thoughts. The mood in this place is always on edge after a death. People might pretend they don't give a fuck, but of course they do. Every time they're thinking *but there for the grace of God. It could have been me.*

She knows the rules. Suspected homicide, police must be called. She leans back in the seat, shifting to take the pressure off her cuffed arm again, her body sore from the aggressive search they'd carried out before they locked her in here. At least they didn't make her take off her shoes. They'd found the razorblade immediately, so it's not like the murder weapon was missing. They have all they need.

No one is rushing, now that she's secured. It's hardly an emergency – the suspected killer isn't going anywhere. There's no clock in the cell and she has no way of finding out what time it is, but it sounds as if everyone is now awake. The bangs have subsided but there's still shouting, crying, an ululation from a stranger with something left to shout about. Anna remembers the first night she spent inside, the terror that froze her to the bunk. It didn't last, that fear for her own wellbeing. She knew that whatever happened to her was less than what was due.

Despite the three years inside, it's hard for her to take a different view now. The guilt hasn't subsided. There's no sentence harsh enough. This might be unfair, that she's found herself suspected of something she hasn't done, but her original offence was so bad that it doesn't matter. No number of years would be enough – at least this way, she'll be properly punished. Does it matter if it's not for the right crime? Backwards and forwards it goes in her head. What Anna deserves, what she might get.

It's not about that, though. There's something bigger here. Someone else has died, a young woman, in the most horrific of circumstances. Anna can't do a thing to change that.

All she can do is wait. She might as well have handed over the phone. There's nothing else she can do about it. She puts her head down on the table in front of her and closes her eyes.

Deep sleep evades her but she must have dropped off a little, because the slamming of the cell door brings Anna to herself with a snap, sitting up so fast that she hurts her wrist on the chain.

Prison officer number one is standing in front of her, two uniformed police officers behind him. They're all men, the prison officer short, but built like a brick shithouse, his face red, his hair receding. She's never spoken to him before today, though she's seen him in the distance. She also knows his reputation.

'What the fuck are you staring at?' he says.

She bows her head.

The police officers take their time sitting down. There's a big one and a small one, like Little and Large, the latter as wide as he is tall, his body poured into the uniform for just a moment too long so it looks overfilled, ready to burst at the seams. Little is wiry, hungry-looking, his tongue darting out to the corner of his mouth every few seconds. They seem nervous.

Maybe they haven't been inside a prison before – that's always a possibility. Large keeps looking over at the door as if to check that it's locked. Maybe he's imagining that any minute a riot's going to break out, or an inmate's going to rush in and pot him. Anna pictures his face with rivulets of liquidised shit running down it, suppressing a shudder at the thought of the smell.

Not quickly enough. 'What are you twitching about?' Large says. She curls her fingers into a fist.

Little interrupts. 'Anna Flyn, we are arresting you on suspicion of the murder of Kelly Green. You do not have to say anything. But it may harm your defence if you do not mention when questioned something which you later rely on in court. Anything you do say may be given in evidence.' He rushes through it, his lack of interest in the formality evident.

Kelly Green. So that's the woman's name. Anna has never heard of her. A thought strikes her. 'What about my legal rights?'

'What legal rights?' Large says, sneering.

'My right to a solicitor. I am entitled to legal representation.'

The prison officer lurches forward from the door where he's been leaning, his face twisted with rage. 'You're bang to fucking rights. That's all the rights you need,' he snaps, as if unable to control himself anymore. 'Caught red-fucking-handed. What do you need a solicitor for?'

Little sighs, shaking his head. His hair is neatly slicked

down with gel, the teeth marks from the comb almost perpendicular to the parting that's so straight it could have been done with a ruler. 'We need to follow due process, lads. That's the way of it. You know what they can be like.' *They* is hissed with some venom, though Anna isn't sure who in particular incurred it.

'You're only putting off the inevitable,' Large says. 'Solicitor or not, you're staying right where you are.'

They turn to the prison officer and nod at him. 'Let's get the *lady* a solicitor, shall we? Since it's so important to her. Not like there's much of a rush. Custody time limits aren't exactly an issue here.' It's Large speaking. Little laughs, but without humour. He must be subordinate.

The prison officer nods. 'We'll get it sorted.' Turning to Anna, he affects a tone of civility. 'Does madam have a preferred legal representative, or will the duty solicitor suffice?' He bows. Anna clenches her fist even harder. She needs to stay in control.

'Duty is fine,' she says. She never wants to see the solicitor who represented her last time again.

'As madam requires,' he says, sneering even more, his face contorted with contempt. With that, he and the police officers leave the room, the door slamming shut behind them.

CCTV

There are two women, one young, one old, inside the kitchen – let's call the young one Scylla, the old Charybdis. Their real names don't matter. They're monsters, after all.

It's a dark room with a low roof, two small windows set deep into a stone wall. Scylla stands at a Rayburn stove, stirring a pot. Charybdis sits at a table made from rough wood. She is weeping, her face contorted, picking at the skin on her arms. They are both very thin.

Scylla brings the pot to the table and ladles out its steaming contents. Plant matter sticks out from the top of the bowls, which looks like nettles. The liquid slops over the sides of the bowl as she pours it.

She puts her hand on Charybdis's arm, strokes it. She then picks up her spoon and brings it to her lips, which pucker as if the contents are sour. She gestures to Charybdis, bringing her spoon up and down to her face as if to say, *Eat up.*

Charybdis pushes the bowl away, hard enough to spill the contents on to the table. She starts banging her head on the table, a rhythmic movement. Scylla stands up and attempts to restrain her, but Charybdis slaps her in the face. Scylla's head snaps back and forward.

She sits down. Scylla is crying now too. There is a dark mark on her cheek.

8

The wait goes on for several hours. Anna is seized up in her seat, her arm throbbing from being trapped in the same position by the handcuffs. She's hungry, thirsty too, and desperate to pee. To distract herself, she counts down from 1,000: 999, inhale, count on the exhale, 998 . . .

She's nearly at 666 when the door crashes open. She's not going to take it as a sign, even though the prison officer is wearing an expression that's particularly demonic. He's at the front, followed again by Little and Large, with another man in a suit bringing up the rear. It must be the duty solicitor. Anna sits up, straightening her hair with her left hand, attempting to create some impression of order.

The police officers sit down opposite her once more, while the solicitor sits to her left. The prison officer props up the door again.

'Right, let's start again,' Large says. He launches straight back into the caution. Murder, that word again. Anna can feel herself freeze.

The solicitor puts his hand up. 'I'm going to have to stop you there,' he says. 'I want to have a consultation with my client on her own beforehand.'

Heavy sighs from round the table, but they all troop out, leaving Anna and the solicitor alone.

'I'm Tom Wright,' he says. 'Solicitor from Douglas Kemp and Co. They've called me in to represent you.'

Anna nods. 'I'm Anna Flyn,' she says.

He nods back at her. 'I know.' He pulls a pen out of his jacket pocket and puts it down on the table next to his notebook. 'Can you tell me what this is all about?' He's brusque in his manner, off-hand.

'I don't exactly know what happened,' she says, 'but when I woke up she was dead. She'd cut her throat with a razor, slit her wrists too.'

'Who was dead?'

'My pad mate – cell mate. Her name is Kelly Green, that's what they've just said. I didn't know her, though.'

'Are you sure about that? They told me she was living on the streets in Oxford in the last few months, staying in hostels. You haven't come across her?'

Anna stares at him blankly. 'I've been in here for the last three years. How would I have met her?'

He leafs through his notes, reads down through a page in front of him. 'Oh yes, sorry. Of course.'

Anna tries not to sigh. She shouldn't have bothered with a solicitor – he's clearly not interested. She takes a deep breath, continues.

'I've never met her before. It was late at night when she was brought in. I was asleep before she came in – I went back to sleep straight afterwards. When I woke up, she was dead, her throat slit. I was checking to see if there was anything I could do to help, when the officers came in and found me . . .' Anna's voice trails off.

Tom is noting down her reply. She glances over at his handwriting, which is slanting, neat. Too measured for the horrors it's recording.

'What do you think happened to her?' he says.

'I think she killed herself.'

'Right,' he says, his tone non-committal.

Anna raises her head and looks at him, clocking now that he's younger than any solicitor who's represented her before: mid-thirties, clean-shaven, his suit tailored to his lean form. He looks more like one of the associates at the city firm where she used to work, not like a criminal hack. His white shirt is so pristine, it's hard not to assume he's having to restrain himself from wrinkling his nose at the smell in here.

Anna looks down at her hands again. She doesn't want to cry but tears are threatening, the reality of it starting to hit her. Not for herself, but for the dead woman, all the other women wailing and yelling in the corridors outside, a constellation of pain.

'I think you should give a "no comment" interview. Let's see what the police have to say. Even the most open-and-shut case can reveal something unexpected,' Tom says. He mutters the last bit under his breath, but she hears him.

'Open and shut?' she says. 'You think it's as clear as that? Did you even hear what I said? She'd slit her own throat.'

He doesn't reply, doesn't look at her, just adjusts his pen and his notebook carefully.

She slams her left hand down on the table, angry now, exhausted, all the strains of the last hours finally coming to a head. 'She killed herself. I'm sure of it. People do that in prison – all the fucking time. Why would I kill her?' Her voice raises to a shout.

Tom turns towards her and for the first time makes eye contact with her, finally seeing her as a person. 'You make a good point.'

'Yes,' she says, trying not to sob. It's not sadness, just frustration at the sheer bloody mess of it. 'I don't know who she was, why she was in there. Why she wanted to kill herself. But I was meant to be released today, and whatever's happened, it was nothing to do with me.'

The words fall on the table between them, cool as stones. Anna bites her lip.

Tom nods once, twice. 'I didn't realise that you were due to be released,' he says. 'I owe you an apology. I made some assumptions about the situation.'

'It's nothing to do with me.'

He takes in a breath, lines his notebook up neatly with the side of the table. 'I believe you,' he says. 'You'd better tell me what happened from the start.'

9

The hatch on the door bangs open.

'Time's up,' a voice says. 'We need to get on.'

Tom looks at Anna – she could argue for more time, but right now she doesn't see what else they can discuss, given how much she's keeping from him.

He's right, they need to see what the police have to say. She nods.

'We're entitled to as much time as we need,' he says, 'but we are ready to proceed at this point.'

'Good of you,' the voice says with a note of deep sarcasm before the hatch slams shut again. After a moment, the door opens and the police officers file in. They don't look friendly. Anna knows if they had their way, they would simply leave her to rot. At least this time they aren't accompanied by the unpleasant prison officer – he must be off shift now. Someone else has unlocked the door for them, locks it once they've entered.

She's exhausted. It's probably been about eight hours now that she's been in here, and they've offered her no food, no water. Nothing. She hasn't raised it with Tom, though, thinking no one would bother with feeding her. But it's the first request he makes as soon as they've sat down, fussing over their notebooks and the device they're using to record the interview. They look at each other and shrug.

'Not a matter for us,' Little says. 'That's down to prison procedure.'

'Then tell the prison to follow their procedure and give my client a meal and some water,' Tom says. 'Otherwise they'll be facing legal action from me.'

Large sighs and lumbers to his feet, pressing the buzzer three times. Anna resigns herself to a long wait, but to her surprise, someone opens the door immediately. It must be a secret police code, she thinks. Three rings and you're free. Not that it would work for her.

Large passes over the request, and shortly after, a bottle of water and a sandwich are produced for her. It's a nice-looking sandwich, too, bits of salad poking out of the side – Anna hasn't seen food that appetising since she was put in custody. It must have come from the staff canteen. Little comes round and unlocks the handcuff, freeing her right hand. She shakes it to get the blood flowing through it again, wincing as the feeling comes back into her fingers, then starts ramming the food into her mouth. Little sits back down, fixing her with a hard stare. She's too busy inhaling the sandwich to care.

'Interesting,' Little says. 'I'm not sure I'd be able to eat if I were facing a murder charge.'

There was a time when a comment like that would have made Anna freeze. But now she's too hungry. The case has already been determined, no matter what she does. The verdict of guilty is as clear to her as if the foreman of the jury had stood up and shouted it in her face. She swallows what's left of her food and washes it down with some water.

'Well?' he says. 'Don't you have anything to say?'

She's still under caution, she knows that, and she's not being caught out in that way. She leans back in her seat, savouring the last of the sandwich flavour.

The problem she's got, as far as she can see, is that either way, the prison is potentially in a lot of trouble. Tom's mention of litigation was on the nose. They'll be sued for not taking care of the dead woman's emotional needs if it's suicide; they'll be sued for not keeping her safe if Anna killed her. There's fractionally more chance they'll get away with it if they can prove it was Anna.

Large slaps the table. 'Enough of this,' he says. 'A woman is dead. A nineteen-year-old girl, to be precise. Do you think that because she was a homeless drug addict she doesn't matter? Did you think we wouldn't care?'

Tom holds his hand up as if to protest at the questions but Anna shakes her head. The words cut deep. If she shuts her eyes, she can still see the body in her mind, the bloodstains. It's engraved in her memory for good. She doesn't want to show that to these men though, the pain of it. Trying to distract herself, she twists her right hand round in circles, releasing the residual cramp from the long period in handcuffs. Then she catches sight of the nail of her index finger.

It's filthy, a dark ring at the base of the nail and underneath. She stares at it, transfixed. The blood on her left hand has mostly rubbed off, as she's had it free during the day, but her right hand is pretty much as it was when she was first locked up. The thought of what's encrusted under the nail surges up in her mind: the drying blood. Sharp bile hits the back of Anna's throat.

'Of course she matters,' she says, her voice low. Of course she cares about what's happened. But she's got to stick to 'no comment'. She and Tom have a plan – 'no comment' to any question asked, regardless of what they say to her. She takes in a breath, puts her chin up. Mask on. They're not going to get to her.

Little snaps open his notebook, writes a couple of lines. He shows it to Large, who smirks, nods.

Here they go. This is where it starts. The questions, a relentless tide of them. The charge. There's nothing that she'll be able to say to make this go away. Even if she could, she won't get rid of the smell of it that's lingering in her nostrils: the blood, the sweat.

Large slaps the table again. Little clears his throat. Large leans back.

By the end of the interview, Anna feels like she's been clubbed round the head. She's reeling from the force of it. They haven't spared any details in their description of how the corpse was found. Even though Anna saw it for herself, there's an impact in the retelling that winds her. By the time they come to asking her about why she was found leaning over the body covered in blood, she's almost ready to throw in the towel and scream out that fine, it was her, she'd cut the woman's throat.

'It must be very frightening,' Little says, leaning over towards her, his voice dripping with honeyed venom. 'To be facing release, I mean. I know how chaotic it is for you girls on the outside. No wonder you wanted to commit a further offence and make sure you never had to face reality again.'

Large nods, mock sympathy on his face. 'Especially given what you're inside for.'

She clenches her nails into her hands. Even though she should have been expecting it, it hits her with the force of a blow.

'Your nephew, wasn't it?'

Head down. *No comment.*

'Drunk driving.' Not a question, his beefy fingers leafing through the file.

No comment.

'Nasty thing to happen. A kid of that age. Can't imagine you've got much of a relationship with your family now.'

No comment. Her breath's coming faster now, her heart rate accelerating.

'Nothing left for you on the outside, is there?'

The voice fades out, the prison cell too. Anna's standing on a beach, totally alone, her feet moving slowly towards the water, pockets full of stones.

Nothing left at all.

Their questions asked, Little and Large leave the cell. Anna stays still, her hands clenched on the table in front of her. The final onslaught left her broken. She can barely bring herself to move, let alone meet Tom's gaze. He'll probably walk out at this stage, refuse to represent her any further.

'Anna,' he says.

She can't move. Won't move. Shame pins her to the seat.

'Anna,' he says again. 'Look at me.'

She can't.

But she must. This is part of it. Facing it. What she's done. She raises her head, turns towards him gradually, braced.

What she sees, though, is completely unexpected. No judgement. No disdain. An expression of concern on his face.

'That's tough,' he says, and overwhelmed by the sympathetic tone in his voice, she starts to cry.

OUTSIDE

Watching you watching me. You're not watching me, though, you're watching yourself talk, standing in front of that big mirror above the fireplace in your back room. Practising? That's the way you hold your head in lectures, the way you wave your hand for emphasis. God, you're so VAIN. I love it.

This is all about you.

I know you were looking at me earlier in the seminar. The others would kill me if they knew how close we are. But I understand you better than all of THEM.

Sometimes you walk so fast it's hard to keep up. I manage, though, on your tail, all the way back to your house. It's a challenge. Quick, slow. Quick, quick, slow. Sometimes you stop altogether, like you want me to catch up.

You want me to know where you live. Why else would you wait?

I need to be alone with you. I can't concentrate when there are too many people around. It's better when I'm here, outside. Looking in at you like this, nothing else to distract me.

It's peaceful here, surrounded by leaves. I like that you've left it all so wild, a special corner just for me. You want me to be here, keeping you company, waiting for my time to come inside.

10

The police are gone for what feels like hours. Once she stops crying, calms down a little, Anna realises just how hungry she still is. The sandwich has barely made a dent. She's tired now, too, and in pain. With no clock and no access to natural light, she has no way of knowing whether it's evening yet. It's the time she's enjoyed the most inside, watching the sunset that she could sometimes see from the corner of her cell window, as the light sank down into the west. Not tonight.

She could ask for more food. She should ask if she can go to the loo. But she's too tired now. She's going to be charged with murder, she knows it, and she'll be convicted. No matter that it's obviously a suicide, there's no motive, no reason why she should have done such a thing. They don't care that someone has died in horrific circumstances. They don't care that she didn't know the woman. She's already inside, a convicted prisoner. Of course it was her.

Tom seems tired, too, his precise edges dulled after an afternoon in the cells, a wilt to his stiff collar. He looks defeated. It's a formality now, the charging, the starting of the legal process for the prosecution of her for this homicide. She'll appear in front of the magistrates' court in the morning, video-link of course – at least she won't have to go in the sweat box to court.

It would almost come as a relief to get this over with. Anna is so tired. All she wants to do is lie down and close her eyes. She can only think as far as tonight. The prospect of spending years more inside means nothing to her now.

'Is there anyone I should contact?' Tom asks, the first thing he's said in hours.

'No,' she says. 'I don't have anyone.'

The words fall between them, bleak and cold. He looks her straight in the eye, a touch of sympathy flickering across his face.

'I'm sorry to hear it,' he says.

'It's not surprising,' she says.

There's nothing else to say. After a moment, his gaze drops and he starts to fiddle again with his pen.

'I imagine you know the procedure by now,' he says. 'If they charge you, most likely you'll be housed here in a secure wing in isolation. They might do that immediately, or else they might want to remand you for further questioning before they charge you. You'll stay in custody, either way.'

'I get it,' she says. 'I get it.' She doesn't, not really, but she's heard enough. She wants them all to stop talking, to leave her alone in a cell. She doesn't want to think anymore. At some point, she knows this is going to hit her properly and then she won't be able to fight it off, the fear and the horror, but for now, she'll settle for peace and quiet.

The door slams open. Anna jumps before slumping back into her seat. It's not Little and Large, though. It's the angry prison officer, pure fury radiating off him.

'You're out,' he says. When Anna doesn't respond, he leans over into her face and speaks even more loudly. 'Get up. You're out.'

'I don't understand,' she says.

'What's to understand? You're due to be released today. That's what's happening.'

She looks up at him, still unclear. 'A few moments ago I was being questioned on suspicion of murder. Now you're letting me go?'

'I'm not the one who makes the decisions round here,' he says, spitting out the words.

'But—'

'Listen, sweetheart, if you want to get out, I would suggest that you do exactly what you're told. Otherwise I'll have you up on a charge of assaulting a prison officer.'

'But . . .' She knows she's repeating herself but it's making no sense. She's still covered in a dead woman's blood.

'Listen, I'm serious,' he says. 'If you don't shut up and do exactly what you're told, you will be facing a much worse situation than a murder charge. Do you understand?'

His words are hyperbolic, but it's clear he's about to blow, veins popping on his forehead. He's bright red, more furious than Anna has seen him. Which, for this officer, is saying a lot.

'You're free to go,' he says. 'No charges.'

'But the police . . .'

'They'll be in touch,' he says, ominously. 'Now shut up and follow me.'

Anna glances over at Tom, who looks just as bemused. He shrugs.

'Better do what you're told,' he says.

Anna stands up, wincing as the blood returns fully to her

feet. Once she's on her feet she realises how much she needs to pee, the urgency overtaking even her confusion.

'I have to use the toilet,' she says.

The officer sighs loudly but signals out of the cell door. 'On the left,' he says.

She goes out as fast as she can, stumbling slightly as her legs start to work again. The phone is crushing her toes now, pushing them out of shape. Still, where it's hidden is better than the alternative.

Maybe she's being too complacent. Maybe they'll search her again before she leaves, just to make sure. It's a chance she'll have to take.

After she leaves the cubicle, she goes to the sink. There's a mirror of sorts above it, reflective plastic glued to the wall, and she glares at herself, her pallid reflection, as she washes her hands. She's grateful to finally have the chance to get the blood off, soaping them repeatedly under the water, even as it becomes too hot to bear.

11

The way out is the same as the way in, all that time ago. Anna remembers it like it was yesterday, the newness of it, the smell hitting her for the first time. The noise. Now she barely notices it, the occasional screams and cries nothing more than background buzz.

She's given a quick pat down, nothing more thorough, to her relief.

'Sign here,' an officer says, and thrusts a holdall at her, the one that she handed over on the day she first checked in. She remembers packing the tatty old thing the night before sentence – she'd had a choice of this or a smarter one that her sister had given to her as a birthday present only a few weeks before the accident, tags still on. Taking it into prison just hadn't seemed right.

It's half full of the clothes that she wasn't allowed to bring into jail, though she can't remember now what was wrong with them – too smart, too short, too fitted, most likely. Her corporate uniform, a skin she shed years ago. She looks down at the regulation grey tracksuit bottoms she's worn virtually every day since being inside, the fresh blood spatters encrusted now into the tired fabric.

'Can I get changed?' she says, looking at the officer behind the desk.

'Toilet's that way,' the woman replies, gesturing to her left.

Anna hoists the bag on to her right shoulder and picks up the clear bin bag containing the rest of her belongings with her left hand. She hadn't planned for this, for needing anything – she'd only packed her clothes to allay any suspicions from Naomi that she might not be planning a life on the outside. No one was meant to know what she was going to do next. But now? Now she doesn't have any idea what to do. This collision with death has broken her resolve, thrown everything into disarray. She could walk away now, stick to the plan. But the image of the dead woman persists. Kelly had put the phone under her pillow for a reason – the least Anna can do is attempt to find out what that reason was. Maybe it was just to hide it, but maybe there's more to it. Maybe there is something Kelly wanted her to do with it, something Kelly wanted her to find out.

On the other hand, she could get clear. The moment she's out, there's nothing to stop her from doing exactly what she wants, whether that means ending it all, or making a new start. Kelly Green is just a name to her. She doesn't owe her anything.

The memory is still there. The glassy stare of the dead eyes, the bloodstains on the wall. The pain in the woman's voice as she pleaded on the phone. Pity surges through Anna.

She's too tired to think straight. She'll sleep one more night. Then she'll work out what comes next.

Locking herself into a cubicle, she rummages through the holdall, holding up skirts and blouses that she remembers wearing in a different world. What was she thinking when she picked them for prison? She'll never need to wear anything like this again. She pulls out a pair of jeans and a stripy top and changes into them. She quickly sorts through the remaining clothes, keeping one blouse and skirt and scraping everything else into the bin bag before leaving it in the corner of the bathroom, the stained tracksuit rammed in along with them.

She sits down on the toilet seat and tips the phone from her trainer, looking at it properly for the first time. It's tiny. The logo under the screen says 'Zenca', and it fits easily into the palm of her hand. She locates the power button and presses it on, hoping that it still has power.

She's seen phones like this before, kicking round the prison. They're so small that they're easy to smuggle in – she heard about a man who was able to squeeze four up his arse. Anna winces at the thought. She's never tried to get hold of an illicit phone. She has no one to talk to, after all.

The screen lights up just as sadness is threatening to overwhelm her. She shakes the feeling off with relief, navigating her way through the limited menu. The absence of any security code surprises her slightly, but less so when she sees there's only one number stored. She looks at it for a moment, trying to commit it to memory. Just then, someone comes into the toilets and locks themselves in the other cubicle, sniffing and coughing as they pee. Anna stays silent, holding her breath until the flush goes and she's finally alone again.

She's about to explore the phone further when there's a thump on the door into the corridor. A voice calls. 'What you doing in there? Get a move on!'

Anna turns the phone off, pushes it deep into the holdall before going back out into reception.

The officer looks her up and down. 'I was expecting you in a ballgown, you took so long about it.'

'Sorry. Got distracted looking at my stuff.'

'Hmm. Well. You need to get going. There's only one more bus tonight. Or are you being picked up?'

Anna shakes her head. The officer doesn't ask further.

A few more signatures, nodded agreement to the probation appointment she'll need to keep in the afternoon. 'Make sure you're on time.'

'Thank you.'

Bus, train, probation office. Back to the beginning again.

It's a short step to freedom. The gate clangs shut behind her, and for a moment it's just her and the sky, the trees. She looks over at the dual carriageway, the cars rushing along at speed. She takes a step towards the road, then another, wondering if it might be simpler just to step out in front of one of the cars, throwing herself into the hands of fate.

She takes a deep breath, picks up her bag. That would be the easy way out, she knows it. So tempting, to cast off all the guilt and self-loathing. One step, two, that's all it would take.

It would satisfy the author of those hate-filled notes, the family to whom she's already dead. Something's changed, though. She'd convinced herself that an eye for an eye was the only reasonable response to her guilt, the debt to them payable only in blood, but Anna owes more than that now. The dead woman in the cell, begging for her help. Anna's not going to turn away.

She turns, walks along the pavement towards the bus stop. With any luck, she hasn't missed the last one into town.

Once she's at the stop, she drops her bags, and leans against the bus shelter. Looks like she's still in time, according to the timetable. She fishes a note, hopes the driver will give change.

Dusk is falling, the spring sky fading to dark blue. The cars have their lights on, streaking bright through the twilight. She looks further along the carriageway in the hope that she might see the bus. The urge to jump out has subsided, a tired resignation in its place. It all seems so fast. She guesses she'll get used to it, but for now—

Lights are coming towards her, straight for the bus stop. She bends to pick up her bag before stopping, frozen – this isn't a bus. It's not slowing down, either. She waits, transfixed, and then they're upon her, the car on the pavement, heading straight for her. The lights are blinding. She holds up her hands in supplication – it roars and it bangs and it hurts like it's happening to someone else, and she's in the air and—

CCTV

Charybdis is turning a bottle of whisky over and over in her hands, a manic smile on her face. Scylla shakes her head and reaches over to take the bottle from Charybdis's hands, but she pushes back at her so aggressively that Scylla falls from her chair. Her companion might be thin but she's very strong. She opens the bottle and takes a swig, another, holding it out to Scylla with a mocking expression. Scylla turns away with disgust on her face, but Charybdis doesn't stop, waving it under the other's nose until she gets up and walks away from the table. Charybdis opens her mouth, laughing, then drinks until the bottle is half empty.

She puts the bottle down and gets up, picking up a glass from the table and throwing it at the wall, followed by another glass, another glass. Next, she takes the chair and smashes it against the table until a leg breaks off. All the way through this, her mouth is open. If there were sound, you would hear her scream.

Scylla reappears. The women wrestle over the chair leg before Charybdis hits Scylla with it, as Scylla shields her head with her arms.

Suddenly, Charybdis throws the chair leg away from her. She's crying. Scylla turns away, walks off screen.

12

'Are you all right? Wake up! What the hell just happened?'

There's a man yelling in Anna's face, and she wants it to stop so she can go back to sleep. But he keeps screaming, shouting, pulling at her.

More noise, more shouting. Anna is becoming increasingly aware of her surroundings, the sensations that slam into her body as she comes round. Judging by the pain in her head, she must have been knocked out. She's lying on hard ground, her leg at an awkward angle, torso twisted. Everything hurts. Slowly, she moves her hand out, turning it from one side to the other.

The man jumps back, catching his breath. 'You're alive.'

'Sort of,' Anna says, every word an effort. She shifts her head round to face him, blinking.

'Are you OK?' he asks.

Now that she knows her hand works, her neck too, Anna thinks she should risk trying to sit up. She pushes herself up very slowly and carefully so that she's in a sitting position, pleased to find her back isn't broken.

'How many fingers am I holding up?' the man says.

Anna blinks again, too distracted to concentrate. 'Three,' she says, without bothering to check.

'That's it, you've got concussion. We need to get you to a hospital immediately. I'm going to call an ambulance.'

Anna still hasn't looked at him properly, too concerned with working out what the hell just happened to her, but at this she does. It's Tom, the solicitor.

'Please don't,' she says. She catches the glint of his mobile phone and lurches forward towards it, but not fast enough. He slips it back in his pocket.

'You've just been hit by a car,' he says. 'You need to go to hospital.'

As he says it, her confusion fades. She hears the roar of the car echoing in her ears, so real she flinches. It might have been an accident. But it might not . . . She squints up at Tom.

'I don't want to go to hospital. How do you know I was hit by a car?'

'You don't remember?'

Anna shakes her head. She's checked her toes, her ankles and knees. The children's rhyme runs through her mind – she puts her fingers up to her face. *Eyes and ears and mouth and nose.* She's still in one piece. Just about.

'I walked out of the gate to wait for the bus,' she says. 'I was standing on the pavement . . .' Her voice trails off. She thinks back: the dark, the lights, the crash. Was the car coming straight at her?

I WANT TO KILL YOU. The letters of the note dance across her mind. Only words, though. Surely?

'That could have been really nasty,' Tom says. He reaches

his hand out to her and she takes it, allowing him to pull her up to her feet. She lets go of his hand once she's upright, seeing if she can balance on her own. Wobbly, but not terrible. One step, two. She can walk, the shaking of her legs as much down to shock as anything else.

Tom's wandering round the area close to the bus stop, looking at the ground. 'Tyre tracks. Where the car mounted the pavement,' he says, pointing at the edge of the kerb, a short distance away, 'and hit you there.' He turns around, Anna following his gaze. 'You must have been thrown clear. I came out of the gate just after it happened. If you'd hit the bus stop, you might have been a goner. Do you really not remember anything?'

He's right, Anna can see that. She's in an area of scrub that runs alongside the road, behind the bus stop. She shakes her head, not sure how much she wants to say to him, the blaze of the headlights still lingering in her mind.

'I bet they thought you were dead,' he says.

'Maybe that's why they did a runner. Could have been a drunk driver.' The words stick to her tongue. This will be the moment he shows his contempt for her, for what he learned about her in the police interview.

'Maybe,' he says. Nothing else on the subject. 'There's some smashed glass there – the impact must have taken out their headlight. Not much for the police to go on.'

'No police,' Anna says.

'But—'

'No, I don't want to speak to the police. I've talked to them enough today to last me a lifetime.'

Tom opens his mouth as if to argue, closes it again. Anna takes a couple more steps, surprised to find that most of her is still working, bruised as it might be. He keeps his hand held out to her as if worried she might fall at any moment.

'So what do you want to do?'

'I don't know. I guess I want to go home,' she says, laughing, though it's a sound devoid of humour. 'But I don't have a home. Not anymore. I have an assortment of cardboard boxes somewhere, and a family that's disowned me. So what I want to do now is to get to a station and from there to London, to the hostel where probation has booked me a place for the night, and then get some sleep. That's as far as I can go right now.'

Tom shifts his weight backwards on to his heels, rocking slightly from side to side. His mouth twists. 'A hostel?'

'Yes, a hostel. They've done well to find me a place. Do you know how stretched resources are?'

'Yes, true. It's very late, though. There's nowhere else you can go?'

'There really isn't,' Anna says. 'But it's not your problem. I'll sort myself out from here. Please stop fussing over me.'

'I'm sorry . . .'

'Don't be sorry. I don't need an apology. I need to sort myself out from here. Thank you for picking me up. And thank you for representing me earlier. You can go now, though. Your work here is done.'

With as much dignity as she can muster, Anna brushes down her jeans, dislodging various bits of earth and dead leaves that have stuck to her arse and her thighs. She looks around for her bag, gripped with a sudden fear that it might have been stolen in the drama, but it's still lying by the pavement where she dropped it. She picks it up and settles herself down by the bus stop to wait.

'What are you doing?' Tom says. For a supposedly intelligent man, he's slow on the uptake.

'I'm waiting for the bus.'

'I'm not letting you go off on your own,' he says. 'You're not thinking straight. You might have a head injury.'

Anna puts her hand up instinctively to her head, traces the bump she can feel above her forehead. He's probably right, but she's finding it very hard to care. She just wants to get on to the bus and rest her face against the cold glass of the window.

Tom reaches into his pocket and pulls out his phone. Anna lurches towards it again.

'I'm not calling the police,' he says. 'I'm getting a taxi. You're staying at my house tonight.'

'I don't want to.'

'I don't care.'

'What about the hostel? They're expecting me.'

'I'll call them, let them know that your legal representative has made a new arrangement.'

He's got an answer for everything. Anna looks at him closely, trying to make out his features in the dark. He's keen to help. Instead of this making her trust him more, her suspicions harden. She can't even be sure that someone has tried to run her down – she doesn't have any clear memory of what happened. Even the details she thought she had are slipping away.

While this all loops round her mind, ever increasing circles of paranoia, Tom's been tapping away at the screen of his phone. He could be contacting anyone. She scrabbles for her bag and moves away from him, ready to run.

'What are you doing? I've got a taxi on the way,' he says.

She's being ridiculous. He doesn't look dangerous. He looks like a schoolboy, all smooth cheeks and concerned eyes. She should be careful. But she's so tired now, so beyond tired, she can't face running.

Shortly afterwards, a black Prius pulls up. Tom ushers her into it and takes her bag to the boot. Anna leans her head against the back of the seat, relief washing over her. She's exhausted; the twenty-four hours of hell are almost over. She shuts her eyes, the fragments of the day laid out in her mind like shards of broken glass.

13

Tom starts making calls as soon as he gets in the cab, but Anna tunes out every word. After the cacophony of prison, the sound of a single voice isn't that annoying, his deep tones almost soothing. She watches the lights flash past the window, trying and failing to take it all in.

She should just go to the hostel. She knows what men are capable of, the stories she's heard over the last years. He's a total stranger.

The car radio is tuned to Magic FM and there's a comfort in that, the fact that even after all these years, the playlist is unchanged. If she shuts her eyes, it could be any journey she took back before it all went wrong, 'I Don't Want to Miss a Thing' segueing into 'Got My Mind Set on You', same as it ever was. Between that and the rumble of Tom's voice, Anna finally goes to sleep, her head leaning against the car window.

She doesn't wake until they draw to a stop and Tom shakes her gently by the shoulder. 'We're here.'

She's too out of it to do anything other than follow him sleepily out of the car, feeling the lumps on her head again as she does. Her legs are stiff as she leans against the vehicle, waiting for Tom to take her bag out of the boot.

'Here we go,' he says. 'This is me.'

As the car pulls away, she looks at the long street of neat, terraced houses with gardens at the front, suburban and entirely peaceful. Nothing bad could ever happen here. She laughs at the delusion. Net curtains hide the worst crimes.

'Come on,' Tom says, pulling her out of her reverie. 'Let's get you inside. I've sorted things with probation.'

He leads her up the front path, through a red door and into the house, stopping at the bottom of a flight of stairs.

'Tea? Something to eat?'

She shakes her head. 'I just want to go to sleep,' she says.

'Of course,' he says, and takes her upstairs to a small bedroom at the back. There's a single bed covered in papers and a desk piled high with books. He sweeps the bed clear and pulls back the duvet.

'Here you go,' he says. 'I'll show you where the bathroom is, then I'll leave you to it.'

Within minutes Anna is under the duvet, light off. Peace at last, but now her mind's spinning, flashes of death and handcuffs, the jeering faces of the police officers, the bloodied throat of the woman in the bunk below. Despite the homely smells of washing powder and books, she suddenly tastes that strong iron tang in her mouth.

She turns from one side to the other, trying to dislodge the thoughts, picturing the viscous blood on her hands. But it's too quiet now, the bed too soft, the duvet smothering her, heavy in its warm embrace. A fox screams in the distance and she sits bolt upright. She shouldn't be here; she shouldn't have let this man talk her into coming home with him. He's lulled her into a false sense of security, catching her when her guard was down.

There's a creak outside the door and she's out of bed immediately, taking a fighting stance in the middle of the floor, feet wide, fists clenched. The door opens and, with a shriek, Anna launches herself on the intruder, kicking hard.

'What the hell?' Tom shouts. 'Calm down, Anna. It's me. Tom. It's OK.'

He takes hold of her by the wrists and after a few moments Anna stops, sitting down heavily on the bed. He lets go, backing away to the door.

'I'm sorry,' he says. 'I didn't mean to scare you. I just wanted to give you a clean towel, check to see if you're OK. I'm worried about your head.'

She looks at him, at the chaos in the room, the scratch on his face where she lashed out at him. Slowly her heart rate starts to come down, her breathing slows.

'I'm sorry,' she says. 'I thought . . .'

'I know what you thought. I'm sorry. I should have knocked. I should have told you I'd be checking on you, come to that. It's the concussion. I mean, in case you have concussion.'

'I know,' she says. 'It's just . . .'

Freeze, flight, fight. She used to freeze, but once flight stopped being an option, fighting became her default response, the only way to shut a situation down before it got out of hand. There's so much she's going to have to unlearn.

'I'm sorry,' he says again. 'Go back to bed. I'll do my best not to disturb you. But if you don't mind, I do want to check in on you through the night. Just in case.' He puts the towel on a chair by the door.

She looks him up and down, the dark hair now dishevelled, his cheek marked with her scratch, a small smear of blood where he's wiped at it. He's harmless. Mostly.

'OK,' she says. 'OK.' It's been so long since anyone looked out for her, she doesn't quite know what to do with it. But the idea of leaving now, walking out into the cold night – it's too much. She sits back down on the bed. Tom leaves the room, shutting the door behind him, and after a couple of moments Anna gets back under the duvet.

Whether it's safe here or not, she has nothing left. This final altercation has left her spent, out of all reserves. For all she cares now, Tom can murder her in her bed. Just make it quick. She rolls over, tucking the duvet tightly around herself, and this time the warmth doesn't oppress her, but soothes.

14

the little boy is running towards her laughing the sun shining and the sky blue overhead follow me follow me he says and he leads her through the trees down the shore to the sea and he's running through the surf spray making rainbows in the air and she's laughing too until a bigger wave knocks him off his feet pulls him in and fast as she tries to catch him he slips through her fingers falling falling into the depths of the sea—

This is when she always wakes up, heart pounding, slick with sweat, tears sliding down her face. Anna lies still for a moment, trying to collect herself, work out where she is.

The scent of coffee and toast in the air, the clink of cutlery on china. A faint murmur of voices from a radio. Anna rolls over in bed, only half-awake. The bed is comfy – she stretches, cat-like, calming down as the effects of the nightmare wear off.

She has no idea what the time is, but it's light outside, a grey sky apparent above the rows of houses opposite. Memory returns. She's in Tom's house. But she can't keep lazing here, smelling the coffee. She needs to get on. She'll have to go into London to keep her probation appointment – that's a necessary chore. But after that . . . she swallows a lump in her throat. One thing at a time.

Getting out of bed, Anna looks out over the gardens from which she heard the fox yowl the night before. Suburbs.

Once upon a time, this would have been her idea of hell, obsessed as she was with the bright lights of the big city, working every hour she could, slipping into a taxi in the small hours through London's deserted streets to her Shoreditch flat, surrounded by concrete and glass. Now she's transfixed by what she can see out of the window, trees bursting into blossom, the April sky a vibrant blue dotted with ragged white clouds.

The past is a different country, but sometimes Anna looks back on the person she was and feels like she was living in a completely different world, its customs alien to her now. All she cared about was advancement through the ranks, her professional success. She cancelled on her friends, her family, and saw her colleagues more in a day than she'd see those dearest to her in a year, maybe two. If only she'd known. If only she'd had any idea what was to come, who she would become. She'd have turned her back on the training contract in an instant. All those hours spent in pursuit of her career, time robbed from her family, from everything that really mattered.

Sometimes, she'd look out of the window of her newly developed apartment, floors above the ground, and her head would swim. Not just because of the height of it. The vertigo came from a sense of unmooring, nothing connecting her to reality. She'd thought this was the way to guarantee her rise through the corporate ranks, nothing to hold her back. What it meant was that there was no one there to catch her when she fell.

Not like here. There's a breeze coming in from the open sash window. It carries a scent of earth, greenery, overlaid by the coffee coming from downstairs. The house where she grew up used to back on to a garden just like this, the cherry tree at the bottom of the lawn opening out its snowy blossom.

The quiet, the birdsong, the green leaves and white flowers and the smell of the earth. It's dangerous, she realises. She can't afford to forget her reality, no matter how tempting the surroundings she's in seem. She doesn't even know where she is – it could be any suburb, any town. She wasn't paying enough attention the night before – so stupid of her, so risky. It's a trap, too good to be true.

It's time to get out, before it's too late. She knows how people operate. Even if Tom is one of the good guys, she doesn't want him involved anymore. She's got a job to do, before her one-way trip to the sea. Throwing her clothes back on, pushing her feet back into her trainers, she picks up her bag, ready to sneak out of the house before he can stop her.

She's about to creep down the stairs when she catches sight of the bathroom door, which is standing slightly ajar. She should leave, but it's the last bathroom she'll see for hours. The room acts further to allay her fears, a clean, soothing space with a scent of sandalwood in the air. Homely, reassuring – there's a fern on the windowsill, a soap shaped like a fish hanging from a rope in the shower.

Checking the cabinet above the sink, she finds some moisturising cream and smooths it on to her right hand with relief, the itching soothed for once. Then she brushes her teeth with her finger and a squeeze of toothpaste she takes from the tube on the basin. Her eyes leer back at her in the mirror, the furrow between her brows seemingly permanent now. Only thirty but she feels about fifty. Looks it, too.

Now she's just wasting time. Who cares what she looks like? Such things ceased to matter a long time ago. She needs to get out of here. She shuts the bathroom door noiselessly behind her.

One step down, the next. A creak on the third and she holds her breath, unsure if the noise will travel through the muttered chatter she can hear coming from the radio in the kitchen. She could take Tom on in a fight, but everything is hurting, all the bruises and scrapes from the day before, the place where she hit her head on the wall still throbbing.

It would be so easy to sink back into that comfortable bed, to go back to sleep. But she can't risk it. She's got to keep moving.

Next step down, then the next. She's nearly there. Bottom step, on to the hall carpet, moving as quietly as possible. Her hand grasps the latch of the front door, freedom a second away—

Barking, a drawn-out burst of it, and something warm and furry throws itself at her.

'Anna,' Tom says, following behind the small dog. 'You OK?'

Anna is frozen in place, hand still up to the latch of the door. She smiles, a tide of red surging up her neck into her cheeks. 'I was just . . .'

'Why do you need to leave? It's all under control.'

She turns the latch to pull the door open but Tom blocks it, his hand firm above hers.

'I want to go,' she says.

'You haven't had any breakfast.'

'I don't want breakfast. I want to leave.'

'What's so important?'

She turns her head, looks up at him, still with her hand on the latch. He couldn't begin to understand. She wants to push him out of the way, make a run for it.

'Come on, I'm going to make you an omelette. Then I'll take you to the station.'

'I don't want an omelette.' Her fist clenches at her side, the other hand still on the latch. Her breath's coming so fast she's soon light-headed. Why the hell is he bothering with her? Why can't he leave her alone?

'There's coffee,' he says, smiling. The dog is now sitting at his feet – it's fluffy and brown, a pink tongue hanging out the side of its mouth. Totally unthreatening. Flight diminishes in her. Fight, too. The smell of coffee returns, and she hasn't got the strength to resist anymore. She lowers her hand from the door, smiles.

'Yes, please,' she says. 'But I can't stay long. I don't even know where I am. I really appreciate your hospitality last night, but I need to get to London. I don't know how long it's going to take.'

Tom starts to laugh. 'Didn't you see where we were going last night? We're in Oxford.'

'I didn't see, no,' Anna says. The sense of security engendered by the dog, the coffee – it's disappeared now, a cold chill in its place. She's not where she thought she was. She swore she would never set foot here again.

'Are you sure we're in Oxford?' she says, conscious immediately that it's the stupidest question, hoping still that he'll

76

tell her it's a sick joke. Her mouth is drying out, her heart rate rising. There is drumming in her ears, sweat breaking out on her neck, the back of her hands.

'Yes, Oxford. I'm sorry – I assumed you realised. It's the nearest city to the prison, after all.'

'I wasn't thinking . . . I've got to get out of here. Before anyone sees me . . .'

'We're quite far from the station,' he says. 'You can't just walk.' He's still laughing.

'This isn't funny. I promised I'd never come here again. I promised her. I can't be here.' She's trying to control it, but the panic's got full hold of her now, her hands shaking as she tries to make him understand.

The dog gets to its feet and walks over to her, its head by her hand, leaning against her knee. She's about to push it off, but the warm weight gives her pause. She puts her hand into its fur, taking in a deep breath, another.

'I was asleep all the way here,' she says. 'I guess I should have realised, but I just wasn't thinking.'

'I understand,' he says. 'I'm sorry for laughing. Please, have some coffee, and let's work out what you need to do together. I'm not your enemy, Anna. I'm your friend.'

A friend. It's been a long time since she had one of those. One she could really trust, at least. She never let anyone get close inside, tried to keep it safely transactional, however good the intentions of those around her might have been. You scratch my back, I'll watch yours – though she only ever pissed off one inmate enough to need protection, the woman furious at the legal advice she'd forced Anna to give her. It wasn't like a defence could be magicked out of nowhere, however hard Anna scoured her basic criminal law knowledge to find one. Hard to explain away a kilo of cocaine in your coat pocket.

'You can't tell me you don't need a friend,' he says. It's as if he's read her mind, her lonely thoughts laid out bare in front of him. She rubs the dog's head, speechless, before she walks into the kitchen and sits down at the table.

15

Tom takes a mug out the cupboard and pours coffee into it from a cafetière on the table. The mug has a picture of Snoopy on it wearing sunglasses, and the sheer incongruity of it makes Anna smile, albeit weakly. Proper coffee for the first time in three years. She used to throw double espressos down like they were water, not taking even a moment to relish the flavour. Now, she rolls the rich brew around her mouth, appreciating every nuance of its taste, aroma.

'I've missed this,' she says.

'I'll bet. I don't think there's any way I could do without coffee.'

'It's surprising what you get used to,' Anna says.

'I guess so,' he says. There's silence between them for a moment as they savour their drinks. Tom puts his cup down on the table at last, an air of decision about him. 'About what you were just saying,' he says.

She knows immediately what's coming, puts up her hand, turning away from him.

'What you said just now, about swearing never to come back here. Why was that? Is it to do with your original conviction? Do you have family in Oxford?'

Her head's down. She's tracing a pattern in a splash of coffee that's on the table in front of her, pulling it out into long spikes like a firework. 'I don't want to talk about it.'

'I know you don't,' he says.

'One of the first rules of prison. You learn not to ask.'

'You're not in prison now, though.'

She glances up at him. The panic she was feeling before has subsided, but it's left its trace, her heart still pumping faster than it ought to be, her breathing still ragged. He meets her gaze and for a long moment they look at each other, the tension seeping out of the air. He's right, she's not in prison anymore. She remembers his words in the cell, *that's tough*, a kinder judge than she's ever been to herself.

She takes a deep breath. 'Yes, I have family in Oxford. My sister. I nearly killed my nephew. The last I know of him, he was on life support. I didn't mean to, but I did all the same. It was when I was a newly qualified solicitor. At one of the magic circle firms – you know what they're like?'

Tom nods. 'I escaped from Linklaters myself. I needed to get my life back.'

'Then you know exactly. I spent my life cancelling on my friends, my family. I practically never spent time with my nephew. Sally – my sister – she insisted I commit to a weekend with them, to take Toby out for the day while they went to a wedding. But my boss was equally insistent I come into the office on Saturday, to finish up work on a contract. I told him I couldn't, that I'd finish the document on the Friday evening and there was no way I could work longer. But I was so stressed, I fucked it up. I mean, fucked up completely.'

Tom nods again.

'I couldn't bear it. As soon as I realised what I'd done, I

walked out. I went to the nearest pub and drank myself stupid. I don't even know where the night went. I came round in my flat on the sofa, with my sister calling me to wake me up. I shouldn't have gone. I shouldn't have agreed to drive. But I'd let them down so many times before . . .'

'Those years I was at Linklaters were the worst in my life,' Tom says.

A humourless laugh. 'I'd have said that before I went to prison.'

He doesn't reply.

Anna suppresses a feeling of guilt – he's trying to be understanding.

Now for the hardest bit. 'I got to Oxford, got straight into the car with him. I was meant to be taking him to a bird sanctuary near Chipping Norton that he loved. I didn't check the car seat properly. So when I lost control of the car on one of those country roads, he wasn't strapped in.'

'What happened?'

'I don't know exactly. I was knocked out by the impact. The other driver said that I was well over on the other side of the road, going too fast for the bend. It was a head-on collision. Because the car seat wasn't properly secured, he went through the windscreen. He broke his neck in the impact – they told us he'll never walk again. Not to mention the other injuries he suffered. He might never even regain consciousness.'

'What's his name?'

'Toby,' she says, barely forcing the word out.

Tom reaches out, takes her hand in his. She pushes it away but he persists, taking hold of her again.

'You don't have to be nice to me,' she says. 'I don't deserve it.'

'I can't imagine having to live with something like that.'

81

She stares at his hand, the shape of the veins under the skin, the dark hairs on his wrist.

'I don't know if I can,' she says, her voice lower still. There's a long silence. She's looking at Tom, but it's not him she's seeing: it's Toby, smiling at her from the back seat of the car as they drove off. It's his grieving, angry parents immediately after she was sentenced to six years for her part in his injuries.

'Do you know what you're going to do now?' Tom says. 'Now that you're out.'

She starts laughing, can't stop, a choking sound more like tears. There's a long pause. 'There isn't much family. Only my sister Sally. My dad died years ago, and my mum just after I went into prison.' She pauses, swallows. 'My fault, too – Sally told me, the last letter she sent me. I haven't heard for years how Toby is doing. He could be dead for all I know. It's unbearable.'

Abruptly, she pushes herself up to her feet and empties the contents of her holdall on to the hallway floor. Pausing only to tuck the miniature mobile phone into a pair of socks, she picks up the sheaf of letters she's kept tied up with string, takes it into the kitchen.

'This is what my family thinks of me,' she says, unfolding the letters one by one, placing them in front of him, her actions stiffer and stiffer as the poison from the words leaks on to her fingers, back into her bloodstream.

IT'S YOUR FAULT. ALL YOUR FAULT
YOU DESTROYED HIS LIFE
NO ONE WILL CARE IF YOU KILL YOURSELF
I WANT TO KILL YOU

Tom looks through them, his expression grave. He pulls out the last one, puts it on the table in front of him.

'That car last night? Do you think . . .' He taps the letter, not finishing the sentence.

Anna bites her lip. She's been avoiding the thought. For a moment the headlights shine in her mind, heading straight for her. She shakes her head.

'No,' she says. 'It was an accident. It wasn't deliberate.'

He raises an eyebrow but she shakes her head. 'I refuse to accept it. He's not a killer. Nor my sister. They're family. They're furious, but they wouldn't try and hurt me.' She's not sure she believes it – saying it may make it so.

'If you say so,' Tom says, his voice sceptical. 'I won't push it. Tell me about these.' He points at the pile of notes again.

'These were the only letters I got when I was inside,' Anna says. 'For three years. One would turn up every couple of months. I don't know how they got past the censors, maybe because they used envelopes from my sister's company so they looked official.'

'They're horrible.'

'They are. But I deserve them,' she says.

He shakes his head. 'This is why we have a criminal justice system,' he says. 'Otherwise we'd have the justice of the mob.'

'Maybe we should,' she says. She takes the letters back from him and folds them up, putting them back into their pile.

'Your sister wrote them?' he says.

'Her husband. Toby's dad. I know his handwriting. But it's her office on the letterhead. It's a joint effort.'

'Have you tried getting back in touch?'

'I ruined their son's life, Tom. There's nothing for me to say. The only news they want to hear is that I'm dead.'

She's said it now, matter of fact as she can.

'That can't be true.'

She smiles at him. He has tried to understand, but still grasps so little. 'I've come to terms with it. I had it all planned out.' This last sentence said in a mutter.

He hears it, though. 'What? What did you have planned?'

She's not ready to reply. His phone starts to ring and with a sense of relief, she slips the letters back into her bag.

The relief is short-lived. He ends the call almost immediately, turning back to her, his expression sharp. 'What did you have planned, Anna?'

She looks him dead in the eye, and something crosses the space between them, a communication of some sense of the bleakness she's inhabited since the fatal crash all those years ago.

She's out of words, exhausted by the revelations. Tom must sense this. Without asking, he makes another pot of coffee, busying himself with rinsing out the cafetière and boiling the kettle. He gets her a clean cup and opens a packet of chocolate digestives before sitting back down at the table and pushing the packet towards her.

'What's changed?' he says.

'What do you mean?' The question startles her.

'If that's what you were going to do, why would you bother jumping out of the way of the car last night when it was heading straight for you.'

'I . . . well, I guess it was instinctive,' she says, noting his interrogative tone.

He nods, as if he guessed already that was what she was going to say. 'Or why didn't you just tell the police it was you who killed that poor woman? If you're so keen to punish yourself, confessing to something you didn't do would work well.'

84

Confronted with her twisted logic, Anna's cheeks burn.

He continues his attack. 'What were you planning on doing? You talked about going to London – were you going to throw yourself off a bridge or something?'

The words come unbidden to her tongue. 'I was going to go to St Leonards and walk into the sea.'

He shakes his head, barely able to control a laugh. 'Seriously?'

'We used to go there on holiday when we were kids,' she says with dignity. 'I wasn't just trying to copy Virginia Woolf.'

He shakes his head again, but the smile is fading. 'I'm sorry,' he says. 'I know it's not funny.' He leans back on his chair, drumming the fingers on his right hand on the table.

The noise drills into her – she wants to slap his hand quiet, wipe the stupid smile off his stupid face. 'It's not funny at all.'

'I'm sorry,' he says again, and with that her indignation drains out. 'Are you still thinking about it?'

'It's not like I have anything else.'

'There's always something else.' He must be able to read her expression, because he continues, 'Don't worry, I'm no God-botherer. But I do believe that. Do you really believe that your time here on earth has run its course? There's nothing unfinished left for you?'

Slowly, she shakes her head. 'It's how I was feeling then. Before.'

'And now?'

'I'm not sure.' A voice rises unprompted in her head. *I'm begging you. Help me.* She swallows hard. 'I think there might be something.'

OUTSIDE

Some people are incapable of listening.

You should tell that bitch to shut up. It took all my self-control not to punch her in the throat. All her stupid questions, over and over and over.

They're all so fucking STUPID. We're not here to talk, we're here to learn – learn from the master.

My heart was thumping so hard I was sure you'd hear it. I was ready to explode as she kept yapping on. You're too polite. They all take advantage of you. I want to build a tall, wide wall between you and all those people who keep taking up all your time.

It could be just you and me. You'd get all the work done. I'd protect your time, your assets. No need to share. I won't take up your precious attention with stupid questions. I'll research for you, index for you, type for you, anything for you.

And when you're tired and you're stressed and you've had enough, I know exactly what you need to calm you down, my hands starting on your back, a massage, just the way I bet you like it, down and down and down.

Oh professor, I'm blushing again. You need to stop putting these thoughts into my head.

16

'Kelly Green?' Tom says.

'Kelly Green. I can't leave it like that.'

'You should, though. It won't do you any good, poking round there. You've been questioned on suspicion of her murder.'

She looks at him, shakes her head. 'They let me go. You didn't see what it looked like. The blood . . .' she says. 'I should have helped her. If only I hadn't taken that pill . . .'

'Pill?'

She swallows. 'I took a pill before she was brought into the cell. Something my pad mate gave me – sorry, my cell mate. A tranquilliser. Just to help me sleep.'

'Why didn't you tell me that before?'

'I was worried for a moment that it had made me kill her – people do weird shit when they're on that sort of medication, don't they? I was scared the police might think so. Or you.' As she says it, she sees for the first time the full absurdity of the idea.

'I told you I believed you,' he says. 'I still do. More, if any-thing, having spent a bit of time with you.'

'Yeah, I present so well. Filthy, exhausted, trying to sneak off first thing in the morning. Such innocent behaviour.'

'It's not that,' he says, not rising to her sarcasm. 'It was what happened last night.'

'What about last night?'

'The car,' he says. 'The car running you down.'

'It was an accident,' Anna says. 'Wasn't it?'

'I wasn't sure what it was I was watching, but I saw it happen,' he says. 'I saw the whole thing, just as I walked out of the gate. You were standing next to the bus stop, on the edge of the pavement. I saw the headlights of the car. It seemed to slow down before it turned, very deliberately, and drove straight at you.'

'What do you mean?' Anna says, her fingers tightening into the dog's fur.

'Someone ran you down, Anna,' Tom says.

'It was just an accident,' she says. 'You know what drivers can be like.' Her words fade away.

'I saw it, I tell you. A little white car, heading straight for you, revving its engine.'

'Who would have wanted to do that?'

'I don't know. Is there anything else you're not telling me?'

A ripple of that terror she felt in the cell runs through Anna, the whispered words *I thought I could trust you* an echo in her mind. Tom's face is guileless, his eyes bright. She could go through the hidden phone with him in search of any clues. Maybe he could help her work out who Kelly was talking to.

At the thought of that conversation, something tugs in Anna's brain. Kelly said she was nicked at the Westgate Centre. There's a Westgate Centre in Oxford – Anna's sure of it. She remembers it from her university days. It makes sense that Kelly would have come from somewhere round here, given the proximity of the prison to the city. She mentioned a hostel, too.

Tom lives in Oxford. Maybe he'll know where the hostels are where Kelly might have stayed. She opens her mouth to ask him, shuts it again.

On the face of it, she can trust him, but her gut's telling her not to. This isn't her secret to share. Yes, he's open, maybe too much so. She remembers the girl she bunked with, back at the start of her sentence. She was open, too, full of useful information, warnings about who to avoid in the prison, who to befriend. Anna told her everything, only to find rumours of it everywhere she went, twisted and distorted and used against her throughout the rest of the wing. Her former friend smirked in the background when Anna was jumped in the shower by the resident hard nut screaming 'CHILD-KILLER!', punching her in the face in time to the yells. She made no effort to help Anna or point out that the accusation was false, that Toby had not in fact died.

Tom doesn't seem untrustworthy, but nor did that early pad mate. Anna is going to figure this one out on her own.

'If you take my advice, you'll leave this one alone. It's nothing to do with you. Just keep your own side of the street clean,' he says. 'Promise me you'll keep your nose out of it.'

She raises an eyebrow at his insistence, keeps quiet. Time to change the subject.

'I'm going with you,' Tom says again. She had tried and failed to convince him that she could manage her trip to London alone.

'I can look after myself,' she says. She's trying to withdraw from him, though he's not making it easy for her.

'It's probation. I don't want you to get in any trouble for not staying in the hostel last night,' Tom says.

'I thought you said it was sorted.'

'I left a message,' he says. 'I'm sure it's fine. But we don't need any problems with your licence before it's even begun.'

Anna glares at him, about to have a go, before remembering how tired she'd been, how little she'd wanted to fight her way into London and find the bed she'd been allocated for the night.

'It would have been too late anyway,' she says. 'By the time I got out. It was a total shitshow.'

'You could say that,' he says, and suddenly they're both laughing, the mundanity of the words in the face of the horror she's faced so ridiculous it's the only possible response. 'I'm serious about coming with you,' he continues. 'I want to explain what happened to probation. The important thing is that you're there on time, but just in case . . . What will you be doing? Do you have a job lined up?'

Anna looks at him, the moment of mutual understanding now gone, collapsed to earth. He has no idea.

'A job? Me? That's the last thing on my mind.'

'You'll need to support yourself somehow,' he says.

He's right. She knows he's right, but having any kind of future, taking care of herself in any way – that hadn't been the plan. She hasn't caught up with the change yet.

'Look, I know it seems a bit remote given what you were thinking, what you were going to do when you got out. That was before, though. You're not going to find out about Kelly overnight.'

She opens her mouth to argue.

'Hear me out,' he continues, without giving her a moment to speak. 'I know what we've just discussed about that car, too. You might be at risk, there's no way of knowing for sure. But one thing is certain: you're safer here than out there, in a hostel – or worse, sleeping on the streets in London.'

She nods. Maybe he's got a point.

'So. You were a lawyer before you went inside,' he says.

'I was. A former solicitor. Now, with a disciplinary record. Not to mention prison. There aren't many firms that would take someone on with a conviction like mine,' she says.

There's another pause. The conversation has become awkward, all elbows and knees.

'We can give you a job,' he says.

'What are you talking about?'

'We have stacks of work that we need to have done. Case preparation, sorting out bundles, writing up statements. Going through the unused material that the prosecution invariably dump on us at the last moment. Everything.'

'I can't work on people's cases. I've got a serious criminal conviction. I'm on licence for the next three years. Not to mention the fact that I've never done any criminal work other than what we covered at law school and my own case.'

'None of that matters. Not if you work under my supervision. I mean, obviously you wouldn't be able to appear in court or anything like that, but I can't see any reason why you shouldn't work for us in the office.'

'You must be desperate,' Anna says. It's a tempting offer, she can't deny it. The letter she received from the Law Society striking her off as a solicitor was one of the worst moments of the last few years for her, although it was a punishment she knew she more than deserved.

'To be perfectly honest, we are desperate. You may not have realised how bad things have got, but the system is in meltdown with all the cuts to Legal Aid. I mean, we won't be able to afford to pay you much, but we need someone starting yesterday, even.'

'Prisoner slave labour, eh?' Anna says, but she's smiling, at least for a moment, indulging the fantasy of it before reality hits again. 'I'm meant to be in London, though. That's the terms of the licence. Maybe working in a café or something. I don't know exactly.'

'If we turn up there and tell them you've got a proper job already lined up and somewhere to stay, too, they'll be overjoyed. I can assure you of that.'

'I don't have anywhere to stay, though,' Anna says, before realising that his face is pregnant with meaning. 'No. Absolutely not. I can't do that. I can't stay here.'

'Why not?'

'It's obvious. You don't know me. I've been in prison for three years. All the reasons.'

He holds his hand up. 'I know what you did,' he said. 'I know it's bad, but it's not dishonesty. I've spent several hours with you yesterday and today. I'm a pretty good judge of character. I think we can risk it.'

Anna sighs. He's not making this easy for her. 'You're my solicitor. Not my friend. You're getting over-involved.' The irony of this hits her. 'Keep your own side of the road clean.'

Tom grimaces. 'Touché,' he says. 'Fair point. I've got a good feeling about you, though.'

She's getting nowhere with him. Besides, the thought that there might be a future for her in which she could use some

94

of her experience, some of her skillset, is too tempting. It's a fantasy, but a hard one to refuse.

'I'm going to find myself somewhere to live, though,' she says. 'You can't argue me out of that.'

'I wouldn't dream of it,' he says. 'Look, we'll give this address for now, OK? Then we'll find something else. There's a charity helping women prisoners – I'll put you in touch with them when we get back from London. Maybe they can help you find somewhere.'

'Thank you,' Anna says. 'You're too kind.'

He flushes pink, his hair flopping down over his eyes. Anna feels a sudden urge to reach out and smooth the lock back. She grips her hands behind her back.

'We should get on,' Tom says, not acknowledging her thanks, his tone now brisk.

She's lost all energy for the fight.

Bus, train, tube. Finally, it's happening: a bus to Oxford station, a train to Paddington, a tube to Camden. They navigate using Tom's phone, which he's used to pay for her ticket, too. She's still got the money stuffed in her bra, moulded to her like a talisman. Thoughts slide into her mind – the secret phone, being hit by that car the night before. She's still carrying the bruises. When a bus honks its horn at her as they cross the road to the Probation Service, she nearly jumps out of her skin.

They step back on to the pavement, and it's only then that Anna sees how shaken Tom looks, too. He's clutching on to her arm so tightly she can feel his fingers jabbing hard into it. It's affected him, too, finding her knocked out like that the night before. She's already put him through too much.

They find the office easily enough, and Anna announces herself at the front desk. The appointment isn't until 4pm and they're ten minutes early, an efficiency for which she's grateful as she watches another woman rush in, dishevelled and upset, to be told that she's likely to face sanctions for being half an hour late.

As she looks around the waiting room, it hits Anna just how lucky she is. Straight out of a three-year stretch and she's come up smelling of roses, job and accommodation sorted, a nice young man catching her arm and saving her from possible death under the wheels of a bus.

Not that it's real. She doesn't deserve this, any of it. There's blood on her hands, on her conscience, dripping into every part of her that was once clean, that was once real. She imagines her sister standing in front of her, head bowed, watching, waiting . . .

'Anna Flyn?' Her spiral is interrupted. It's time.

17

'I told you it would be OK,' Tom says on the way out.

'How the fuck would you know?' Anna says, but the hostility isn't real. She's flooded with relief, the grey street in front of them more like an oasis of green trees and glittering water than its reality, the bleak brick facade of a bingo hall, concrete-coated in the miasma of a north London afternoon.

'She was more understanding than she might have been, given the circumstances yesterday,' he says. 'But look, the important thing is that the terms of the licence are varied, you can work at the office, you can stay at the house . . .'

'I'm going to sort something else out,' Anna says. 'I mean that.'

He turns to look at her, the smile fading as their eyes meet. 'Whatever you want.'

He's close, so close she can smell the scent of his soap, the same she washed her hands with only this morning. It yanks her back to reality, reminding her of what she was washing from her hands, the way the dried blood itched her skin. The grey sinks back into the street in front of her, the graffiti glaringly obvious, scrawled swear words and a collection of random tags. She can't keep running; she needs to get back now, find somewhere to live that's within her own control, rather than being beholden to this strange man with his compulsive generosity.

'You must be a crap solicitor,' she says, turning away from him and striding towards the tube. He trots to keep up with her.

'Why do you say that?'

She stops, so suddenly that he crashes into her. She pushes him away. 'That's what I mean. I insult you and instead of telling me to fuck off, you ask me why. You're so soft. You treat me like a charity case when I'm still a murder suspect. An ex-con.'

'I don't think you killed her, I said that. Neither do they, otherwise they wouldn't have let you go.'

'They don't give a shit. What does another dead junkie matter to them?'

He holds his hand up but before he can tell her to hush, she's crying, raw sobs sagging out of her, snot streaming from her nose. She leans her head against the wall, the bricks rough, a stench of piss creeping up from the pavement beneath her, but she doesn't care. She's beyond all that now, blood in her head and on her hands.

After a while, she gets her breath back under control. He hasn't said anything, done anything, moved forward to comfort her or to tell her it's all going to be all right. She's grateful for that, at least. None of this should have happened like this; she should already be dead, not being handed a lifeline by a solicitor who looks like he's barely old enough to drink, let alone sort out all her problems.

She resents him for it, the ease with which he's negotiated the system, smoothed her passage, all the privileges that others would kill for. She should walk away now, go back in and tell them that it's not happening, she's not going to work for him, she's not going to let him rescue her. She's going to do it on her own.

But she can't. He's got her trapped, dependent on his help. Help she hasn't asked for. Help she doesn't deserve. It doesn't make any sense to her, why he'd be going out of his way like this. She looks up to see him watching her, his eyes fixed on her.

That must be it. He's not being selfless. He wants something from her. There's only one thing for it. At least she can give it to him, pay him back with the only coin she has. She takes one step towards him, another, reaches her hand out to his shoulder, ready to take hold of him, kiss him, her face tilted towards him. But he steps away.

'What are you doing?'

'Isn't this what you want? Isn't this why you're doing all this, because you want to fuck me?'

He looks at her with such pity in his eyes that she nearly vomits. She knows he's going to speak, and she can't bear it. Spinning round in humiliation, she walks into the station, only to be reminded again of her helplessness as she comes up against the barrier. She goes back to the ticket machines but the only one that's working doesn't take cash; the grubby notes in her bra, the only thing of value she has left, won't help her.

Tom stands behind her, and when she turns to him, he hands her a ticket without saying a word. They get on to the tube together, the train, the bus, and it's not until they get back to his house that she's recovered enough to speak to him.

'Do you have a computer I could use?' she asks when they're back inside.

'Sure,' he says. Without another word, he leads her into

99

the front room and switches on the computer that's sitting on a desk in the corner. She waits until he's left, opens a private browsing window and enters the words *Kelly Green* into Google.

Immediately, she's confronted with a sea of green colour samples. She stares at it with confusion before registering. Kelly Green. Obviously. God, the poor woman's parents must have had a dismal sense of humour. She scrolls past all the useless colours, finding little of note. *Kelly Green dead* elicits nothing but an obituary for a woman in the US and various items of clothing in garish hues with the word DEAD stencilled on them.

It's hopeless. No way will she be able to find something on the poor woman. Most people don't produce more than a couple of Google hits, especially ones whose names are tiresome puns. She's going to have to try another way, though she has no idea where to start.

All of a sudden, Tom swoops in behind her and turns off the screen.

'I told you to leave this alone.'

Her shoulder smarts where he's pushed her aside. 'You can't just manhandle me like that.'

'It's not your business. I'm serious. Don't go poking into what doesn't concern you.'

Alarm bells. 'You can't tell me what to do.'

'That's exactly what I'm doing. I'm telling you to stop digging into this. You'll only get yourself in trouble.'

Her eyes narrow. 'What are you trying to hide, Tom? Do you have something to do with this?'

'Don't be ridiculous. As your legal representative, I am

telling you that you must not get involved any further with this. It is not your fight.'

'And I'm not your pity project.'

They face off.

'I'm warning you, Anna.'

With that, she hits her limit. She can't do this anymore. Straight upstairs, and she rams her remaining belongings back into the holdall. Enough time wasted. She needs to get out. She hauls her bag up on to her shoulder and runs back downstairs.

'I'm going,' she says to Tom. He's standing in the front hall, his brows knitting together in confusion.

'What?'

'I'm going to find somewhere else to stay. This isn't working out.'

'But what about the job?'

'I'll see you there on Monday morning. What's the address?'

'Jesus, OK. It's 501 Banbury Road. But you can't leave now. What about the conditions?'

'Fuck the conditions. I'll deal with it. I need to get out of here. Nine o'clock on Monday?'

He nods, out of words. Anna's not surprised. It's the most decisiveness she's shown since she's met him. But she can't sit around helplessly anymore. She needs to do this on her own.

'Where are you going to go? It's nearly dark.'

'I'll find somewhere. Don't worry. I'll see you on Monday morning.'

'What about your family? You said you'd promised never to come back.'

She looks at him, doused in acid, the words cutting down to her bone.

'You're putting on this brave act,' he carries on, 'but you're a coward. Holding on to those threatening letters, wallowing in self-pity. Digging around in someone else's business instead of dealing with the most important matter at hand. If it were me, I'd be straight over to my sister's house. I'd want to find out exactly what I'd done, what their lives look like now. Killing yourself, that's just running away. Totally selfish.'

She opens her mouth, shuts it. There is nothing she can possibly say to counter that. She pushes past him in the narrow hall, opens the door and slams it shut behind her, before walking away down the path, her heart pounding with unexpected speed. It's only once she's around the corner, well out of sight of the house, that she allows herself to slow down, take in some deep breaths. She's still on high alert, waiting for his footsteps behind her, but the longer it's quiet, the calmer she gets, her conviction still burning, anger and shame equally so.

A bus is approaching. She fishes the cash out of her bra before climbing on. The driver makes a face when she hands him a note but gives her the change she's owed before they trundle into Oxford city centre.

It's so familiar to Anna, yet completely unknown, the years she spent there as a student so far away now that they could have happened to someone else. It wasn't this Anna who paced under the dreaming spires, this sad, guilty woman. It was a girl, still full of optimism, dreams for the future – a ghost now, a girl who ceased to exist a long time ago. It would have been better if she'd never attended, if she'd failed the exams and the law course, failed the interviews and the training, failed to impress the solicitors at her firm – until the day she didn't, the day she could never impress anyone ever again.

Wallowing in self-pity. Tom's words ring in her ears. She's full of it. But it's all she's got.

The if onlys take her all the way to St Aldate's, where she comes back into the real world enough to remember to get off the bus. She's kicking herself for not looking up where the Jericho hostel is that Kelly mentioned, but she'll find out. Oxford isn't a big place – someone will be able to direct her. They'll know who Kelly is, where she came from. If she believes she can sort it out, it'll happen. She's not going to consider any other possibility. She's in control.

With a deep breath, she steps off the bus into the evening air. Now it begins.

18

The last time Anna walked round Oxford city centre she was a student, high on life at the end of her finals. She tries not to imagine herself among the packs of young women who are out for the night, skirts too short for the chill that's biting into the early spring air. No one looks at Anna as they pass her, swerving to avoid the bag she's holding as close to her as possible. She might feel like everyone is staring, seeing 'PRISON' tattooed across her face in bright red letters, but of course they're not; they're just getting on with their own lives, eyes sliding over a frumpy woman in her early thirties in a smelly Puffa with a tired holdall on her arm.

Anna finally spots two people in high-vis jackets, a man and a woman, outreach workers for the homeless. They're speaking to a man huddled in blankets in the doorway of a boarded-up shop. Anna hovers until they've finished and then waves hesitantly for their attention.

'You OK?' the man says.

'I'm looking for somewhere . . . um, somewhere to sleep tonight,' Anna says. 'The Jericho hostel – do you know it?'

'That's a night shelter. It's not too far from here. They might still have some space.'

'Can you tell me where it is?'

'Sure. We'll walk you there if you like.'

They take her through the darkened streets. No questions asked, no small talk, but the atmosphere is friendly. They'll have seen it all before, the worst, most tragic manifestation of humanity.

At last they get to their destination, an unprepossessing building on the corner of a side street with an institutional, disinfectant smell. She's come full circle, the brief freedom of the last twenty-four hours forgotten now. The volunteers leave her at the door and she goes in, lucky to negotiate the last bed for the night.

Not bothering even to take off her jacket, she lies on the small cot, her bag tucked up beside her like a small child. She's surrounded by strangers, the room full of sighs and creaks as other sleepers shift in their beds. She's too tired to worry about who they are, too tired to ask questions about Kelly – that'll have to wait. Even more immediately, she needs to pee; she should rinse her mouth, even if she can't brush her teeth. But she does none of it, felled by an immediate need for sleep that drowns out all the noise of the surrounding area.

She is completely out of it until the following morning, surprised to find herself waking at dawn. The room is filled with the sounds of sleep: snores, grunts, the occasional cry. It's like being back inside, the background noise more familiar to her than the calm of Tom's house the morning before.

She gets up, finds the bathrooms and washes as thoroughly as she can without having a full shower, unable to face the thought of going out into the cold morning with wet hair. Picking up her bag, she walks back through to the reception

105

area, where two young women are sitting, different from the night before.

'Sleep OK?' one of them says, smiling at Anna.

'Yes, thank you,' she says. Hoisting her bag even further up on to her shoulder, she makes her way towards the door, but the other woman calls out after her.

'We're doing a Sunday roast here later on, has anyone told you? It's the culinary highlight of the week. For me, too!'

Anna smiles. She hasn't eaten properly since the sandwich Tom handed to her wordlessly at Paddington station the day before, when they were on their way back from the probation appointment. Plus, it'll be a chance to ask around about Kelly, see if anyone knows her.

'Yorkshire puddings?'

'Sounds delicious. What time?'

'From twelve. Get here early to get your pick of the roast potatoes!'

She nods. 'It sounds good,' she says. She's at the door when she turns abruptly and returns to the desk. 'Actually, I do have a question. I'm looking for someone,' she says. 'I wonder if you've heard of her. Kelly Green? I think she might have been living on the streets here for a while, dealing with some addiction issues. Did either of you ever come across her?'

The women look at each other, shrug. One of them replies, 'I'm afraid I haven't. I'm only on duty occasionally though – she might have been in one night I wasn't here.'

'Same with me,' the other says.

'Tell you what,' the first woman says. 'We'll ask around, see if anyone has any idea about her. There are a couple of volunteers who come in much more frequently. If you're back at lunch, you can check in.'

Anna nods her thanks, leaves. Now there really is an incentive to return.

It's so early the streets are still empty, curtains drawn for Sunday morning lie-ins. She's wandering aimlessly, her feet taking her along streets that she used to know.

She stops for a moment by the Radcliffe Camera, looking at its rotunda. She spent hours working here at its wooden desks, soaking up the atmosphere of centuries of learning while other students hung out with each other, building friendships for life. Another chance wasted.

Down Magpie Lane now, a wave to her old college as she goes. In theory she could go in, claim alumna rights and wander around, but she balks at the idea of trying to prove herself to the porter. Her sister would laugh to see her so fallen – she always took the piss about Anna's decision to go there rather than Sheffield, where she herself had *the best time ever, Anna. Modern, not the rod up your arse Tudor shit you're obsessed with.*

Her sister. The thought winds her. She wanted to reject Tom's words. She can't. He's right. She has been running away from it. When she thinks now about her plan to kill herself off the south coast, she shrinks with shame. Prompted by what? One letter returned to sender?

Anna thought she was doing the right thing, wallowing in misery, polishing her guilt like a warped trophy on a shelf. It would solve nothing, though. Her death wouldn't show her sister how sorry she was – it would just compound misery on misery, a further blow to a family already wounded beyond repair.

She can't blame her sister for ignoring her letter. It was too little, too late. Anna's going to have to go in person, apologise, tell them how much she's changed. And if they won't listen, if they don't accept it, even if Marc attacks her, as he threatened to do so many times in the letters that he sent – all of that would be fine. At least she'll have said it to their faces.

More importantly than anything else, though, she might be able to find out if Toby ever recovered. If he's off life-support. What kind of life he has left. If any.

OUTSIDE

Leaves all around me, the wind in the trees. It should be quiet but I can't stop crying.

How totally fucking stupid I was to think that you'd understand how important it is.

I saw her. HER. She came into the garden while I was there. I had to move so fast to get out of sight but what the FUCK?!

You didn't tell me this.

HOW WAS I MEANT TO KNOW?!

Maybe you can't get rid of her, maybe she's clinging on like some fucking PARASITE.

You know what they do with parasites . . .

All I want is for you to tell me she doesn't understand you, that's all I need. I know how that works, living with someone who makes it so hard.

Now I'm feeling sorry for you. Isn't that funny? Only a few minutes ago I was so angry I was ready to kill you, but now I understand it properly. It's not your fault. You knew her before. I guess you weren't to know that there would be someone better out there for you, someone perfect. The other half to your whole.

I'm not sure you've realised it yet. Men don't always know what's best for them.

It's as well I do know. And I'm going to make sure it happens.

19

Decision made, but she's still not ready. Bracing for the rejection she's sure to face. Instead of heading straight there, she walks around Christ Church Meadow, wandering past the boat houses, dodging hefty blokes in tight Lycra. She stops in front of the one that belongs to her old college, trying to scrape back through the years to remember how it felt to stand on the terrace as she allowed herself to do occasionally, plastic glass of Pimm's in hand, cheering on a boat to do she understood not what, bump another boat or something – but that was never the point, only the drinking and the laughing and the disco that followed, a sense of belonging that normally eluded her.

The doors are open and she can see a man using the rowing machine, a couple of other men in training gear and a girl in tight jeans, laughing. The girl's laughter stops the moment she catches sight of Anna, her face shutting down.

'We don't have any change,' she calls out, before Anna can even open her mouth to speak.

Anna blinks. She wasn't expecting this. She's just looking, that's all. 'I used to be at the college,' she says, 'a long time ago.'

The girl laughs again, a bitter sound this time, then swallows it. 'Sure you were.'

Anna could argue, there might be enough fire in her belly to take this little cow on, but she's past this now. She doesn't have anything to prove to anyone. She did her time – Oxford *and* inside – and no one can take either from her.

More's the pity.

Resisting the temptation to croak out a curse, a warning, *this could be you in ten years if you don't watch it*, Anna turns and walks back along the stretch of boat houses before turning along the path up the tributary that leads into the River Cherwell.

It's quiet here, fewer runners, only a mother walking along slowly, holding a toddler by the hand. Anna overtakes them easily. Round a bend, another, and there's the bench she remembers sitting on with a boy she liked, their knees almost touching in the dark. They used to sneak over the wall from college after the gates were locked at night.

Sunlight breaks through the clouds, rays of it slanting down through the big willow that overhangs the water to Anna's right, and a duck swims past, another, the light catching the flash of green on the mallard's head. The tightness in Anna's chest eases, slightly, though the weight of memories remains.

She leans back against the bench, closing her eyes in the slight warmth the sun provides. Despite a full night's sleep she's exhausted, images of the events of the last two days flickering into her mind. A bloodied face, Little and Large, Tom's hair flopping down in that irritating way. The lights of the car as it barrelled into her, the pain when she came round. Tom's high-handedness, the way he tried to stop her finding out about Kelly. The smell in the hostel that took her straight back to the day that she was first arrested.

All of it lies on her chest, adding to the guilt she constantly feels. She's almost winded, unable to take in a proper breath, watching the shadows dance around her mind, wishing she could give it all up . . .

A bark breaks her stupor. God, Tom was right. She's stuck in a loop. She opens her eyes and watches a small brown dog jump into the water in an attempt to chase the ducks, unable to control a smile at the indignation with which the ducks take flight. She's got to pull herself together. There is one thing she's got going for her: she's still alive. Not like that poor woman in the bunk below.

She pulls the phone out of her bag, delaying the walk to her sister's house. It's quiet around here. She holds the power button down, but the tiny phone does nothing, the screen blank. It might not even have charge left. She jabs at the condom encasing it with her fingernail, trying to break it loose. It won't shift, so with a grimace, she raises it to her mouth and rips into the rubber with her teeth, trying not to think about where it's been. Once she's ripped enough of a hole, she peels away the latex, freeing the phone, before stuffing the broken condom into the side pocket on her bag.

She tries pressing the power button again, almost unable to isolate it, it's so small, and with a surge of triumph, she watches the screen light up as the phone turns on. Her search through reveals nothing new, however.

Only that one phone number. One that's not even saved in the memory of the phone, but just logged as the last call. There are no other numbers in the call records, either. Anna was hoping to find a photograph, maybe. Nothing.

113

She turns the phone over and over, flicking at menu options and settings until the phone beeps. She's hoping that by magic something useful will appear, but of course it doesn't. There's just the phone number. Should she call it?

Her finger's hovering over the call button when suddenly the phone rings, a shrill noise so loud it startles a pigeon by her feet into flight. Anna's hands are shaking now, the jolt of adrenaline rushing through her lightning fast. Should she answer? It's buzzing in her hands like an angry hornet. Holding it as lightly as she dares, Anna waits for it to stop ringing, the noise beating relentlessly on her ear drums.

It stops. Anna looks at the screen to see if it shows the number of the caller, but then it starts to ring again. She jumps so hard she nearly drops it, the water only a couple of metres away from her, then she takes a firmer grip, both on it and on herself. It's a phone, not a snake. It won't bite her. It's not a sophisticated phone, either, so the chances of someone tracking it are small.

She squints at the screen, seeing the number pulsating away in time with the rings. It looks like the number that was already in the call log, the one entry that had no name, but she can't be sure. Putting the phone on the bench beside her, she digs through her bag and takes out a pen and an old paperback, scrawling the digits down as the phone continues shrieking at her.

Written down, checked. All details correct. It stops ringing and she takes her chance to check whether the number calling is the same as the one in the call log, but before she can read it fully, the phone rings for the third time. They're not going to give up.

The phone isn't secret anymore. Someone knows now it's

still out there, still in use. They'll start looking for her, she can feel it. She picks up the phone and presses the power button until the ringing is muted. Looking over at the river, she thinks about throwing it in, but something in her balks at the idea. It's the only clue Kelly has left her. She tucks it firmly down into her bag.

Enough delay. Her sister's face comes into her mind one more time, contorted, weeping, *my son* . . . the sunlight through the trees loses its heat suddenly, a cloud passing over the sky, chilling the air. She shivers, picks up her bag. She can't put it off anymore.

20

It doesn't take long for Anna to walk over Magdalen Bridge, take the turn off into Divinity Road. She wishes it did.

Her steps slow to a halt. The adrenaline has gone, slipped away, any residual courage drained. She could go. She doesn't have to see this through. No one knows she's here, not even Tom – there's nothing to stop her getting on a coach to London and disappearing.

Her sister might hate her. Her sister might even wish her dead. But Anna knows, right to her core, that her sister would never actively do anything to harm her. Her brother-in-law, Marc, though – that's a different story. He's made his feelings entirely clear over the years. If she knocks on the door and he answers, she's not entirely sure she'll survive the encounter.

Headlights in her mind again, the force of the impact as it knocked her off her feet outside the prison. She's still sore from it. Could that have been Marc driving?

Fuck's sake. He's an accountant. How dangerous could he be? Easy for him to send threats, safe in the knowledge that he wouldn't risk running into Anna at any point while she was inside. A different matter to see those threats through in person, abusing her face to face. He wouldn't have the guts.

She's nearly sure of it.

The emotions are pulling her this way and that, a few steps closer to the house she used to know so well. A couple of passers-by stare at her, or at least she thinks they're staring, and she scowls furiously until they back away, scurrying round the corner.

She's pacing now, forwards and back, sloughing off the bits of Anna that have emerged since her release and putting them back inside, hardening up again to her old prisoner number, the number by which she was designated inside for so long. She's not a name. A number can't be scared. A number has no feelings at all.

She walks back to the house, pushing her way through the gate and ringing the doorbell. She moves fast, not hesitating for a moment, because she knows if she stops, she'll turn and run, never looking back.

No reply. She rings the doorbell again, stepping back a little so she can peer through the frosted glass panels to see if there's any movement inside. Nothing. She bangs on the wood this time, knocking so hard her knuckles ache.

Now she's got time to look around her, get her bearings. It's a nice house. Or rather, it was. She remembers how it used to look. There were roses growing up the front and a hydrangea in a large pot in the middle of the small front garden.

They're all dead now, the petals brown and withered, a pile of debris blown against the house. The front garden doesn't look like it's been tended in years. Same with the house, the paint peeling now, the windows filthy. She glances round the side to see a mass of greenery where once there was a side passage to the back garden, everything overgrown and wild.

Maybe they've moved away. Her heart sinks. If they've gone, she has no idea how she'll find them.

One more bang at the door, then she'll give up. Then, at last, she hears footsteps approaching.

Time stands still. This is what she's here for, this is why she's come. It's too late to back down now, to run and hide. She's going to have to see this through. The door opens and, as it does, she raises her chin, tightens her lips, feet in a boxer's stance.

'I'm on my way!' a man's voice bellows as the door opens fully – and it's him, Marc. He's already hostile, aggression bristling. He looks at her, and for a moment his face is blank, before a glint of recognition hardens his features further, veins corded in his neck.

'Jesus fucking Christ,' he says, and everything in her retreats at the fury in his voice. She's about to take a step backwards but forces herself to stand her ground.

'What the fuck do you want?' With that, he reaches out and seizes her arm before she has time to protect herself, pulling her hard across the threshold and slamming the door shut behind her.

Part 2

21

Nervous, jittery. Ants crawling under Lucy's skin, a prickling in her gut. The last moments before the last part of the promise she made to herself comes true. She's played it through so many times in her head.

When she sees the professor in person for the first time, it'll be like she's known him for years. He'll know her, too. It'll be the way he looks at her, nods his head to welcome her in. *Ah yes, you, I've been expecting you.*

She's been expecting him. Always.

Some rules are made to be broken, that's what she'll tell him later, in his office. Or maybe he'll say it to her – it doesn't matter. She'll pull her shirt up over her head, unhook her bra, hooking him in. He'll be hers, caught tight.

She checks her thoughts, nodding at the porter as she passes through the gate into the front quad of her college. That's the dream. She'll be grateful for anything, any crumbs from his table. It'll be enough to be in the same room after all those years online. That's what she's trying to tell herself, anyway.

From the first moment she saw him on her computer screen she knew, in those terrible days after the funeral when she was searching for answers and finding nothing. In his TED Talk, he spoke passionately about the need for prison reform, the toll it took on female prisoners to be incarcerated in such a punitive way – he seemed to understand exactly what Lucy was going through, somehow. His eyes were so piercing as he looked out of the screen that he might have been staring into her soul. She was only seventeen – she swore to herself then that she would do whatever it took to study under him.

The years have passed. She's followed everything he's done, watched every talk, read every publication. Every time he posts online she's there, watching. His words inspired her at first, but it's more than that now, when she allows herself the fantasy. She knows he's the one for her.

Is she crazy to think so? She thinks about him at night, hard flesh in soft sheets. It started with his mind, the way she connected with his thoughts, his theories. But it's grown, bigger, stronger, almost out of her control.

Now it's only a matter of minutes before the image of his face becomes flesh, before she's there in the same room as him. Will it have been worth it?

The stone walls of the quadrangle are mellow in the January sun. Borders of crocuses are starting to emerge, snowdrops too. There's a wind cutting through Lucy's thin coat. She wraps her arms around herself. It doesn't bother her, though – it's grounding, reminding her that she isn't in a dream. The novelty still hasn't worn off, the beauty of the place. Nor the disbelief at the fact that it's hers.

Through the cloisters to the garden at the back, and there are more bulbs flowering here, bright white among the evergreens. Over a high wall, she can see down to a meadow surrounded by trees, their branches silhouetted against the blue sky. Rural. Not like the city in which she grew up, has only just left. Different worlds.

The seminar is due to start soon. The course she's been waiting for since she first arrived in Oxford. She's done a term already, hard at work in the MSc in Criminology she's studying. But this, this is why she's here.

She thinks back now to her arrival in the autumn, how she had to lecture herself before she got off the coach from Manchester, a freshly minted first-class law degree in her back pocket. She wasn't to let anyone intimidate her. Anyone at all. It was good to be a postgrad, she saw that from the moment she stepped off the coach and wheeled her suitcase along St Giles and down the side street to her new college. If she were still eighteen, she'd have wondered if she was good enough when she saw the kids unloading mountains of belongings from their parents' SUVs. She's from another world, Primark to their Carhartt and Supreme. She's the one who needed the full scholarship, after all.

She travelled light, all she needs in her head. It's served her well over the last while. As has her holiday job for the last few years in a pub in that northern town, pulling pints for a series of drunk men who would never believe that someone so young and pretty could be a law student. Let alone at Oxford.

She wouldn't believe it herself if she wasn't here, bang in the middle of the dreaming spires. She knows exactly how she got here, though. That degree in law was hard won. But worth it. One step closer to her dream.

Some might call it obsession. She knows it's more than that.

The first term went in a flash. Battels, blues, the Bod,

college bops, the hacks running round trying to get slates together for the Union elections – the obscure terminology a mystery wrapped in an enigma. Or, more likely, a load of bollocks.

She loves it though, nearly everything about it. The room with its view across the rooftops, the short walk down staircases and through cloisters to breakfast. She's lucky to have got a room in college – most postgrads have to live out, in purpose-built blocks on the Cowley or Iffley Roads, but she hit the jackpot. It's a bubble, a chimera, golden stone against blue skies, trees towering over her as she walks down to the river, past the boat houses, but for this year the illusion is hers, and she's going to relish every moment.

Eyes on the prize, though. She never lets that slip from her mind.

The core subjects of the course are fine. She's blasting through them, head down. It's the optional courses she's interested in: Victims; Race and Gender; Sentencing: Victims and Restorative Justice. And then there's the core reason she's here. Bringing the personal to the principles. She's studying Prisons, with the professor.

'Lucy,' a voice says, interrupting her reverie. She looks round. It's Ben, bouncy and expectant as a puppy waiting for her to throw a ball. She swallows hard, trying to get her irritation under control. It's not his fault she was lonely that night at the start of the course, that she let him in before she realised what a foolish mistake it would be.

'I didn't realise you were doing this option,' she says, forcing a smile.

'It's Prisons,' he says, and for a moment she's completely lost, the relevance of this to him out of her mind. Then she remembers. He'd said something to her about his dad being a prison officer. She didn't share her own story, though, and now he's seen the expression of confusion that's just passed quickly across her face. He turns from her, his shoulders hunched. He's tried to message her a couple of times, to attract her attention at the end of lectures, but she's blanked him. A pang of regret as she looks at the back of his head – his hair was so soft under her hand.

'Come on then, what are you waiting for?' One of their fellow students, a hearty woman called Alexandra. She's doing the course purely because she didn't get the pupillage she wanted first time round – this is meant to be making her more attractive to future chambers, or so she hopes. Opportunistic. Lucy doesn't have time to waste on her.

The three of them walk together across the quad to a wooden door set into the stone wall. There's a low step, the edge shiny, worn down by hundreds of years of students stepping inside, and for a moment Lucy feels herself not herself anymore but part of a chain, a continuum through the centuries, seekers of truth and knowledge.

They weren't seeking the knowledge she wants, though. She knows she's unique in that. Nor is she like past students – or present ones – in any other way.

Through a short passageway and through another wooden door, and then they're into the seminar room. It's bright, the light dazzling her after the gloom of the hall, and she can see the chairs around the big table are nearly full. Alexandra and Ben sit down, leaving only one seat free, next to the big chair at the head of the table that clearly belongs to the professor. She takes a deep breath and sits, looking around as she does.

The walls are lined with shelves of books, old statutes, leatherbound King's and Queen's Bench Reports, copies of Hansard, textbooks on prison law and criminal justice.

The window at the far end of the room is open, the frame latched open and surrounded by dead leaves from the ivy that covers the back of the college building. Lucy closes her eyes. This could be some mansion, some posh hotel, she could be a visitor here—

'Welcome,' a deep voice says, a hand slapping the table. Lucy's eyes snap open.

He's arrived. She looks at his profile. Late fifties, dark hair frosted through with grey – the very definition of a silver fox. Perhaps he feels the intensity of her stare, because he turns directly to her and they hold each other's gaze. The feeling of instant familiarity grows stronger. He nods at her again, breaks the connection. Raises his head to address the room.

'Someone murdered your mother. They broke into her house, tied her up and stabbed her to death. You've caught them red-handed. What do you want to do?' He looks round the room as if issuing a challenge. No one looks up. 'Come on, she's died in agony. Don't you want revenge?'

Alexandra is studying her pen. Lucy squints past her to see Ben staring fixedly down at the table in front of him.

'No one?'

Alexandra slowly raises her hand. 'I'd want revenge.'

'What kind of revenge? Would you like to take the same knife and make him suffer in the same way? Would you like to twist it into his guts just like he did to your mother?'

Alexandra nods, a small, decisive movement. 'Yes. I would.'

The professor nods too. 'Of course you would. Anyone would.' A pause, then. 'Right, what if you *didn't* catch them

126

red-handed? What if someone told you that *that* man was the culprit, pointed him out in the street? Would you still want to twist the knife?'

Alexandra opens her mouth, closes it again.

Ben raises his hand. 'I suppose it would depend on how close to my mum's death it was. If it were immediately afterwards, I think I'd still be so fraught, I'd go for him. But a bit later on . . .'

The professor smiles. 'Right. And this is why we have a criminal justice system. Mob justice might be one way of getting criminals off the street, a way of enacting revenge, but it's not real justice. The danger of getting it wrong is too great.'

He looks round the room, catches Lucy's eye again. She feels his gaze as strongly as if he's laid his hand on her.

'Let's take it beyond street justice. Let's say your mum's killer has been arrested, tried, convicted. They're about to be sentenced. What kind of sentence do you want them to receive?'

Jessica, a mature student sitting at the bottom of the table, raises her hand. 'I'd want to lock them up and throw away the key.'

'Whole term imprisonment? That's an entirely human response,' he says. 'Prison works. None of you were alive at the time the Conservative politician unleashed his famous mantra. "Prison works." Do you agree with him?'

Jessica thinks for a moment. 'Yes,' she says. 'I think I do.'

The professor gets to his feet, strides over to the window. He's animated, as impassioned as Lucy has ever seen him, even in his most emotional speeches online. Her heart is pounding.

'Then I'm not sure you have any place in this class.'

Jessica recoils as if he's slapped her. 'I didn't – I mean . . .'

The professor's eyebrows are raised to his hairline, his expression frozen. Jessica shifts uncomfortably in her seat. Lucy's holding her breath, the tension thick as smog. She could punch a hole in it.

His eyebrows fall, his face returning to a more relaxed position. He returns to his seat. 'Whatever you think you know about prison, you're wrong. It's worse than you can imagine, and stupider than you'll ever believe. The purpose of it might be to punish, to rehabilitate, to keep dangerous people locked up and to deter others. Well, guess what? There's precious little rehabilitation going on, and judging by the way the numbers are rising, it's not serving as a deterrent, either.'

Jessica raises her hand. She's got her fight back. 'Some crimes deserve punishment. Why should someone who murders someone else get to live in comfort, given what they've done?'

A flicker of something passes across the professor's face and he pauses before he speaks. 'An eye for an eye, a tooth for a tooth? Blood for blood – is that your philosophy?'

She reddens but holds her ground. 'I'm not arguing for capital punishment,' she says, 'I just feel that some crimes deserve more punishment than others, that's all.'

'Perhaps,' he says. 'Or else we could think of it in the way Sonia responds to Raskolnikov when he confesses to murder: "What have you done – what have you done to yourself?" Don't you think we have a duty to find out *how* this has happened, to discover what breakdown in the social contract has led to the destruction of not just the victim's life, but the murderer's, too? The reverberations of murder are loud and ring through the years – do we hear better by stopping our ear against the murderer's cries?'

Lucy is breathing hard, swept up in his words, even though she couldn't paraphrase them if she tried. She knew this about him. He's always been passionate about rehabilitation, believing that prison as an entity should be abolished as not fit for purpose. She's listened to his podcasts, read every one of his articles. This is why she's here.

'Sorry sir, but who's Ralsonikon?' It's a boy, sitting next the hang 'em, flog 'em Jessica He's got his laptop out, ready to tap it all down.

'Raskolnikov. The protagonist of one of the greatest novels ever written – *Crime and Punishment* by Dostoevsky. I suggest you run away and read it before next week, all of you.'

Alexandra thrusts her hand into the air, barely waiting to be invited to speak before the words burst out of her. 'Dostoevsky is crucial to any study of prisons and prison reform. He was the one who said, "The degree of civilisation in a society can be judged by entering its prisons."'

Lucy looks over at her. Alexandra's arms are crossed, her cheeks flushed. Maybe Lucy's been unfair on her – maybe she also has strong feelings about prison reform.

But Alexandra keeps talking. 'I can't believe anyone here hasn't heard of Raskolnikov,' she says, glaring at the poor boy sitting next to her. The tips of his ears have gone bright pink.

'Dostoevsky didn't actually say that,' Lucy interjects.

'Didn't say what?'

'That the degree of civilisation in a society can be judged by entering its prisons.'

'Yes he did,' Alex says. 'It's from *The House of the Dead*.'

'Have you read *The House of the Dead*?' Edgar asks, interrupting the argument. He's asking the question of Alexandra, but looking closely at Lucy.

Now it's Alexandra's turn to go pink. 'I haven't, no. But everyone knows that Dostoevsky said that. It's, like, his most famous quote.'

Lucy puts her chin up. 'He didn't say it. Look.' She picks up her phone and scrolls through, eventually lighting on the article she's saved about the misattributed quote. 'Look.' She hands her phone to Alexandra, who flicks at it crossly before pushing it back towards Lucy.

'Well, he could have said it. That's more important.'

'More important than quoting him correctly?' Lucy says. She knows she's being pedantic, but Alexandra has irritated her with the bumptious self-confidence the woman displays without any grounding in actual knowledge.

Alexandra subsides into her chair, her shoulders slumped. She's muttering something to herself. Lucy can't make out the words, but she doubts they're complimentary. On the other hand, Edgar is still looking at her, a warmth to his expression as if he's proud of her performance.

'Lucy's right. It's a common misconception. Very good.' She catches his eye and he nods at her, smiles. Lucy glows inside. 'So, back to the original discussion,' he continues. 'Does prison work? What do you think?'

No one responds, no one puts up their hand. A roomful of confident law graduates reduced to silence by this man. Lucy can feel the charisma radiating from him. She needs to show more of herself. She'd been too focused on imagining how she would seduce him, undressing herself for him at some private tutorial, but now she sees how foolish she's been. That's not the nakedness he needs from her – what she must give him is deeper inside.

'When I think of prison, I think of my mother,' she says, not bothering to raise her hand.

He turns to her. 'In what way?' he says.

'It was where she died,' Lucy says. Their eyes meet, and this time it's not a spark that's lit. It's a flame.

22

It's been over a fortnight since that class. She thought then that the professor might have asked her to stay behind and explain to him what she meant. But he watched her walk out of the seminar room without any attempt to hold her back.

Ben hasn't talked to her either, not since she walked straight past him at the end of the class. It's as if she's surrounded by a forcefield, or something at her core that repels all the other students, although Lucy sees them watching her when she turns her head suddenly and catches them staring.

She doesn't care about the other students. She's isolated, not lonely. The workload is steep, no time for dwelling on things. At least forty hours a week, and that's with only selective reading from the list. Lucy is reading everything, not just the books on the list, but the books referred to in the footnotes, too, and all the articles.

Perhaps she should be worried that the professor hasn't tried to engage further with her, but she's not. She knows that he's hooked, that he wants to know what she meant, what she was talking about. It's only a matter of time.

Sure enough, as the year edges into early spring, her moment comes. At the end of the seminar, he asks for volunteers for a

research assignment, a paper he needs to prepare unexpectedly for a conference at the weekend.

'A keynote speaker is ill,' he says. 'So they've asked me to step
in. I'm going to need some help, though. It's nearly my area, but
not quite, so there's some work to do. I need someone to provide
a synopsis of all the main points of any relevant research. Could
be a couple of all-nighters, but you'll learn a lot.'

Lucy shoots her hand up before looking round the room to
see that nearly everyone else has, too. Not like school, when
volunteers had to be dragged kicking and screaming to read
aloud, or even answer a simple question. Every student is as
keen as she is. Though not quite.

She sits still, an image of what's going to happen clear in
her mind. He's going to look round the room, and after a
show of hesitation, he's going to lean over and—

'Lucy, you said something in your application about the
Nordic model of incarceration, if I'm not mistaken.'

She nods, unable to speak. It's exactly as she'd hoped it
would be.

'I think this will be right up your alley. Stay after class and
we'll discuss.'

Daggers from round the room, but they bounce straight
off her, the forcefield around her now glowing gold.

'Come over to my office,' he says at the end of the session.
She's the last student left at the table.

'Now?'

'I'll show you what I need you to do,' he says.

They walk through the quad together, their shoulders nearly
touching as they approach the narrow arch that leads to the
building where his personal office is situated. Lucy jumps back

at the proximity, stumbling as he gestures for her to go through. She might be twenty-two, not some squeaky undergraduate, but now that the moment's come and she's in his presence, she's all thumbs, her feet stuck on the wrong way.

As he unlocks his office door, Lucy's cheeks start to warm. He gestures her through but she steps back – *no, after you.* She wants to get her blushing back under control. It really is like it was at school when she had such a crush on Alan Mackenzie, who was in her history class. They snogged once after a disco one Friday night and every time she saw him after that, she turned red as a tomato, much to her friends' glee. Shouldn't she have grown out of it by now? She could kick herself for the stupidity of it. It's time to stop undermining herself.

He's noticed her. He knows she could be the other half to his whole, the partner in his already illustrious career that he doesn't know he needed. The work they'll do together, the advances in prison reform . . .

'Come on through,' he says, and she lands back down on earth, shaking her head free of the nonsense of it all. She follows him.

'It's these,' Edgar says, handing her a sheaf of printouts. 'I need to get these summarised as soon as possible, so that I can see if I should address them in the paper.'

Lucy takes them from him, starts to leaf through them.

'It's more general than my usual area,' he says. 'More of the criminology aspect, less of the specific prison considerations. Of course, I keep up with all of this, but it's good to know what peers are proposing.'

Lucy nods enthusiastically, like a bloody dog. Nothing useful to say for herself. Now she's alone with him, the idea of bringing up anything unsolicited feels almost impossible. He sits down behind his desk and turns on his computer, the light catching his cheekbones, emphasising the clean lines of his profile. Objectively speaking, despite his age – perhaps even because of it – he is ridiculously handsome. It's not just his reputation; in some ways she knows she's responding to that, too, in her blushing and her fluttering and the way that she keeps touching her hair, flicking the strands across her eyes.

He catches her gaze and looks away, his expression resigned. It must happen all the time, students flinging themselves at him. Lucy is filled with a sudden urge to blurt out that she's not like them, she's different.

'You said something about your mother,' Edgar says, breaking the silence.

Oh God. Not here. Not yet. She's not ready to talk about it. Her mouth can't form the words.

'She died?' he prompts.

'I . . .' She can't say it. He turns his face away, but not before she's seen something pass across it, a shadow, so fast she's not even sure now that it was there.

'Never mind,' he says. 'No need to discuss anything you're not comfortable with. Tell me about your first degree. Manchester, wasn't it?'

Now she's on more comfortable territory, the words start to flow. She tells him about her studies, her first, the fact that she had visited Strangeways every week as a volunteer in a literacy charity throughout her degree.

'That's fantastic,' he says. 'My wife's interested in literacy in prisons, women after their release, that kind of thing. Maybe you could volunteer with her organisation?'

Her nails dig into her hand. She'd known he must be

married, but it's difficult to hear. 'I'd love to,' she says after a moment. 'It's great that you both work in the same field.'

'To a point,' Edgar says. 'She volunteers from time to time, that's all. Though at least she has views about prison welfare. It would be tricky if she were completely uninterested. I mean, it's . . .' He doesn't finish his sentence.

He looks at Lucy with such intensity that she almost quivers, his gaze searing through to her core, as if he can see the very heart of her. His charisma level is almost through the roof. She'd thought she would have the upper hand as a young woman; she was wrong.

'I'm glad you're able to help me with this,' he says, and for a moment he stands close to her, his blue eyes locked to hers, and it's hanging in the air between them, the question *will they won't they*, and even though Lucy knows how much there is to say, and how much this is not what this is about, all she actually wants is for him to lean forward and—

'Do you think you'll be able to get the work done in time?' He turns away from her and the moment is broken.

'Yes, it's no problem. I'll have it done by Friday morning.'

'No boyfriend or anything to distract you?'

'No.' She blushes again, glad that he's got his back to her now.

'Good. Sensible. Devote yourself to your studies.'

She shuffles the papers together and puts them into her bag. He's sitting at his computer, absorbed by something on the screen. She raises a hand in farewell and he tilts his head towards her without looking.

She's dismissed.

But she knows when she returns that the door will be open for her, and that he will be waiting. Next time, she's going to be ready.

CCTV

A Scottish loch, the water clear and unbroken by waves, mountains reflected in the surface.

A small motorboat comes into view at the end of a wooden jetty, one man aboard. He climbs up the ladder, a cardboard box in his hands. It's full of groceries. A head of celery sticks up from one corner, two bottles from the other side.

The man puts the box down further up the jetty before returning to the boat and starting the engine. The boat leaves the picture. Some hours pass where only a few birds come into the screen and fly away again – a heron and two ducks.

At last, Scylla appears. She seems out of breath. She pulls one of the bottles out of the box. Now we see that it's whisky. She unscrews the lid and starts to tip the contents into the loch. Moments later, Charybdis comes into view, her teeth bared in a silent scream. She pushes at Scylla, trying to get hold of the bottle, but then stops, catching sight of the full bottle that's still in the box.

She snatches this and runs away up the jetty and out of shot. Scylla watches after her before putting the bottle in her hands up to her lips and draining the rest of the contents. Then she, too, moves out of shot.

23

The next weeks go by in a blur. Work, research for the professor, more homework of her own. He asks her to complete a number of tasks for him – a paper that he needs to write, a presentation he's giving online. Checking his references for a paper he's submitting to an academic journal.

He makes his latest request at the end of their usual Thursday seminar. He doesn't ask for volunteers anymore, nor even ask her to wait. She's there, hovering, knowing that soon enough he'll turn the beam of his attention to her and she'll light up like a beacon.

'It's a lot of work,' he says. 'I'm sorry to spring it on you last minute.'

'I'm happy to do it,' she says. She means it, too. He hands over the work, his gaze lingering on her, their fingers meeting. She tries not to show the electric jolt she feels – it's the first time they've ever touched, and her hand is burning. Her cheeks, too. She turns away in a hurry, goes straight to her room to get on with the work.

It is immediately clear that this task will be harder than most. The data is badly presented, the pages out of any logical order. Lucy's usually good with numbers, but tonight

138

she's getting a headache, the black print dancing on the page before her. Even when it turns midnight, she's still got pages left to go through. She puts on her kettle to make some coffee for the final push, sitting on her bed for a moment as she waits for it to boil.

When she wakes, it's after six in the morning.

There's no way she can finish it now.

Even as she hands over her rushed notes to the professor later that morning, she knows she's broken something, the invisible chain of trust that was building between them. She's let him down.

'I'm surprised,' he says. 'Clearly I've been asking too much of you.' His voice is light, tight, an edge to it she hasn't heard before.

'I'm so sorry. I don't know what happened.'

'I expected too much,' he says. 'I forget you're only an MSc student.'

She's winded by the blow.

'I'm sorry,' she says again. 'Please give me a second chance. I'm up to it.'

He ponders for a moment, shakes his head. 'This work is too important. I can't risk giving it to someone who doesn't take it seriously.'

She stands in his office, mute. It's raining outside, the sky iron-grey, the clouds dark, ominous. 'I can do better.'

'I hope so.'

Back in her room, the weekend stretches before her, dull, empty, no one to talk to, nothing to do. She picks up her phone, scrolls down to see who she could call.

Friends from school?

She doesn't talk to any of them now.

From uni?

There was no time for friends back then. Between studying and her work in the pub, not to mention the long commute back to her family home every morning and night. She was barely on nodding terms with her fellow undergraduates, even after three years. And, of course, there were those long months online during the pandemic.

Other postgrads at college?

She leans back on her bed with a laugh, a barking sound that could be a sob. She's not going to cry, though.

There is one option. She scrolls back up, presses call. The phone rings out for a long time, twenty rings at least before it's picked up.

'Who's this?' A gruff voice.

'Me. Lucy.'

'Lucy? I haven't seen you in a long time.'

'That's because I'm away at college, Dad. You remember.'

'College? Oh yes, college. Not good enough for you at home, was it? You had bigger ideas. Has it all gone wrong for you, then? I told you it would.'

She places the phone down on the bed beside her, swallows hard. It's after six – she should have checked the time first. She should have thought about how many tins of Stella he'd have drunk by now – it is Friday, after all. His voice keeps talking through the phone; even without the speaker turned on, she can make out the swear words, the rise of abuse before it falls into the self-pitying whine she knows so well.

Pushing the phone off the bed, she climbs under her duvet

and pulls it up around her ears, but it's many hours before she sleeps.

The week passes. Dull, grey, monotonous. She passes the professor a couple of times in the quad but he doesn't look up, doesn't acknowledge her. It's like she's dying inside, the withering of the dream she's had for so long.

She could kick herself. It's all her fault. The only thing stopping her from packing up her bags and fleeing the place immediately is the presentation she's due to make at the end of the week. She spends every hour in the library – it's going to be the best piece of work she's ever done.

At last it's the day of the seminar, a Friday morning this time. As usual, no one acknowledges her, though Lucy barely lifts her head to register their lack of interest. She's too focused on her notes to care. She needs to be pitch-perfect. It's her last chance – if she hasn't blown it already.

Her turn at last. They've sat through a lacklustre monologue about young offender institutions from the mature student Jessica – no new insights, banal in the extreme. Lucy glanced over at the professor a couple of times to try and read his reaction. Nothing. A flat tone when he asks her to come up.

She looks down the table at the indifferent faces, a sneer on Jessica's face, boredom on Alexandra's, something close to aversion on Ben's. The professor is looking at his notebook with concentration, his brows furrowed. It's like someone's switched off the light, the room dim. She takes a deep breath, and she begins.

When she's about halfway through, the atmosphere changes, a crackle in the air. Ben is looking up at her, Jessica too.

141

There's even grudging respect on Alexandra's face. Lucy is talking about the effect of prison sentences on women offenders' families. An emotive subject, and she's talking from the heart. When she relates the account of a pair of siblings who were separated and forced into care when their mum was sent down for dealing, Jessica winces in sympathy. By the end, they're all leaning forward, nodding at the conclusions that she's drawn.

As she finishes, there's a smattering of applause. More than the usual, muted response – she's pulled it off. She can feel it deep inside her. At last, she dares to glance in the professor's direction. She must, surely, have made an impression.

He's looking at his phone.

24

Lucy wants to get out of the seminar room as soon as the class is finished. No chance she's hovering for the professor's attention today. She's kept her face mask-still for the remainder of the session, but there's a limit to how long she can keep it going. She's damned if she's going to cry in front of him. Or anyone else, come to that.

As she gets to the door, Jessica catches hold of her arm. Lucy's jaw clenches, the tightest of smiles. All the woman wants to do is rub her nose in it.

'You coming to Formal Hall tonight?' Jessica says. Alexandra is standing behind her, smiling.

Lucy tries not to look surprised. 'No, I wasn't planning to.'

'You should – we're all going.' Jessica gestures round the room, taking in all the students. Some of them, Lucy would struggle to recognise outside class.

'I might,' she says. The professor is still looking at his phone as he sits at the end of the table. Time to pull herself together. 'Fuck it, yes. It's been ages since I had a proper night out. Count me in.'

* * *

Little black dress, black tights, black eyeliner. She's pulling out the stops, blending eyeshadow into the crease above her eyes and smoothing foundation and blusher over her skin. She's going to show them all what she's got. *You think the professor's going to turn up tonight and you want to scrub up for him,* a little voice jeers inside her head, and she tells it to fuck off, adding a slick of lipstick and a spritz of perfume as she does.

When she gets down to the college bar to meet up with the others it becomes immediately clear that the group has evolved from mere seminar allies to close friends. They're doing shots of Jägermeister to screeches of laughter, even the staidest of them. Lucy blinks to see it, hesitates over the shot that she's offered before tossing it down her neck so as not to be a spoilsport. They cheer in encouragement as she does so, making room for her in their circle, though Lucy is sure she can feel a little hesitation from Ben and Alexandra, who are sitting a little too close together.

'Not working tonight then?' Alexandra says. She is smiling, but there's no warmth there.

'Night off,' Lucy says. 'Wouldn't want to miss this.'

'Of course not,' Alexandra says. 'Though I'm sure you have more important things to be doing. Say, for the professor?' Her tone is nudging, something nasty at the core of it, though her smile continues to play on her lips.

A stone drops in Lucy's stomach. She fights a snarl into a smile. 'I can't imagine finding anything more important than this. So nice to get the chance to bond with everyone.' She gestures around her in an expansive way at the others sitting at the table, hoping she might flush out an ally. Ben actively looks away from her.

No one else catches her eye, or even smiles at her. She messed that right up. Hang on, that guy over there – he was smiling. Charles, Charlie, something like that? She arranges her features in what she hopes is a winning way and sets out to charm.

By the time the meal is over, she's made some inroads. Charlie takes the seat next to her in the old dining hall.

'Your presentation was excellent,' he says.

'Thanks. I feel very strongly about it.'

'I can see that,' he says. He pours red wine into her glass, filling it almost to the brim before doing the same to his, too. They toast each other, clinking the tumblers together carefully so as not to spill any of it.

Alexandra is sitting opposite Lucy. She's banging on as usual about how much the portraits and wooden panels make her think of Hogwarts. 'I'm in Ravenclaw, you know,' she says.

Lucy catches Charlie's eye and bites her lip. She mustn't laugh.

When they leave the table, he walks by her side back to the bar. She's feeling a lot more relaxed. The shot helped, as did the copious amounts of red wine she had at dinner. She takes a seat in one of the alcoves built deep into the wall of the beer cellar, and Charlie goes up to buy them drinks. She eases off her shoes under the table. The heels aren't even that high, but she's so unused to wearing them that they're hurting her.

The relief is immediate, but lessened when Alexandra comes over and plumps herself down straight opposite Lucy. She's accompanied by Soraya, another woman on the course with a very loud voice, who seems fractionally less of a bitch than Alexandra. At least, that's what Lucy had thought.

Soraya leans forward on one elbow, an air of self-importance to her actions. Lucy can feel her hackles rising, hairs standing up on the back of her neck. Soraya opens her mouth to speak, and for a moment Lucy wants nothing more than to slam her hand into the woman's face and stop her before she says something that Lucy can't unhear.

'Have you asked him about his wife?' Soraya says.

'I know she does some work with prison literacy,' Lucy says, a sense of hauteur running through her. They can't catch her out like that; of course she knows he's married.

'So you know I'm talking about the professor,' Soraya says, smirking.

Lucy feels her cheeks flush red. 'Who else would you be talking about?' she says, trying to get the conversation back under her control.

'He likes to keep his private life private, we all know that,' Alexandra says, joining in. 'But we all know about *this* wife.'

Lucy's heart drops a beat.

'But do you know about the other one? The wife before?'

Lucy looks at her, silent. She doesn't know what to reply.

Alexandra licks her lips, the tip of her tongue darting from one side of her mouth to the other. She smiles again, showing her teeth.

'The wife before?' Lucy says eventually.

'Yeah,' Alexandra says. 'The one who died.'

OUTSIDE

You lied. You fucking LIED, you SWORE it wasn't like that. You said she didn't understand you. You said that in class. To EVERYONE.

I'm such a fool, such a total and utter fool. Did you think I wouldn't find out? You can't hide anything from me.

So I'm sitting minding my own business in my little shed, all tucked up and comfy like you know I like to be, when out she comes, waddling and fat and glowing.

I smile.

You won't catch me going above a size ten.

But then I see her side on and I know it's not fat.

She's pregnant.

She's having YOUR baby.

I should be having your baby. Not her. It's not right. She's trapped you. Maybe she stole your sperm. I guess you only fuck her to keep her happy, not because you want to.

You should only want me.

25

At that moment, Charlie comes back with the drinks, pints of lager and some tequila slammers as well. The conversation gets lost in the melee that ensues, shouts and screams of laughter as the MSc cohort reconvenes round the table.

Lucy joins in, but only superficially. Any sense of relaxation she felt before has disappeared, Alexandra's words playing on her mind. So what if the professor was married before? It's not that unreasonable. He's in his late fifties, over twice her age. At least two lifetimes.

At last, it's just her and Soraya at the table. Everyone else has gone to play table football. She looks over at Soraya, who seems now to be looking at her with some kindness.

'His wife died? Is that such a big deal?' Lucy says. 'I mean, it's very sad. But people do die. It happens.'

'You'll have to ask Alexandra,' Soraya says. 'She knows the details more than I do.'

Lucy looks over at Alexandra, who is flashing a lot of cleavage as she manoeuvres the knobs on the football table. Her face twinges with dislike.

Soraya clearly picks up on it. 'She's not so bad, you know. You should give her a chance.'

'What about her giving me a chance?'

'I'm sure she would, if you didn't spend every waking moment either with the professor or doing his work. She hasn't exactly had the opportunity to get to know you. None of us have.'

'I'm not here to make friends,' Lucy says. Soraya laughs, so she smiles, but she's not joking. There's only one friendship she's been interested in building, and it's not to be found in this bar.

'All I'm saying is – be careful, Lucy,' Soraya says. 'I don't know much about you—'

'You certainly don't,' Lucy interrupts.

'Let me finish. Underneath the piss-taking, Alexandra is a bit worried about you. I am too, to be honest.'

'Are you trying to imply he's like some kind of Bluebeard? Dead wives in the attic?'

'No, not that. But there are rumours.'

'Rumours?' Lucy says.

'He's got this lovely wife,' Soraya says, in an apparent non sequitur, 'but you know how things can be.'

'Things?' Lucy says, not making it easy for her.

'Oh, you know what I mean, Lucy. I don't have to spell it out for you.'

Lucy raises an eyebrow, still not helping.

Soraya takes a deep breath, her expression crosser than usual. 'OK, if you're going to force me. There's this dead wife in the background, and now, despite the lovely *current* wife, the handsome Edgar is allegedly in the market for distractions. There are at least three affairs that I've heard about. And if that's the tip of the iceberg . . .' She pauses, pouts in a coquettish way. Both she and Lucy start to laugh.

'Good to know,' Lucy says. 'Good to know.'

She finishes her drink in one go, Soraya too, the chill between them melted now.

'I mean, *I* would. Wouldn't you?' Soraya says, tongue darting round the corners of her mouth. Her lips are wet, her tongue fleshy, and the moment of unity passes. Lucy feels a surge of revulsion, her gaze drawn irresistibly in by the red maw, like a fly at the edge of a Venus flytrap.

'I mean, he's gorgeous, wife or no wife. Plus his professional position. Everyone might be watching him, desperate for him to fail, but that's only because they're jealous. He's made himself the undisputed expert, the first person justice ministers consult whenever they bring in a new policy. Who'd be able to resist?' Soraya's voice continues relentlessly, working its way into Lucy's ears, seeping into her skull. The fact that this is just what she's been thinking herself only makes it worse, that she's complicit with this leering fool, brought down to a level that she can't deny is exactly where she belongs.

She leaves shortly after this conversation, having sobered up entirely. Charlie was making hopeful faces at her before she went, edging his thigh closer and closer to hers, but the buzz has gone. She's full of confusion now, not infinite potential; the professor she's idolised has feet of clay, a cheat and a liar, infidelity and lies dripping off him. If she's honest with herself, though, that's not the issue. The issue is her. He's found other women attractive. Why not her?

She's washed up, a failure. She had one goal, to impress the professor, and she fucked it up.

She's sober, but too wired for sleep. The flagstones are cold under her bare feet, but after the heat of the beer cellar, it comes as a relief. She's heading towards the garden to sit under a tree for a moment and try and find some peace. This can't be the end of all her dreams. There must be something she can do to save the situation.

As she walks through the cloisters, she hears footsteps coming from the opposite direction, and looks up automatically.

It's him.

She puts her head down and spins around, heading back the way she came. If she's quick, he won't notice her.

'Lucy,' the professor says. 'Glad I've caught you.' His voice is entirely normal. No sign of the anger that he showed last time they spoke. 'Do you have a moment?'

She blinks. The shoes she's carrying in her hand feel as if they've turned into clown shoes, with massive toes and flashing red lights. She lifts a hand up to wipe away the eyeliner smeared under her eyes.

Without waiting for an answer, he leads the way into his office, holding the doors open for her as they go. Once they're in, he gestures for her to take a seat in one of the leather armchairs by the fireplace while he goes to a side table and pours them each a measure of whisky from a heavy crystal decanter.

Wordlessly, he hands the drink to her and sits down in the chair opposite. She sips from it, glad that the stink of alcohol already emanating from her will be masked soon by the peaty liquor. Talisker, maybe, or Laphroaig. It's delicious, the glow of it warming her from within.

He sips, clears his throat. Here it comes, some comment about last week, a warning maybe, another reproach.

'I hope you don't mind this extra work – I probably shouldn't be asking you to do it,' he says. It's as if none of it has happened.

'But last week . . .'

He puts up his hand. Clearly nothing to discuss.

'I don't mind the extra work at all,' she says. 'I'm learning from it all the time.'

'I'm beginning to wonder what I did without you. Your assistance is invaluable.'

'Don't you have anyone else who can help you?' She knows she's fishing, but she can't help it.

'Not as good as you,' he says with a smile.

She smiles back. 'You said there was something else?'

'Yes, I've got this talk next Saturday in Cambridge. It's going to be a lot of preparation – they've begged me to do it as a favour, as one of their speakers can't get a visa to come over.'

'That's a bit shit.'

'Totally shit.'

She flushes at his repetition of the swear word – she shouldn't have said it. Too casual. Too familiar. 'Terrible, I mean.'

'No, shit is exactly the word.' He smiles, a moment of complicity between them, the air shifting closer. 'It's a travesty. He's a Nigerian professor, highly respected in the field. It's outrageous that it can't be sorted in time. It may be possible still, but the organisers don't want to risk leaving a gap. He's meant to be a keynote speaker.' He stops, wanders over to the window and looks out at the big horse chestnut tree in the garden behind. Lucy stays quiet, not sure whether he's finished speaking or if there's more to come. 'So I need to prepare a keynote speech, which is great in principle. It needs to be good, though.'

'It'll be brilliant.'

'It will be if you help me.'

'I'd love to help you, professor.'

'Please, call me Edgar,' he says.

26

Lucy has the work finished by the middle of the following week, and she emails through her summaries to the professor – Edgar – heart in mouth. Objectively, she knows what she's done is good, but she's still anxious, keen to impress. Keen to get inside his head, at least a little. She checks and rechecks her emails for the next couple of hours, twitching every time a notification comes up, before finally she receives a reply.

Good job. Thanks. Do you want to come with me? You might find it interesting.

Does she want to come? She almost laughs at the question. It's a no-brainer.

Yes, please. Let me know the details and I'll be there.

This time, his reply doesn't take so long.

Great. I'm driving, so come to the house at 8am on Saturday morning. See you then.

He includes his address and she googles it. Not far, just up the Woodstock Road. She won't even have to get up that early.

Lucy rolls her eyes at her optimism on Saturday morning, having had the worst night's sleep she's had since she started

154

the masters. She'd been on the cusp of sleep for hours, blurred figures crawling in and out and over her as she hovered on the edge of consciousness. It's a relief to get up finally, blast herself with a hot shower, the water easing the tension in her neck and shoulders as she shaved her legs, her armpits. After a moment's hesitation, her bikini line, too. Not for any reason, of course. It needed doing. That's all.

It's going to be fine. There's nothing to worry about. All she's doing is sitting in a car with a man for a few hours, listening to some papers about penal policy and the criminal justice system. She knows it'll be fascinating – she enjoyed the articles she summarised, found lots of useful information for her own research.

She's not fooling herself with this reassurance. There's more to it than that. She wants to impress, entice, draw Edgar into her. She might have started out wanting his expertise, but now she wants a whole lot more from him, rumours or not.

Hair dried and styled, she paints her face carefully, emphasising the hollows under her cheekbones, the slant of her eyes, the red of her lips. Too red. Like Soraya's the other week. Fleshy, lascivious. Grabbing a piece of loo roll, she scrubs it off her face, before applying lip gloss in a neutral shade. She checks herself up and down in the mirror, the dressed-down version of the little black dress: black trousers, black top, black shoes, black eyeliner. Nude lips. Nude . . .

Fuck's sake, it's as if Soraya's moved into her head. She shakes herself free. It's time to go.

'You found us all right, then,' Edgar says.

Lucy nods. It was easy enough to find his house, a neat semi-detached set back behind a privet hedge. Very domestic.

155

Not quite the setting she'd imagined for him, but then he has the kind of face that would look best in a dark bar, cigarette hanging from his lips as candlelight lent shadows to play across his perfectly chiselled features.

Soraya is back again. Lucy's IQ is dropping in real time the more she looks at him. How the hell does anyone get any work done around him? It must drive him mad. She looks away, staring out of the window as they drive out of Oxford in silence.

After a while, Edgar clears his throat. 'Sorry, I know I'm being very quiet. My wife's had some bad news about a woman she's been working with. She's relapsed, been arrested for theft and assault. Rachel is worried about her.' He pauses. 'Not much we can do about that right now, though.'

'Sorry to hear that.'

He nods. 'Anyway, this really does promise to be fascinating,' he says, keeping his eyes on the road ahead.

He drives well, Lucy thinks, a smooth ride, the steering wheel held lightly between his hands. Perfect command of the road . . .

Fuck's sake . . .

'Yes, I'm looking forward to it,' she says, pleased that her voice manages to come out sounding normal.

'All the speakers are great, but I'd particularly recommend Alison Liebling. She's doing a session on prison suicide. One of our finest criminologists.'

The thought of Soraya is ousted, all triviality gone from Lucy's mind. She's breathless, dunked into a vat of cold water, the shock of the word *suicide* reverberating around her.

Finally, she recovers herself. 'I've read some of her stuff,'

Lucy says. Edgar doesn't reply, and a silence stretches out between them. It's oddly comforting.

The traffic has ground to a halt, an accident ahead. He coughs, clears his throat. 'You said something a few weeks ago, when I asked what came into your mind when you thought about prison. You said your mother.'

Another sucker punch, head back under the ice.

She looks straight ahead at the brake lights of the car in front. This wasn't how she was planning on telling it. But maybe now, maybe it is the right time.

Deep breath. Another.

'She was in prison. When she died.'

'How did she die?'

'She hanged herself with a sheet. They hadn't picked up what a bad state she was in.'

'I'm sorry,' he says, and he turns to her, only quickly, but for long enough for her to see the concern in his eyes. 'My mother died five years ago. I thought I'd be able to cope, but it's changed everything. How old were you?'

'It was five years ago. I was seventeen. Not that young.'

'Young enough. Hard at any age, really. Is your dad still around?'

'He is. Sort of. It hit him very hard.' She can't bring herself to mention the drinking. She's too ashamed.

'I'm not surprised.'

She watches the fields pass in the window, the hedgerows, the trees battling to absorb the exhaust from a thousand different vehicles. Thoughts of a car journey long ago come into her mind unbidden, her mother laughing, *I spy, I spy, I spy with my little eye, something beginning with . . .*

'Do you mind telling me what happened?'

'She should never have been in prison,' Lucy says. 'We always knew that. She was having a breakdown – she wasn't herself.'

'Was there a trigger for that?'

'My little brother died. He had cancer. It was too much for her. She started drinking to numb the pain of that, got hooked in.'

'I'm sorry,' Edgar says. He sounds sincere. 'Why did she get sent to prison?'

'Shoplifting. Repeat offending – she kept trying to take booze from the supermarket. No sooner was she out of court than she'd get nicked again. She needed help, though. Not prison.' The words tumble out of her, a little pile of vomited stones she's pouring on to Edgar's lap.

'That's terrible,' he says. 'Everything about it.'

He reaches his hand out to her from the steering wheel and puts it on her arm. It's warm. Her heart jolts in her chest at his touch.

'I . . . Oh, shit.'

Lucy jumps at the exclamation. She'd almost forgotten they were driving, but thankfully Edgar hasn't. The cars ahead have started moving, someone honking at them from behind.

He lets go of her arm, grips the steering wheel. She stops talking. There's nothing else to say.

27

As soon as they arrive, they're swept up into a throng of delegates for the conference. Edgar seems to know almost everyone who passes them – not just superficially, but enough to have any number of in-depth conversations about the status of X's grant application, or Y's upcoming publication in a prestigious journal.

The enthusiasm is infectious, as is being in the orbit of such a star. Lucy is sparkling in his wake, introduced to any number of people as his brilliant MSc student who's done such a great job helping him prepare for this. Every time he says it, she grows pinker, more flushed, buzzing with the excitement of being a part of this.

At last, he makes his way to the podium, and Lucy flushes again with the excitement of the thought that out of everyone here, she is his student, studying directly beneath him. There's a ripple of anticipation in the auditorium, as if to say here he is, the one we've all been waiting for, and Lucy watches with amusement as half the women in the room start flicking at their hair as he passes.

Not that she can talk. The reactions he's eliciting have changed her perception of him, no doubt. She thought he was attractive before, charismatic; now it's turning into something even more profound.

Edgar quotes from the articles that Lucy herself summarised – she recognises the information. He's so passionate about the subject, though, it's as if she's hearing it all for the first time, with a new clarity as the pieces fall into place: her mum's mental-health issues, the addictions, the crimes committed to fuel her habit once her relationship with Lucy's father broke down. They had all tried to help her, but she was beyond any assistance they could give.

A tear trickles down Lucy's cheek, another, the horror of it, the tragedy of the waste fully hitting home, before Edgar's speech reaches its crescendo and she's filled with a hope, an inspiration she's never known before. She's found her vocation now. She's not alone – the room rises to its feet in a standing ovation, a ringing endorsement of the prison abolition that Edgar has outlined as the starting point of his vision for the future, and now Lucy is standing too, her hands stinging as she claps them together to join in the applause.

The rest of the day passes in a blur. Even the keynote speech by Alison Liebling, brilliant as it is, fails to have the same impact on Lucy as Edgar's did earlier, the power of it still reverberating through her. It's plain it's had the same effect on most of the other delegates, too, and the hair-flicking increases wherever he moves.

At last they get to the end of the lectures, and Edgar takes her by the elbow, leading her through to the bar where the delegates are congregating. At nearly every step, he's sought out, women stopping him to congratulate him on his work, his speech, his research. Some men too, though fewer of those, Lucy notices. Despite the attempts to distract him, Edgar shows an admirable level of determination to get to the bar, replying to each new greeting only with a nod and a smile, his grip on her arm unchanged as he uses her almost as a battering ram to make his way through.

Now they're at the bar, leaning against it. It's still a crush behind her, but at least there's no one standing in front of Lucy now. She takes in a deep breath, relishing the head space.

'What do you want?' Edgar says.

'Red wine, please.'

He orders her a large glass, the same for himself, and when the drinks are poured, he holds his glass out to her as if in invitation. She raises hers, a little hesitantly, and he clinks his off the side of it.

'Cheers! Thanks so much for your help.'

'I barely did anything.'

'That's not true,' he says. 'I can see how much work went into those summaries. You got to the heart of each of the articles in a way I haven't seen done for a very long time.'

She's about to argue, dismiss her contribution further, but she stops herself. A man wouldn't minimise the work he'd done, so why should she?

Mind you, he might not be leaning quite so close if she were a man, nor looking quite so intently at her. She knows she should object to it, but she can't help responding, leaning in closer herself, flicking her hair in exactly the way that she's been observing in the other women around him. It's different in this case, though; he is genuinely interested in what she has to say about the speakers they've heard today, laughing at her jokes in exactly the way she'd hoped that he would.

She doesn't need to attract his attention – she's got it. The room might be crowded, but it could be empty for all it matters to them, enclosed as they are in a bubble that excludes everyone else.

She can smell the red wine on his breath, a hint of cologne, and underneath that, a scent of sweat, warm and earthy. She's moving in closer and closer, ignoring the chatter around them, people coming over occasionally and attempting to pull him free, defeated by the magnetic bond between them. Lucy has never felt so understood, so heard, as she does this moment, the intensity of Edgar's gaze not intimidating her but instead drawing her even further out of herself. At this moment, there's nothing she wouldn't share, no fantasy too dark, no secret too buried—

'There's something I've been meaning to talk to you about,' he says, and she thrills at the words.

'What is it?'

'It's a project I've been working on,' he says. Her heart sinks a little, rises again. Work is his passion, after all. The rest will follow.

'What's the project?'

'That's the thing. It's highly confidential. I've been working alone on it, but I need some help. I was waiting to see . . . well, I was waiting to see if you'd be suitable. But I think you will be. It's—' He turns away from her abruptly. 'Fuck,' he says, and a man appears in front of them, his hands held up in front of him as if to say he comes in peace. Lucy looks between the two of them, Edgar's face wary, the other man's challenging, one eyebrow raised, before the men wrap their arms round each other, in what could be an embrace or a death grip.

Lucy feels light-headed. The bubble has burst, and for a moment the noise in the bar threatens to overwhelm her.

'I can't believe it,' Edgar says, stepping back from the embrace, his hands still on the stranger's shoulders. The anger has faded from his face, but there's still a trace of suspicion. 'You're the last person I expected to see here.'

Lucy swallows her disappointment. She was hoping to have Edgar to herself.

'Why didn't you tell me you'd be here?' Edgar says.

'I thought you might try and avoid me.' The man speaks with a slight accent. There's a shake in his voice. The sense of disappointment Lucy was feeling shifts, makes way for something different. She's still in the inner circle, still privileged, witnessing what is clearly a deeply personal moment.

'Forget all that shit. This is you and me. You know I'd always want to see you.' Edgar turns to Lucy. 'Lucy, meet Victor. One of my colleagues from – God, I don't know, about ten years ago? Victor, this is Lucy, one of my masters students, though you would think she was a post-doc. She's brilliant.'

Victor reaches out his hand and Lucy shakes it, taking him in at the same time. He's younger than Edgar, she reckons, though not by too much. Less grey in his hair, fewer wrinkles. Also very good-looking. The hair-flicking around them has doubled in intensity. Lucy catches herself doing the same and grips her glass with both hands to stop it.

'Hi,' she says. 'Nice to meet you.'

'You too,' he says, smiling at her.

'Let's get out of here,' Edgar says. 'We need to speak properly. Let's go and get food somewhere.'

'What about the conference dinner?' Lucy says.

'Fuck the conference dinner. This is more important,' he says. He takes each of them by the arm and pulls them through the bar. The bubble is back around them, now expanded to include Victor. As Lucy clocks all the envious glances darting in her direction as she leaves with the two men, she's happy to welcome him inside.

CCTV

Charybdis walks into the kitchen, bottle in one hand, a bunch of lilies in the other. She's grinning, more a grimace than a smile. Drinking from the bottle as she goes, she takes a large jar and fills it with water before putting it on the table.

She arranges the lilies in the jar before sitting down at the table, bottle in front of her, waiting for someone.

A while later, Scylla comes into the room. She looks tired. When she sees the flowers, her face tightens, her mouth disappearing into a straight line. She goes straight for the jar and pulls them out, bashing their heads against the table until all the petals have been knocked off.

Charybdis laughs. She continues to drink from the whisky bottle, though it's having no visible effect on her, other than the growing sneer on her face. Scylla lunges, grabbing the bottle and taking a long swig, coughing after she swallows before taking another swig. Charybdis tries to get the bottle back from her – Scylla takes two more deep swallows before handing it back.

When she has the bottle safely back in her possession,

Charybdis goes through the door at the back of the kitchen and out of shot. Scylla stands in the middle of the room, swaying, before she sits down at the table and bursts into tears.

28

Although it's Saturday night, the three of them manage to find a table at a restaurant easily enough. Edgar leads the way in, seating Victor opposite him and Lucy to his right. She's pleased that she still gets to sit next to him, until he and Victor become engrossed in conversation. She might as well not be there. So much for her nonsensical fantasies of how the evening would play out.

A waiter appears beside them to take their order for drinks, and Lucy interrupts the men to draw their attention. Edgar turns to her almost with confusion when she taps at his arm, mouth still open, mid-sentence. He asks for a bottle of red wine without even checking what the other two are drinking, before waving the waiter away.

Lucy raises an eyebrow at his presumptuous behaviour, half-irritated, half-entertained, and Victor catches her eye, a similar expression on his face.

'Still the same Edgar,' he says, interrupting their conversation to include Lucy. 'I haven't seen him for ten years but nothing has changed.' His words might be critical, but his tone is far from it, a fondness that's survived all this time. Lucy is impressed; it's yet another virtue of Edgar's that he can inspire loyalty and friendship like this, not just the lust that so many have shown him.

Including her. She sits on her hands to stop them from reaching up inadvertently to her hair, smiling back at Victor.

'We need to include our friend here in the conversation,' he continues, gesturing at Lucy. 'There will be plenty of time for all this.'

Edgar nods, no sign of annoyance that he'd prefer not to be interrupted. 'Sorry, Lucy. Of course. It's just been such a long time . . .'

'How come so long?' Lucy says. 'I mean, pandemic aside.'

The men look at each other with rueful expressions, almost shame-faced, as if they've been caught doing something wrong. Then they speak, both of them at once, before Edgar prevails.

'Victor is one of the finest thinkers I've ever met,' he says. 'He's got a wealth of experience from universities in the US, specialising in prisons in Central America. He worked with me in Oxford for a couple of years, gave me some incredible insights.'

Victor is nodding, his face lit up with enthusiasm. 'It was a brilliant time. Cross-pollination of ideas, some truly revolutionary concepts that we were working on. I remember it so fondly.'

Lucy has finally put two and two together. 'Wait, you're Victor Machado? Sorry, I've only just clocked. I've read your book about prison and philosophy. It's brilliant.'

Even more enthusiasm on his face, if that were possible. 'I can't believe you've read it.'

'Lucy has read everything,' Edgar says. 'I told you she was brilliant.'

The love-in is getting silly. Any minute they'll be suggesting a threesome. Lucy almost snorts at the thought, glancing between the two men and thinking, on balance, she wouldn't be entirely averse to it. At that moment Edgar catches her eye, and she blushes to her hairline, paranoid suddenly that he can see what she's thinking.

Mercifully the waiter arrives at that moment to pour the wine. Victor holds his hand over his glass, muttering about driving, but Edgar and Lucy's glasses are filled. Lucy takes a huge gulp to cover her confusion, but in doing so, she ends up spilling half of it down her shirt before slopping the rest of it over the table when she puts her glass down too fast.

'Let me help you,' Edgar says, dabbing at her front with his napkin, his arm grazing dangerously close to her breasts. She jumps to her feet, muttering something about going to the ladies', before escaping to lean her head against the cool wooden door once she's locked it behind her.

She's behaving like a fucking idiot, all clumsy and adolescent. They're academics. Criminologists. Not rock stars. When she's out of the cubicle, she splashes at her face with cold water, willing herself to cool down, reminding herself of quite how ordinary they are, how ridiculous she's being.

It's no good though. She can't fight it anymore. She's obsessed. She thinks about the way he's described her to Victor – *brilliant*. Surely it must mean he's got a thing about her, too, that he's noticed she exists not just as a tool to summarise his work for him, but as something more than that, someone real.

Only too real. Her face is still flushed, her shirt stained with wine, and the eyeliner that she applied that morning is long gone, only a trace of it remaining to enhance the shadows under her eyes in the harsh light of the bathroom. She dabs at her shirt, drags her fingers through her hair, wipes off what's left of the eyeliner, before giving it up for a waste of time. Edgar is so good-looking, his age a badge of honour that suits him more than she can say. He doesn't need her to be beautiful, just brilliant. That's how she'll reel him in.

But the mood has changed by the time that she gets back to the table. Victor's face is drawn, all smiles gone, while Edgar's is flushed red, distress almost palpable in the air. Anger, too. She slips back into her chair and looks from one to the other before checking the bottle of wine which is almost empty. Edgar's been hitting it hard, or so it looks by the flush on his face.

'Is everything all right?'

Edgar is staring down at his glass, no reply forthcoming. Victor steps into the silence.

'We were . . . We were talking about why I went back home,' he says. 'When I left Oxford.'

'I was wondering about that, if you'd thought of staying on,' she says.

'There were reasons I needed to get back,' he says. 'Family stuff. Plus visas. My tenure was uncertain, and they wouldn't extend the visa past the end of the last term of my contract. I was under threat of deportation if I didn't get out.'

'I did try,' Edgar interrupts. 'I did try. But there was so much else . . .'

Victor picks up the narrative again, looking at Lucy yet past her, his eyes sliding away.

'Gabriela,' he says, and at the name Edgar seems to shudder, huddling into himself. 'That's what was going on.'

'Who is Gabriela?' Lucy says, her voice low. The skin is crawling on the top of her scalp.

'Gabriela was my wife,' Edgar says, sitting upright. 'She was killed.'

Victor puts his hand up. 'Murdered. She was murdered. By an evil bitch of a stalker.'

'We're not going to agree on this, Victor. I know what you're telling me, but . . .' Edgar leans back into his chair, head slumped. His shoulders move up and down as he inhales deeply. 'She was killed. That I will say.'

Soraya's words, *this dead wife in the background*. No one said anything about her being killed. Or anything about stalkers.

Lucy's scalp prickles. 'She was what . . .?'

No reply.

She looks from Edgar to Victor, back to Edgar. Their faces are still. Too still. Lucy can see the tension sparking between them. Any minute, one of them is going to leap out of their seat, grab the other by the throat.

The waiter comes to the table, asks if they're ready to order. The moment passes. Victor's face relaxes, slightly. He shakes his head to food, orders another bottle of wine.

'I think they're going to need it,' he says.

Victor starts the account. Edgar is too far gone, still hunched over, his face pinched now in a way that robs it of all pretensions to beauty. This is how he'll look when he's old, Lucy can picture it: the deep lines that have formed from nose to lip, the pallor that's overtaken him.

'I went to see Gabriela this morning.' Lucy takes a moment to catch on; Gabriela's grave is what he means. An image of a headstone comes into her mind. Flowers. A man standing, his head bowed. 'She was perfect,' Victor continues. 'The kindest woman you could meet. Everyone loved her. She was truly—'

'She was my wife,' Edgar interrupts, 'and I didn't look after her properly. It's a short story, really, though there's no end to the pain it's caused. One of my students – she became obsessed with me. I didn't know. She was bright, I was help-ing her with her dissertation. Anyway, she found out that Gabriela was pregnant, and she lost her mind. I came home from the university one evening to find Gabriela dead. Killed.'

'It was all planned. She was stalking her. It was murder,' Victor says, his face grim. 'Premeditated murder.'

'It wasn't *planned*, Victor. She didn't know what she was doing.'

'Who is "she"?' Lucy says, but they ignore her.

'Edgar,' Victor says, as if in warning. 'You know that's not true.'

'I still can't accept what you told me,' Edgar says.

She can't look away from him, from the way he's glaring at Victor, his face full of anger.

'Wait till you see the notebook,' Victor says. 'Then you'll change your mind.'

'I have seen it. I got the scans you sent.'

'It's different when you see it for real. The way the pen digs into the paper, the anger . . . it's obsessive. It changes everything.'

'I will not change my mind. You're the one who's changed. This goes against everything I've ever taught. We can dress it up in academic theory as much as we want, but it comes down to forgiveness. Redemption. Without them, there's nothing,' Edgar shouts, sitting up now. He's practically standing, hands clenched into fists as they rest on the table.

Lucy is finding it hard to breathe; so much emotion in the air she wants to shut her eyes, cover her ears. Make it all go away. Edgar shakes his head as if to throw it off, at least the worst of it. Gradually, he sits back, unclenches his fists. Then he drinks some wine, his eyes closed.

'What happened next? After the . . . death?' Lucy says, finally getting her breath back enough to be able to speak.

Victor takes over again. 'As I said, the woman confessed. No need for a trial, that was something. Sentenced to life.'

Without stopping to think, Lucy says, 'Ten years ago – does that mean her killer is out now?'

A tremor runs through Victor – she can feel it, as if there's a source of tension in the air. 'No,' he says. 'That's why I'm here. I want to make sure she never gets out.'

Lucy digs her nails into the palms of her hands. Edgar doesn't reply, drinking what's left in his glass and refilling it before sitting back down. The bottle is empty, and he waves it in the direction of the waiter, who swiftly brings a replacement. Edgar glances down at the menu before ordering quickly, shared platters of tapas and chips.

The subject is clearly closed. There's so much more that Lucy wants to know, wants to ask, but she's not going to get anywhere. At least for now.

29

The mood lifts when the food arrives. They've had a decade to deal with this, Lucy reminds herself as she finds herself judging Edgar for the alacrity with which he's throwing food into his mouth, trauma apparently forgotten. Victor eats less, she notices, but he's still chatty. The conversation moves on to his work, what he's been doing since his return to Bolivia, his subsequent move to the US, the difficulties he faces in getting either country to reconsider the punitive nature of their penal systems.

She's more shaken than either of them, the weight of the revelations lying heavy on her. She's trying to make sense of what the men were discussing, what new information Victor thinks might change Edgar's mind. She doesn't dare ask for it herself.

Despite all the wine, she feels totally sober. She can't be, though. Edgar has drunk the lion's share of it, but still, they've got through the second bottle, nearly finished a third. She's relieved when Edgar says no to an aperitif, orders coffees instead and asks for the bill. It's still early, not yet nine, but she's exhausted.

Victor pulls out his wallet to pay, but Edgar waves it away.

'This is on me,' he says. 'Now look, you can't go vanishing without telling me where you're going. I'm not losing touch with you again.'

'I'm going back to Oxford tonight. I need to get back for something,' Victor says. 'I'm staying for a few more days, but I really wanted to see you. I went round to your house earlier but obviously you weren't there – I only came here because I saw you were on the programme for this conference.'

'What's so urgent?' Edgar says, though there's a resigned note to his question.

'You know what's so urgent,' Victor says. 'I want you to look at this. Please.' He reaches down into the bag by his feet and pulls out an A4-sized brown envelope containing something small and rectangular.

'Is that . . .?'

'The notebook. Yes.'

Victor holds it out to Edgar. After a moment, he takes it, holding it by its edges, as if he were handling a snake.

'Promise me you'll read it, at least. And you'll think about it. That's all I'm asking.'

Edgar nods. 'You're trusting me a lot with this. What if I decided to destroy it?'

Victor laughs, a short, dry cough that twists his mouth. 'You could destroy it if you wanted to. But we both know what it says. I think if you actually look at it, though, if you see the anger . . . It's disturbing stuff, Edgar. The parole board needs to see it. She can't be set free.'

Edgar nods again.

'I'm due back at yours on Monday evening. She invited me for dinner.' Victor's eyes slide away from Lucy as he says *she*. Are Lucy's intentions that obvious? She lowers her head.

'You'll come?' Edgar asks.

'Of course I'll come. Maybe we can talk about it all, if you have a chance to look at it before then.' Victor gestures towards the envelope, which Edgar has left on the table beside him.

Talk about what? Look at what? Lucy is bursting with questions, but she bites her tongue.

'I'm happy to show you how you've misinterpreted it.'

'Or you could accept you're wrong – and do something about it,' Victor says, his voice surprisingly gentle considering the aggression there's been between them during the evening. The men stare at each other for a moment, a muscle twitching at Edgar's jaw.

'I'm not wrong,' he says. Silence for a beat, two.

'I'll send it to the parole board myself, Edgar. You know I'll do it. But I'd rather we worked together on this.'

Edgar shakes his head, his lips compressed. A moment later he says, 'Anyway. Won't you stay tonight?' A lighter tone, an effort to get himself under control after all the outbursts of emotion.

'I'm sorry, I can't. I need to get back. I borrowed a car and I need to return it.'

Edgar looks at Lucy. 'How about you? You could get a lift with Victor if you want? Or there's a hotel room available for you. I spoke to the conference organisers about it, told them you were my researcher. Do you need to get back for anything?'

Time stops, a breach. A primrose path to hell to her left, Edgar smiling up at her; a steep and thorny path to heaven to her right in a rented car with a man she's only just met. She should leave. Even if a long drive in a borrowed car with someone she's only just met is hardly tempting.

And there's the wife. Edgar's wife. Lucy's never even met her. They're not friends. Lucy owes her nothing. But at the same time, she should do the honest thing, the more sisterly thing. Anything else will come back to bite her.

On the other hand, from what little Edgar has said, it doesn't seem their relationship is in great shape. He hardly spends any time at home, is always working or at conferences. His wife doesn't sound as if she has much in common with him. Lucy would be doing them both a favour, hastening the end of something that should have been put out of its misery long ago.

Oh, who's she trying to kid? The only person she'll be helping is herself, to someone else's husband. But dear God, she wants him.

Victor looks at her as if to say he can't help her, she's on her own with this. Edgar has one eyebrow raised, his good looks fully returned by now, a saturnine twist to his mouth. She knows what she should do; she knows she's not going to do it.

'I'll stay,' she says. 'I left my coat in your car.'

Victor is kind enough not to smirk at the paucity of her excuse. He squeezes her shoulder in farewell as if to tell her to be careful, although she knows she's most likely projecting thoughts into his mind. He and Edgar embrace, less of a death grip this time.

'I'm going to come and see you on Monday,' Victor says. There's an emphasis on the last word, though Lucy might be imagining it. She feels very young all of a sudden; there's a distinct sense of *pas devant les enfants* lurking there. 'We'll discuss it then.' He nods at Lucy, smiling at her before he turns and leaves, taking some of the warmth of the room with him.

Edgar sinks back down into his chair. 'Sorry, that was a lot,' he says.

'It's OK,' she says. 'I understand. I mean, my mum . . .'

'Yeah. We both know what it means to lose someone so suddenly . . .' He stops for a moment, clears his throat. 'I've got much better at keeping it all under control. But seeing Victor . . .'

'He seems like a lovely man,' Lucy says, and Edgar nods in agreement.

'The best. It was hard for him, too. I think for both of us. Seeing each other brings back a lot of bad memories.'

Death, deportation. A murdered wife, a mother hanging by a ligature from the end of a bunk in a prison cell.

'Are you all right?' Edgar says, leaning forward and putting his hand on hers. 'You look very pale.'

'I don't know.'

'What a waste,' he says. 'But time moves on. We adapt. Look at you. If you keep going like you are, you could really be someone. Make a difference.'

She looks at him, her eyes bright with tears.

'I remarried,' Edgar says, 'I've made a new life for myself.'

Lucy looks at him. His expression is blank despite the positivity in his words. 'Is it one that you're happy with?' she asks.

He takes a deep breath, straightens his shoulders. 'Can I be totally honest with you?'

She nods.

'I've told you so much already, I may as well tell you this, too.' Another deep breath. 'No, I'm not happy. Not like I used to be . . .'

He stares into space. Struck by sudden decision, Lucy doesn't wait for him to finish the sentence. If she could make a difference, then what could they achieve together? She leans forward, puts a finger to his lips to hush him, then moves closer still, taking his face in her hands and pulling him in to kiss him, any thought of those around them completely out of her mind.

He kisses her back, but only for a moment before pulling his head away. She blanches, drenched in shame.

'I'm sorry,' she says. 'I thought . . .'

Leaning forward, he takes her hand in his. 'Not here. Not like this.'

She's still frozen. However kindly he's putting it, it's a rejection. She tries to pull her hand away. His grip tightens.

'Let's go to the hotel. Have some privacy. We don't need an audience for this.'

Without waiting for her reply, he signals to the waiter, pays the bill with a tap of his phone. Then he pulls her to her feet and leads her out behind him.

Maybe it's the darkness, the full moon shining bright above, but Edgar gives up on any idea of caution the moment they leave the restaurant. He kisses her in the street, in the lobby, halfway up the stairs to his room. Forget any audience, she's half naked by the time he opens the door to his room, her top somewhere round her waist. Only a few steps to the bed and then she's under him, the weight of him hard on top of her, all thinking stopped, only a mass of sensations flowing through her mind.

It's only when Edgar's phone buzzes with a message that the spell is broken. He gets up, rummages among the discarded clothes on the floor before sitting back down with it. Lucy's hit by reality again, a cold wave slapping her in the face. It's his wife, she must have guessed, worked out what Edgar's doing. Given him an ultimatum. Faceless, wordless, the wronged woman is in the room with them.

Edgar sighs, slams his phone down on the bed. 'Now, where were we?' he says. Lucy raises her face to his.

The phone buzzes again.

'Fuck. I told her I was working tonight.'

He's not talking to Lucy. He's talking to the ceiling above him, his eyes cast upwards impatiently.

'Everything all right?'

'It's fine. Just my wife.'

'Shouldn't you talk to her?'

'She knows I'm away. It's fine.'

Lucy stays silent. The curtain's been pulled back a little, light harsh on the cracks in the veneer.

'I will explain another time,' Edgar says. 'But I don't want to spoil this. Let's focus on us.'

Despite herself, there's nothing Lucy would like more. She's about to kiss him again when the phone buzzes for the third time. Edgar sighs again, looks at his phone. Slams it down even harder than before.

'I'm turning it off now,' he says. 'Sorry.'

'Your wife again?'

'No, Victor.'

'What does he want?'

'That envelope he gave me. He's asking me to look at it right now. I'm sorry, but I have better things to do. It can wait till the morning.'

With that, he turns to Lucy, his gaze intense.

The phone does not buzz again.

OUTSIDE

Your wife
  Is fucking CHEATING
  That man came round – your so-called FRIEND *– they're in the garden kissing and laughing, his hand on her belly . . .*
  Like it's his child inside.
  You shouldn't have to put up with this, you shouldn't have to put up with this at all.
  I'm going to have to fix this. I won't allow anyone to walk all over you.
  Let alone that BITCH *and her horrible baby.*

Part 3

30

The first year, that was the hardest for Marie. The most shocking, for sure. The weather was terrible – the weather is always terrible – and it was cold when they arrived, bitterly cold, and the holes in the walls not yet filled. Cameras she could see, cameras she couldn't, but they knew all right, they knew everything she did, wherever she went. Pretty much all she thought, too.

The air chilled, the days short. Woodsmoke smouldering from the low stone building she's still learning to call home. Electricity from solar panels, water from a nearby burn, a cesspit for waste – all the basics – but miles from anyone else, a long walk or a boat trip away.

It's safer this way. That's what she's always told herself.

Now it's all she knows.

She's built muscles cutting logs, building fires, rebuilding the walls and patching the roof. The grey has gone from her skin, the softness gone of all those hours confined, motionless, nothing but an endless maw for the processed shit they fed her. Now she's brown, strong, weather-beaten, her hair hacked out of her eyes by blunt scissors.

She's become attuned to the seasons, the rise and fall of the sun. A time to till, to sow, to harvest. To preserve against the winter ahead before spring comes again and the thaw.

That first year was the bleakest, yes. The larder bare, the wood store too, once the few logs that were left for them ready-chopped were burned. It was a long week until a pile of logs appeared at the pier. It took days to chop and carry them back to the house.

Janice didn't help.

Janice never helps.

Other than Mondays – or rather, the days they call Monday, every seventh sunrise. That's when Janice gets up first, paces the kitchen until Marie's ready to go. They walk down to the loch together. She forces herself to think that Janice is being friendly, but she knows it's because Janice wants to get to the whisky first. If they send it. It's not always there, but if it is, Janice isn't going to risk losing it.

Five winters they've been here, the days bleeding into one another, no idea of time or the world outside of this; the movement of the sun and the stars is how she moors herself now. In the spring, the leaves start to appear on the few, bent trees, the scrubby hawthorns that surround the croft softening under a fuzz of green. The days slowly lengthen and, for one month, maybe two, it's as close to peaceful as she could ask, before the midges arrive and render it unbearable.

There's a pattern to her days, a pattern to the months and years, outside of any human control. She's learned to wait, to watch. To expect nothing; to be prepared for anything.

Like Mondays. The delivery always comes, but that's the only certainty. She never knows what's going to be delivered, whether they'll eat well that week or if they'll need to live off the reserves she's managed to build up over the years.

Or whether she'll have to spend the next seven days dodging Janice drunk or cleaning her up once she's sober.

As ever, Janice is ready, waiting. It's only just gone dawn, the sun still low in the sky. They walk down together. Marie looks sideways at her companion, always surprised at the pace at which she can walk when they're going for the delivery. Normally she's stooped, slow. Now she's moving at speed, glee in her face. Today she might be lucky.

Lucky for Janice; not so lucky for Marie.

She doesn't understand why Janice doesn't make a run for the cardboard box on her own, why she always waits for Marie to go with her. One day she won't wait, but until then, Marie's normally the one to win the contest for the booze. Janice has been conditioned never to be alone. Terrified by the huge skies above them, the louring hills. Her fear's even greater than her love for alcohol.

Whisky was Marie's drink, before. Spurred on by her dad's dismissal, *whisky's not for girls*, she'd made a point of drinking it, forcing it down her until she learned to love the taste, the pungent scent of the deep amber liquid. But since that night, so long ago, she hasn't been able to smell it without it taking her straight back to the point where she came round, encrusted with vomit. Blood.

She was free of that sensory trigger for years. Maybe the biggest upside of that time. But now it haunts her, every time she sees the green bottle with its white label, sticking out of the delivery box like a challenge.

The first time she found a bottle in the box, she made the mistake of taking it back to the house with her. She thought she could ration it out to Janice, a small glass a night. It

187

could have lasted weeks. But Janice got hold of it before she could put it away, drank half of it pretty much in one go.

That was a long night. A lot of crying. A lot of vomit, too.

None the week after, nor the week after that, but the third week, a bottle appeared again. This was before Janice made sure to come down with Marie for the collection, so Marie got to it first, opened it and poured it out into the loch. Janice was trailing down to find her when she caught sight of the emptied bottle. It took all Marie's strength to push Janice off her, loosen her bony fingers from Marie's neck.

After that, Marie tried to get down to the collection point on her own every week, but without fail, Janice would already be up, waiting for her, matching her step by step down to the loch.

They're at the pier now and the box is here, as usual. Janice takes one look and spits with disgust, a guttural sound. No alcohol today. Marie hides her relief, kneeling beside it to go through the contents – the lentils she asked for, and a carton of almond milk, too. Nice, Janice'll like that. Once she gets over her fury about the lack of booze. Janice read an article in a magazine that was in the box a couple of weeks ago and now she won't shut up about being lactose intolerant. Marie nearly put some butter in the peas last night just to test her, but then she stopped herself. It's best not to be unkind. They always catch her.

For once, the sky over the loch is blue, the summits of the surrounding mountains clear silhouettes as the morning sun throws purple haze up off the heather. It won't be like this much longer, as the year turns to autumn. Winter is coming.

The kettle's boiling on the old Rayburn by the time she gets back, dumping the box down on the table with a grunt before she starts unpacking it. She freezes when she sees a glass bottle hidden at the bottom of the box under some greens. Janice moves fast as a hawk to pull it out, thumping it down with disgust when she sees it's a bottle of cordial. She stands over Marie as if she's about to hit her. Marie's poised, ready, her hands clenched under the table, but the moment passes. There's another magazine at the very bottom of the box and Janice pulls that out instead, slumping herself down at the table to read.

Only for a few seconds, though, before the colour drains out of Janice's cheeks, and she pushes the magazine aside. Fuck, Marie had meant to check what it was before she let Janice get to it. She picks it up and looks at it. *TRUE CRIME* is emblazoned on the cover, with small headlines shouting *KILLER MUM* and *BETRAYED BY THE TEACHER SHE LOVED* underneath photographs of sad women. She puts it on the table face down, covers it with a tea towel.

'I don't understand how people can bring themselves to read that,' Janice says. 'It's not entertainment. It's people's lives.'

Flashes of Tyburn pass through Marie's mind, the baying mob, the gallows. As it has always been.

'I guess it's how some people deal with their fear,' she says. 'Maybe their way of understanding it.'

'I don't want to understand.' Janice is wringing her hands.

Marie looks at them, her gaze caught for a moment. Those were the hands that . . . but Marie's not going to think about that. She's going to drink her tea. She can't control what they send, she can only control her reaction to it. She's learned the hard way that the worse her reaction, the more they try to provoke her. Janice is perfect for torment, a puppet twitching on their string. Marie, less so.

Later, when Janice has gone back to bed for a little nap after her upset, Marie picks up the mag and reads it cover to cover. All that complexity, reduced to a few paragraphs. She tears it in half along the spine, stuffs it into the Rayburn. It'll be burned up soon, nothing to distress Janice anymore.

Janice comes down, calmer now. 'Let's go for a walk,' she says, 'while it's still sunny.'

Marie stands up. 'That's a good idea.'

'I thought we could wander up the hill. It's windy, though. I need to tie my hair up. It's all over the place.'

Marie watches as she picks at her sparse locks. She's clearly agitated. It's that damn magazine. Still, Marie would rather deal with her like this than off her face, the cycle of laughing to screaming to crying, the dodging of glasses thrown, the long hours spent watching to make sure the woman doesn't choke to death on her own vomit.

'I need a ribbon for my hair. Do we have . . . hang on!' Janice says, as if seized by a sudden plan. She rushes through to the front room. Marie can hear thumps and rustles, as if Janice is digging around for something, and in a few moments the woman rushes back clutching a long piece of pink tape.

'I knew this would come in handy one day,' she says, her voice triumphant.

Marie takes it from her, wraps it round her fingers, forming the fuchsia-pink ribbon into a slipknot, pulling it tight around her thumb. *Hanged by the neck until you be dead.* The last time she saw tape like this was around her barrister's papers in court.

'Aren't I clever to keep it?' Janice says, insisting on praise.

'Very clever,' Marie says, getting the words out with an effort. She's trying not to think about what this particular piece of ribbon was last tied around, the evidence photographs of Janice's children, all three of them, laid out on the slab.

Janice takes the ribbon back and loops it round her head, tying it into a jaunty bow. Marie blinks, wipes her mind clean.

31

Another seven days gone. She's marked them off, the scratch marks taking up most of the wall. Five years, fifty-two days a year. Nearly 2,000 days. The first scratch in each group of seven is the deepest, to mark delivery days, the only external event to disturb the monotony. She calls it Monday, but it's just a name. It could be any day at all.

That aside, the days have passed in their usual way: cooking, chopping wood, calming Janice's fears when they get too much of an evening. She wouldn't want to be in Janice's head, the horrors that visit. Though it's not as if she's immune to them herself, the shadows that creep sometimes under the door she tries so hard to keep locked tight.

At least there's something concrete to do today, walking to the pier, collecting the box of food. They put in their requests the week before – now's the time to find out if they've been met, or if the organisation has gone rogue again. If only she could get used to it, the uncertainty. The unpredictability. She strives for radical acceptance. Easy enough if the stakes weren't so high. If they keep delivering the whisky, there'll come a day when Janice kills Marie. Or herself.

The house is quiet when she sets out. For once, Janice

hasn't woken. Let sleeping alcoholics lie. It's early still, the sun slowly emerging from beyond the hills, a pale disc of grey against the darker clouds. No warmth, though; she's glad of the fleece she's zipped up to her neck, the thick boots on her feet.

Down the hill, past the tendrils of bracken, brown now and dying back. Sheep are scattered here and there, their droppings glistening black on the path in front of her. One of them turns to watch as she passes, the eyes black too, a bottomless void. She shakes herself free of the thought she always has, that sheep are evil, but a sense of it lingers with her even as she leaves the animal well behind, the eyes burning into her back.

The loch opens up before her, vast as any sea, the water a pure mirror of reflection, with the mountains reaching down as far as up. She pauses for a moment to take it in, the peat and the heather, the tang of woodsmoke that's sometimes in the air. So far from everything.

Enough. The box is down near the pier, as it always is. Her heart is thumping. Even after all this time, she's still scared that this week there'll be nothing, or something that will ensure the next week of her life is hell.

At the beginning, it was hunger that dogged them. Scurvy, too. Bags of rancid oats, wizened vegetables, as if they'd pulled together leftovers from compost bins left out on the street. She took to foraging, boiling down nettles and hunting for berries. Funny to think now how alien it was, this corner of isolation of which she now knows every inch. Where bilberries can be found in summer, brambles in autumn, the best leaves to gather year-round.

The first weeks, she'd wandered far. That was before she

clocked the direct effect this had on the supplies they were given. The further she went, the worse they were. The first time that she kept close to the croft, they were rewarded with cheese and bread, tucked up in the box with a heap of fresh fruit and vegetables, and a notebook and pen on which she can make requests, occasionally granted.

Actions have consequences. Sometimes. They like to keep her on her toes.

She's nearly at the box now. No whisky immediately apparent, some bags of fruit. A flutter of excitement grows inside her. Bramley apples were on her list, the idea of crumble taking hold of her as she wrote. There's a hint of green – perhaps that's them, in season now. Assorted tins, a loaf of bread and yet another carton of almond milk for Janice. A flash of white and orange, too, almost like some flowers have been put on top of the box. It can't be, though. She's never added them to the list. They never send her flowers.

But now she's at the box, and she's not wrong. It's a bunch of supermarket lilies, their petals just starting to unfold. She stops dead in her tracks. Lilies. Reaching her hand out with some reluctance, she picks them up, turning them around to see if there's any note on them, any explanation at all for their presence.

Most of them are closed, but one has opened fully, and the scent of it hits her at the back of her throat. Suddenly, she's back ten years, standing at the back of the crematorium, lilies lined up along the sides of the chapel. The scent had clung to her hair then, even after she left, almost causing her to retch every time the wind blew it across her face. It wasn't long after that she was arrested, the police waking her at dawn to bring her in.

The smell is crawling into her brain, orange pollen scattering now across her skin. She throws the flowers away from her as if the stain is acid, wiping her hand furiously on her jeans to get it off her, the touch of it searing into her. She crouches down on the ground beside the box, poking through it gingerly to see if there's anything else lurking in there, any more scorpions hiding in the depths.

Nothing. All exactly as it should be, down to the very last item she wrote on her list. Meat, fish, vegetables, bread, milk. She puts it all back together into the box and walks over to where she's thrown the flowers, picking them up and looking at them again, trying to stay calm. No reaction for the watchers on the other side of the camera; poker face. She's not going to dance.

She rams the flowers back on top of the other groceries and takes it all back to the croft, walking faster than usual so that the exertion pushes all extraneous thoughts out of her mind. When she gets back, she puts the bouquet on the side before unpacking the food. Once the bulk of it is put away, she sets to peeling the apples and rubbing flour and butter together for the crumble topping, ash in her mouth, decay in her nostrils as the scent from the flowers still clings on.

32

Seven days, seven scratches on the wall, again, again, again. There's a rhythm to it, a routine that's developed, the days stretching out endlessly before her. Marie's obsessed with food, with cooking and preserving, finding ways to stretch the ingredients in case the next week the supplies are less than they need. There are jars piled on every shelf, pickles and ferments, cabbages sliced and brined, bramble jam glistening when it's caught by the rays of the rising sun.

She barely recognises herself now, compared to the person she used to be; someone who despised domestic tasks, who only cared about academic success, the validation of her peers. It's a perverse housewifery, mother not to a child but a child-killer.

Janice wouldn't survive without her. Marie knows that. She feels the responsibility deep to her core. Sometimes, she dreams of leaving but the idea of Janice's slow decline stops her in her tracks. Janice might not deserve an easy end, but that's not in Marie's hands. There's enough blood on them already.

For months now, the food delivery has been stable. No alcohol, either. To her surprise, the predictability is sucking the life out of her. She thought she wanted routine, but now she'd do anything rather than unpack the same collection of chicken, cod, broccoli, onions. Over and over again, the repetition of it eating into her brain. *Why do we always have chicken curry?* Janice whines one night, and Marie has to restrain herself from throwing the saucepan she's holding straight into Janice's face, from picking up the chilli powder and rubbing it into Janice's eyes. After all, it would only be serving Janice with her own medicine.

But Marie is above that. Or at least she tries to be.

The monotony disarms her. She gets sloppy. She lowers her guard. Spring's on its way, the hawthorn hedge is in bloom, a couple of the sheep have had lambs. When she and Janice walk down to the pier, she's forgotten to be afraid. Janice is a few steps ahead of her, and Marie doesn't even bother to keep up, enjoying the view, the light breeze.

The peace shatters the moment Janice sees the box. There are multiple green glass bottles sticking out the top, the lids glinting in the sunlight. Janice lets out a yowl, a high-pitched noise that raises the hairs on the back of Marie's neck. There is no stopping her. The woman grabs the drink from the box, all three of the bottles, and turns on her heel, marching back to the croft.

Should Marie go after her, wrestle her to the ground and confiscate the alcohol? She's faster than Janice. Stronger, too. She could take her down.

But something holds her back: a reluctance to foist her views on Janice. Janice is her own person. If she wants to drink herself to death, who is Marie to stop her? She hovers for a moment more, before sitting down on the ground next to the pier, looking out at the loch.

The cameras are always watching, she knows that. Expecting her and Janice to fly at each other. Why give them a show? Two women slugging it out for booze, of all things. Fuck that.

She wraps her hands around her knees, the breeze picking up slightly now, cutting through her jumper. Standing up, she jogs on the spot briefly to get her circulation moving. She's about to turn back up to the croft, brave the consequences of a drunk Janice, when she sees something unusual tucked into the side of the box. An envelope – large, brown.

Eyeing it like she would a cockroach, she reaches out to touch it. It'll be instructions of some kind, maybe some maintenance that's needed; a change to the usual routine.

There are only a few words written on the front. Not an address, not a name.

I know exactly what you did. This ends now.

A thump in her chest, a catch of breath. The predictability shatters. She's so fucking stupid, to have longed for change. How arrogant she has been. Looks like Nemesis has finally caught up with her. Slowly, reluctantly, she opens the envelope, pulls out the papers that are inside.

Watching waiting I'll catch you I'll stop this he's mine you can't have him he's all mine not yours mine mine mine mine.

Garbled words, the odd sentence, capital letters jumping at her randomly from off the page – *watching me watching you watching me* – the words repeating themselves over and over again in her mind.

By the time she's walked back to the croft, she's exhausted, even though the sun has barely reached the top of the sky. She's weighed down by the box, filled with tins of Spam and marrowfat peas. The papers are tucked in on top of the food; they're the heaviest burden of all.

But all thoughts of them go out of her mind the moment she steps over the threshold. It's chaos, chairs lying on their sides, her jars of preserves smashed everywhere, the bramble jam bleeding its juice out on to the floor. Swallowing hard, trying to hold back a scream, Marie walks in further, dumping the box on the table.

Janice is crouching in the far corner, her head in her hands. She's weeping, great sobs shaking her thin body. One of the whisky bottles is lying on its side – the contents look to be half gone already. Marie hesitates, goes over to her, puts a hand on her shoulder.

'Are you all right?'

'I can't go on like this anymore.' Janice picks the whisky up, unscrews the lid and casts it aside. She necks a mouthful. 'I don't deserve to be alive.'

Another long week begins.

Later, much later, when the crying and the screaming and the puking are done, Janice leans over to Marie, her eyes bright, glittering in the light from the single bulb hung overhead.

'When the time comes, let me die, won't you?'

'You're not going to die.' Marie's answer is automatic. Why would she try and stop it? The question goes unasked.

'I want to,' Janice says. 'Seriously. I can't go on like this. Will you burn me?'

'What the hell are you talking about?'

'I don't want the worms to get me. Or the beetles. I picture them at night, crawling through me, picking at my bones. Please, just burn the hell out of me.'

'I don't understand.'

'A fucking cremation, you stupid bitch. That's what I did with the kids. Nobody understood. I was just saving them. What kind of mother would let rats eat her babies?'

Marie's blinking. She remembers the story, the small bodies covered in petrol, scorched to the bone.

Janice is still talking. 'Let me burn. Just let me burn. Ladybird, ladybird, fly away home, your house is on fire, and your children all gone . . .' It's her parting shot. With that, she collapses to the floor, her eyes tight shut.

Marie takes the envelope, pushes it to the back of one of the shelves. There will be a time for her to deal with what it means.

That time is not now.

33

Some mornings, Marie wakes and she's forgotten. Lying in bed, silence around her, only the occasional baaing of a sheep there to break the calm of the morning. She'll watch the sun creeping up the wall, luxuriating in the warmth of her bed, the clean smell of the air washing over her.

But then Janice will cough, or call out in her sleep, and the spell will break. She'll remember exactly who and what she is. She'll remember the photocopies she was sent, and the job she needs to do.

She can't decide whether it's better to start the day like this, with a couple of moments where she's clear of memories, or if she should have them always in her mind. At least she'd then be spared the shock as reality returns. Or as much of reality as she can stand. Always, every time, it stops at a closed door, her hand on the doorknob. Then black.

Another Monday – delivery day. She draws a new stroke on the wall. How many groups of seven are there now? She doesn't want to think about it, the collection of six vertical lines, one horizontal, the only way she can keep a tally of the days. She learned to do this the hard way, when she was a day late for the collection and the milk had turned.

There's normally a cacophony of sounds coming from Janice's room at this time, expulsions of air, a racking cough that speaks of years on roll-up cigarettes until her enforced quitting. But this morning it's quiet. Too quiet. The silence bothers Marie. She puts her feet to the floor, moved by a sense of unease. Janice was drunk again the night before, passed on dinner, leaving Marie to eat the pasta she'd cooked on her own. Marie tried to get her to eat but she got aggressive, told Marie to go to bed. Marie did what she was told. She wishes she hadn't now.

'It's up to me if I want to kill myself.' Janice did say that. It's not making Marie feel better to remember it, though.

Since the delivery of the envelope, the day there were three bottles of whisky in the box, the booze has come, a relentless tide of it. Marie's given up the Monday morning race, unable to deal with the abuse Janice gives her if she tries to interfere. Even if she gets to one bottle, Janice will have another squirrelled away. Janice's body can't take it the way it once could. Too old to be able to handle it in any quantity now.

The silence seems to grow.

Marie jumps out of bed and rushes through to where Janice is sleeping, in the single bed that mirrors her own on the other side of the wall. The older woman is lying still, so still that Marie's heart misses a beat when she sees her as she opens the door. She rushes forward and puts her hand to Janice's cheek, suddenly struck with panic.

She's out cold.

Marie has always been grateful for her ability to sleep through anything, but that gratitude flies out of the window in a heartbeat. She should have known how ill Janice was from the sound of her awful coughing and retching. She should have come to help earlier, perhaps it wouldn't have got so bad. There's a strong smell of vomit and alcohol coming from her, and the bedding is encrusted in sick.

She puts her hand to Janice's neck, feels for a pulse. Nothing. She doesn't think so, anyway. She tries her wrist – a flicker, nothing more. She forces her fingers into Janice's mouth and pulls out gobbets of vomit, trying desperately to clear the woman's throat, to let her breathe. Pulling her into the recovery position she thumps at her back, hoping to dislodge anything Janice might have inhaled.

There is no reaction from Janice, despite her efforts.

Should she perform CPR? Not if Janice's heart is still beating. She thinks she's read that somewhere. The thought of putting her mouth to Janice's, tasting that stinking sick on her own lips, inhaling the stench of whisky so close . . . Marie swallows down a sour bile that rises at the back of her throat.

Let me die. The words that Janice spoke to her that terrible, drunken night come back to her now. *Let me die.*

Think. She's got to think. Janice needs a doctor, immediately. To go straight into hospital. What the hell is Marie going to do?

She looks at the cameras situated around the house. Maybe they'll see, send medical assistance. Maybe it's on the way already. In her gut, she knows they'll be more interested in observing, watching life or death play out without intervention. Like a nature programme. Captive apes.

At least it's delivery day. Maybe she'll be in time to catch someone. She'll run down to the loch, watch out to see in case it's being brought late this week, so she can stop the skipper of the boat and ask for help.

Leaving Janice in the recovery position, Marie secures the

duvet around her, touches her face and promises that she'll be back as soon as she can. Then she takes to her heels and runs.

The sheep aren't used to such activity. They look up as she puffs past, almost startled. She's trying to keep her footing on the uneven path, but finally catches the edge of her shoe on a loose rock, almost crashing to the ground. She needs to slow down. If she injures herself . . . it doesn't bear thinking about. Neither of them would make it through.

A moment of hope when she arrives by the loch – the box isn't there yet. She isn't normally so early to collect it, she can tell that by how low the sun still is in the sky, making its way up from the east. She'll wait, get their attention, make sure that they know they need to come back with medicine. With a doctor.

With any help at all.

She finds a hollow that gives a good view across the landing stage, unwilling to make herself too obvious in case she scares them off when they see her waiting on the jetty. This isn't how it was meant to be. She can't believe she didn't take the warnings seriously.

You'll be pretty much on your own up there. If you need urgent medical assistance, it may not be forthcoming. She hadn't paid any heed at the time. Still young enough, still fit enough to think she was invincible. Not much caring if she wasn't. She didn't think about Janice, though. She should never have agreed to this. The peace of it, the tranquillity – all the factors that once most appealed to her are now fraught with threat.

It's all right, though. Someone will be here soon. They'll be rowing, maybe, or powering in on a motorboat. They'll stop the boat, climb out with the box of provisions, prepare to leave it on the shore, at which moment she'll jump up, run down, catch hold of them before they leave.

She can see it now, the surprise on his face, or maybe hers, the person who's been their lifeline for the last years. *Are you sure you'll be able to deal with the isolation?* When they'd asked her that, she'd brushed the question aside, impatiently. Of course I can, what do you think I've been dealing with for the last eight years? Maybe they expected her to try and find human contact sooner, lie in wait like this years ago. But she's had her fill of human contact, more than enough of it to last a lifetime.

Until now. Now, the idea of something bad happening to Janice is the only thought in her head. *Let me die, let me die,* a relentless drumbeat running through her mind. Marie thought she wanted to be free of the responsibility of caring for Janice, but now the thought terrifies her.

34

The sun's high in the sky by the time she gives up waiting. It's beating down on her, but she can't get warm. She needs to get back, check on Janice, make sure she's still alive, still in bed, safe. Or as safe as Marie can make her.

Maybe it's because she's here. They can sense her presence somehow, won't come until she leaves. Best to proceed on that basis. She grabs the notebook and pen out of her pocket and scrawls a note: *MEDICAL ASSISTANCE REQUIRED URGENTLY, JANICE SERIOUSLY ILL*. That will have to do. She waves it under the camera for a while before she shoves it under a rock on the pier and starts to climb back up to the house.

They should have discussed protocols. They should have put guidelines in place. They should never have delivered whisky to a recovering alcoholic.

Maybe you want her to die. She stops in her tracks. No. That's not right. She's never wanted Janice to die, never resented her care of her. Sure, there've been times she could have done without it, hankering for the quiet of her own company, but it's not like she couldn't leave the room, go and sit on her own for a bit. Or go walking, foraging in the endless wilderness.

I don't believe you. You've always hated her. That's not true. Not true at all. She's not going to accept that. She keeps on walking.

You're going to have to take action when she's gone. Can't keep using that as an excuse to hold back. This one's unanswerable. *Fuck off,* she shouts back at her head. *Not now.*

She's nearly back at the house, but she needs to stop, catch her breath. Normally she's so fit, but panic is driving up her heart rate, making her breaths shallow, not allowing in the oxygen she needs. There's a rattling of stones in the distance; she hears them fall, looks round to see if someone is there, someone who could help, but it's nothing. Only a sheep, staring at her. Accusation in its eyes.

Fuck's sake. She's losing it now. The sheep is not staring at her in accusation. The sheep doesn't give a shit. Neither does the sky, the mountain or the massive rock off to her left, which she climbs sometimes, just for something to do. The landscape is impassive, untouched by her. Filled with sudden rage, she picks up a stone and hurls it at the sheep, screaming as she does. The noise she emits doesn't even scare the sheep, which keeps eating grass regardless. The stone she's thrown lands harmlessly on the ground metres in front of it.

She can't even hit a static target. She's useless. Completely worthless. Nothing she does has any effect. If Janice dies, it's going to be her fault.

Janice isn't going to die. She's got a tummy bug, that's all. Or gastric flu. Marie's cleared her airways, propped her up. It's going to be all right.

'Sorry, sheep,' she says, walking towards the house. It grazes on, unheeding.

35

Forget all the attempts to find rescue – there's none there to be found. No knight on a white charger to carry them away, no helicopter swooping down on its dragon wings. It's up to her. Her and Janice, backs against the wall, as they've always been.

She's up the stairs now and in the bedroom. The air is thick, a stench of whisky hitting her throat. Janice is still slumped in the recovery position and for a moment, just one, Marie thinks it might be all right, that Janice has held on. She takes a step closer, another one.

Even from a few paces away, though, she can tell. Something's different; there's an absence. What she's looking at isn't Janice, not anymore. She takes the final steps slowly, so slowly, and reaches out her hand, takes hold of Janice's wrist.

Nothing. In that short time that she was searching for help, Janice has gone. Marie slumps down on the floor, leaning against the bed, her hand still on Janice, and she weeps. Not for Janice, not really, but for the end of something. The change that's going to come.

But not for long. She knows what she needs to do. Her mind's completely clear now, all the doubts and fears gone. She needs to get out of here – there's no time to waste. Soon, very soon, they're all going to descend. The helicopter, police, journalists. She can see the headlines now.

*CHILD-KILLER FOUND DEAD IN
HIGHLANDS HIDEAWAY.
BRITAIN'S MOST HATED MOTHER
ESCAPES JUSTICE AGAIN.*

Let me burn, Janice said. *Just let me burn.*

If Marie waits for them to arrive, Janice won't get her wish. Not the way she wants. It'll be a midnight burial, an unmarked grave. And for herself, she can't face what'll come. Ghoulish, that's the word. They'll clamber round her, full of questions, unable to understand how she could stay with this woman for so long, in such an isolated way. If she can't explain it properly to herself, how can she ever explain it to them . . .?

There is a solution, though. There's a can of petrol in the outhouse. She found it once when she was rootling through everything, assessing what they had and what they might need. Maybe this is an extreme solution, but the problem is also extreme. She can take Janice out into the hills, carry her to a quiet spot and burn her body. It's not legal, of course, to impede lawful burial. But this way, at least she'll know that Janice gets the respect that she doesn't deserve, but which Marie feels is her due for the past years of companionship. Of friendship, almost.

Steeling herself, she tries to lift Janice from the bed. Fails. Even though Janice has always appeared slight, the body is too heavy for Marie. That won't work.

She goes through to her own room, throws her clothes into the rucksack in which she brought them those long years ago. Janice has a couple of jumpers she likes – she packs them, too. Janice doesn't need them anymore. Once that's done, she goes down to the kitchen and puts what food she has into the top of the bag, as many non-perishables as there are, a bottle of water, too.

Not long now. She needs to get the hell out of here. Standing for a moment in the kitchen, she looks around, checking there's nothing she's forgotten. The envelope. That's it. She moves towards the shelf where she's hidden it before stopping herself. She's seen enough of them, their secrets all revealed to her. She won't be sorry to see them burn, either.

Now she's as ready as she can be. Time for the final step.

The petrol can is still where she remembers, a sound of liquid sloshing when she tips it from side to side. There's not much inside.

But it'll be enough.

In the back of her mind is a lurking suspicion that she might not be acting entirely rationally, but she ignores it, squashing it down fast. Headlines rush through in their place, from Janice's parole hearings, the outcry, her struggle to be freed. Janice deserved a chance then; she deserves dignity now. If it weren't for Marie's involvement, perhaps Janice would never have been released from prison to this place, but she owes the woman a debt, too. Despite all the privations she's suffered here, life would have been purposeless had she not been entrusted with Janice's care; she's going to make sure she carries out her final responsibility.

Holding her breath against the fumes, she goes upstairs and pours petrol over Janice's body, over the bed. There are

210

a couple of polyester garments hanging on the back of the door, a fleece and a shirt, which she tucks around Janice, hoping they're as flammable as they look. Dumping the can at the foot of the bed, she stands in silence for a moment beside Janice, her hand on the dead woman's face, saying her goodbyes.

Ashes to ashes, dust to dust. She might not be able to commit Janice's body fully to the flames, not like a crematorium, but she'll give it her best shot. At least Janice will be spared the prying, cold fingers prodding at the dead flesh of a woman they despise.

Making sure she's well clear, Marie lights a piece of paper that she's scrunched up and throws it on to the end of the bed, before turning and running for the door. There's a *whumph* as the petrol catches, crackling as the flames lick the bedding, the blankets, the piles of paper under the bed that Marie's always told Janice are a fire hazard.

Smoke biting at her eyes, her throat, she retreats fast, down the stairs, and picks up the bag. Taking one last look at the kitchen, she makes her exit. The bed is burning, the sounds from upstairs indicating that the fire has entirely caught hold.

They wanted a show on their cameras, those lidless eyes.

They've got it now, the performance to top them all. She'll bring the house down.

Outside, a good distance away, she turns to look at it. The purification of fire, though she doesn't feel like a phoenix reborn. Not yet. It's a bridge burned, though. With Janice gone, Marie is free. She puts her shoulders back and heads into the hills.

Marie's taken her punishment, served her time. Now to deal with unfinished business. She's got a job to do.

Part 4

36

The door slams behind them and Anna struggles to keep her balance as Marc pulls her along the entrance hall and into a room at the back of the house. He shoves her into a chair at the end of a long table and strides away to the window, breathing heavily. She grabs on to the seat for support.

Anna was already hyperventilating with nerves before she even rang the doorbell, but the way she's just been manhandled has sent her into overdrive. The room starts to go hazy, spinning around her, and there's a buzzing in her ears. Just in time, she realises she's about to pass out, so without thinking about Marc's reaction, she puts her head down between her knees to stop the room from spinning.

'What the fuck are you doing here?' he says again. Three long strides and he's back beside her, looming over her. She can feel his physicality, anger beating off him like flames. Slowly she brings her head up, looks at him straight on. His eyes are piercing, burning with rage that's so white-hot she has to put up a hand to shield her own gaze.

'I could kill you right now,' he says. 'I could kill you right now and no one would blame me. Why the hell have you come to my house?' He shifts from one foot to the other, as

215

if preparing to hit her. Anna braces herself, her head still down.

But after a moment or so, he still hasn't struck her. Instead, he moves away. Anna keeps her head down for a little longer, but the room has stopped spinning, she's got her breath back under control.

'Go on, then,' she says, pushing herself to her feet and holding her hands up to him. 'Go on, hit me. Kill me, if you like. I'm not going to stop you.'

Marc moves back towards her again, his face pale, his eyes blazing. He pulls back his right hand, tightening it into a fist. This is it, finally. Anna's going to receive the punishment that she deserves.

He doesn't hit her, though. Instead, he collapses on to the chair next to her, his head in his hands, and bursts into tears. Anna stands rigid for a while longer, uncertain whether she should say something, put a hand on his shoulder, anything. She opts for the safer option and sits back down in her own chair, pulling it away so that he has more space.

His sobs subside and he looks up at her, his eyes bloodshot, snot running from his nose. He wipes it with the back of his hand, the movement impatient.

'I can't do it,' he says. 'I want to, but I can't. You shouldn't have come.'

'I'm sorry,' she says. 'I'm so sorry.'

'Why are you here?'

'I couldn't keep away. I need to know how he is.'

He looks at her, completely silent, his mouth slightly open. Then he starts to make a barking, painful noise. It's laughter – of a sort. 'I have no fucking idea.'

'You what?'

He laughs again, a sob breaking through. The sound sends a chill through Anna.

'I have no fucking idea. Sally lost it with me – said it was too much. They've gone. Moved away. She doesn't want me visiting, won't tell me what's going on. I thought about taking her to court, but I don't want to make the situation any worse.'

'Why did she lose it?'

'She found out I was still sending you letters. I dropped one in front of her. She said I had to choose, continue the contact with you, or stay with her and Toby. She told me that letter she sent you about your mum would be the last communication you had with us, ever. We had nothing left to say to you, not even words of hate. But I couldn't stop. It's been eating me alive, the idea of you sitting there, getting away with it.'

The words go through her like nails into a coffin. Anna can't look at him – seeing the expression of anguish on his face is too painful. As her eyes wander round the room, look-ing anywhere but at him, she sees the neglect in the garden has spread indoors, too. There's dust everywhere, accumu-lated debris and an overflowing ashtray spilling on to the dining table. Empty sandwich wrappers, crisp packets, rem-nants of takeaways from McDonald's. The room smells of stale food, stale smoke.

Sally and Toby are gone.

She remembers the last time they ate in here together, the first Christmas they celebrated together after Toby was born. Same room, the table bright then, polished, laid with shining cutlery and glasses, crackers and an angel chime.

She broke it all.

'Is there anything I can do?' she says. She's not going to challenge the hate mail.

'Don't you think you've done enough? The only thing you can do to make this better in any way is go back in time and not get in the fucking car in the first place.'

Anna opens her mouth. Shuts it again.

'Get out of my house.' He's standing now, moving closer and closer to her. 'Get the fuck out before I do something I regret.'

He's not joking. The set of his jaw tells Anna that much. She picks up her bag and scurries for the door. But before she goes, she needs to ask one more question.

'Was it you? Outside the prison?'

'Was what me? I told you to get the fuck out.'

'Someone tried to run me down, soon as I was released.'

'Smart move on their part,' he says. 'But no, it wasn't me. You should know that already.'

'How should I know that?'

'Because I wouldn't have fucking missed. You wouldn't be standing here. You'd be in a morgue. Where you belong.'

With that, he moves closer to her, hostility radiating off him so strongly that Anna stumbles as she leaves the house, nearly falls.

37

The walk back to the hostel feels further, her bag heavier, her guilt mingling with panic. She went to find out what she'd done to Toby, and she's no further forward with that, the absence of news still burning a hole in her gut. Worse still, now she has no idea where Sally is.

Anna needs to face facts. The reason she didn't complain about the hate mail was because it felt as if Sally still cared, at least enough to wish her harm. This total absence, this void – all it proves is that Sally doesn't care about her at all now. She can't even bring herself to hate Anna anymore.

Their dad died young, when the sisters were still in their teens – they were so close then, with their mum too. Sally's marriage to Marc, Toby's birth, these just strengthened the bond between them. Until Anna blew it up, smashing it all to pieces.

The shock of the accident, Toby's injuries, Anna's culpability in it all. Their mum's heart couldn't take the strain. It killed her.

Anna thought she'd felt bad before, but it's nothing compared to how she feels now. Everything lost. Then she comes to a halt. Tom's words in her head. *Self-pity.* She might have nothing, but she's still alive. Unlike Kelly.

But Toby must still be alive, too. If he'd died, Anna knows Sally wouldn't have kept that from her husband, however angry she was. And if he's still alive, there's still hope that one day, there might be a reconciliation, even just the brief information she sought in that letter all those months ago. If Anna can show how much she's changed, that she's learned, that she's sorry. That she wants to put things right.

Maybe she can find redemption.

Is that being too hopeful?

It's totally fucking delusional. But it's all she's got.

'Watch where you're going,' someone shouts, and Anna jumps, brought back abruptly into the moment by a sharp thump to her shoulder. It's another set of men in Lycra, spread across the path like a battalion going into war.

Go fuck yourself is on the tip of her tongue but she pulls it back. No sense in taking on this fight. She moves on instead, head down. Once she's at the High Street, she pauses to catch her breath. The sun is back out and the smell of baking cookies spills from the Covered Market. Chocolate, cinnamon, all the smells of home. They turn her stomach.

She could make the trip to St Leonards, as she'd planned from the start. She could take that short walk into the sea. That would put an end to this guilt, this pain. Tom's words flicker back into her mind, though. *Coward.*

That's where he's wrong. She saw Kelly's body; she knows what it must have taken for her to do that to herself. Desperation, yes. But more than that, courage. Anna can't forget the pain in her voice. And if she's honest with herself, she's not at that point now. Not yet.

She might be delusional for hoping that her sister can ever forgive her. But at the same time, she's not going to give up on life entirely. That's the difference that the last few days have made. Kelly felt like she had nothing left. Anna still has something to fight for.

A broken woman fights harder than no woman at all.

Even though there was no connection between them other than those few hours they spent in the same cell, she feels a kinship with this stranger. A responsibility, too. Anna couldn't have stopped Kelly from doing what she did. But there is something she can do now. She needs to find the person on the other end of the phone, the person who stole all hope from Kelly. After all, that phone didn't make its way into Anna's bunk by accident – Kelly chose to put it there. She needed Anna's help.

What Tom told her about the car trying to run her down outside the prison comes into her mind again. Marc seemed adamant it wasn't him. She's barely admitted to herself that it could have been deliberate. But what if somehow, someone had discovered she was in the cell with Kelly? What if the person on the other end of the phone had some connection in the prison, knew that she would be released, and waited for her? It's a stretch, but it's not impossible. Tom was clear that it looked to him as if the car was driving straight at her.

He could be wrong. But maybe he isn't. Maybe there's some link between the woman's death and the attempted assault on her. Maybe someone doesn't want Anna prying into Kelly's affairs. Though how would the driver have known what was happening inside the prison? She tucks her hands into her pockets, chilled.

The thought of Tom brings her back to her immediate surroundings. It would have been nice to stay in his welcoming home, if she could just bring herself to trust him completely. Maybe he'll invite her back after work on Monday, and she'll accept. The hostel isn't a long-term solution, after all.

But what it is offering is lunch. She remembers what the staff member said to her that morning, the promise of a Sunday roast. Someone there might know something about Kelly, too. She gets up off the pavement and makes her way back, hoping there's still some food left.

She's in luck – it smells delicious. Anna loads her plate high and takes it to a table in the corner which is still empty. It's not that she means to be unfriendly, but her brain is too full of the events of the last days. She's thinking about the phone now, its ringing still reverberating in her ears.

She's got the number right there, scrawled into the back of the paperback in her bag. Once she's cleared half her plate, practically inhaling the food, she reaches down into her bag and pulls out the book to have a look. Just as she's about to open it, one of the volunteers approaches, a younger woman, not someone Anna has seen before. She sits down opposite Anna.

'That's a good one,' she says. 'Have you read any of her earlier stuff?'

Anna blinks. Her mind's blank for a moment, before she clocks that the woman is talking about the book in her hand. She thinks Anna is about to start reading, not checking it for secret phone numbers.

'Yes, she's good.' It could be true, too, for all she knows, but she can't even remember who the author is, let alone whether she's any good.

'Let me have a look?' the volunteer says, taking it from

Anna's hand. Her heart rate accelerates immediately. If the woman sees the phone number . . .

Anna's being ridiculous. She watches the woman skim the blurb on the back cover before she gives it back to Anna, not even opening the book at all. She's a book-lover, that's all.

'It's always the husband,' the woman says, with a laugh. 'That's the rule.'

Anna smiles, too hungry for literary discussion. She piles up another forkful of food and sticks it into her mouth. The volunteer settles back in her chair, waiting patiently for Anna to finish chewing before she leans forward, elbows on the table.

'So, what brings you here?'

Anna blinks. It's direct. 'Well, I . . .'

'Sorry, stupid question. Life. That's what's brought you here. The real question is, what's next?'

Anna looks at her, meeting her gaze steadily, taking her in from head to toe. Brushed, clean hair, a jumper that might well be cashmere, gold studs in her ears and flashes of gold and diamond on her left hand. Colour in her cheeks, no sign of prison pallor, none of the grey of days and years spent inside.

Anna takes another mouthful of food, chews it slowly, deliberately, counting the number of times her jaw works, nineteen, twenty, trying to exert even the smallest amount of control.

Despite her caution, her long-held policy against trusting strangers has softened, leaving her defences down. Maybe because of Tom, maybe because she's so tired. Maybe because the way the woman is smiling at her reminds of the sister she hasn't seen for over four years, though this woman is clearly older, closer to forty than thirty.

223

Anna swallows, roast potatoes long turned to mush in her mouth. The food sticks on the way down and she swallows once again, drinking some water. Then she puts down her knife and fork, inhales deeply. 'I only got out of prison on Friday. I don't like asking for help, but I think I might need to learn.'

'A lot of people say that,' the volunteer says. 'You're not alone. And admitting it is the first step. It will get much easier from here.'

Anna laughs, though it catches in her throat like a sob. 'It can't get much worse.'

'Honestly, I've talked to so many women in your situation. Men, too. There's a bright future ahead if you let yourself look for it.'

Straight to the jugular.

'I wish Kelly had seen that,' Anna muttered.

'Kelly?'

Her sotto voce remark had been louder than she intended. 'My pad mate – sorry, my cell mate. She took her own life.'

The volunteer reaches forward, puts her hand on Anna's arm. 'I'm so sorry. For both of you.'

'I mean, I didn't know her. We were just sharing that night. But still . . .' Anna's voice trails off. The pressure of the fingers on her arm tightens.

'Very traumatic.'

Anna swallows, raising her chin. Shifts her arm gently to remove the hand that's clasping it. She'll cry if she gets any more sympathy. 'Anyway. This is a total long shot but I need to start somewhere. Her name was Kelly Green – I know she was living on the streets here recently. There was a mention of a hostel. Has anyone by that name come through here lately? Have you come across her in your volunteering?'

The woman looks thoughtful, shakes her head after a moment. 'I don't think so, no. The name doesn't ring a bell. Are you sure she spent any time here?'

'No. I don't know anything about her. I'm clutching at straws here.'

'You could always ask around, but if I haven't heard of her, not sure anyone else will have done.'

Anna laughs. 'Back to square one. Thanks, anyway. It was nice to talk to someone.'

'Nice to talk to you, too. Good luck with everything.'

38

Anna finishes her lunch. She's completely exhausted now, wiped out by it all, a blood-sugar crash from the food dragging her even further down. If she only could, she'd curl up in a corner and sleep for a week. The volunteer has wandered off, but when Anna stands up to clear her plates away, she returns.

'So, what's your plan? Do you have somewhere to go tonight?'

Anna shrugs. 'I guess there is somewhere I could go. I'll have to do some grovelling, though.'

'Would that be so bad?'

'I guess not.'

'It won't be for long,' the woman says. 'You'll get some money in soon enough, then you can sort out your own place.'

'I'm meant to be starting a job on Monday, actually,' Anna says, half surprised at herself for volunteering this.

'That's great.' The woman smiles broadly. 'Good luck!' She turns to walk away, then pauses and steps back. 'Look, I know you said you find it hard to ask people for help, but you do need to let people help you. I know it's hard, but it's safe to open up, just a little.'

Anna waits.

'So, I want to ask you something,' the woman continues.

Here it comes. Anna knew it was too good to be true, that anyone could be so easy to talk to, so lacking in the sort of prurient curiosity she's been primed to expect. The woman opens her mouth to speak and Anna is bracing herself, waiting for it.

Why did you get sent to prison?

Fuck off, she wants to shout, *mind your own fucking business*, and she's ready to say it, the words at the tip of her tongue, but then she hears what the woman is saying.

'What are you going to wear?'

Not what Anna was expecting. 'Wear to what?'

'Work. You said you're starting a job. Do you have the right sort of things to wear?'

'I hadn't really thought about it. I've got a skirt, a blouse. That's about it,' Anna says. 'I mean, he knows where I've come from. I doubt he's expecting . . .'

'Look, that's as may be. But I think you need to make a bit of an effort.' She looks Anna up and down. 'We're about the same size. Why don't you come round to my house, and I'll dig out some stuff for you. I left my office job a while ago, so I don't need the smarter clothes anymore.'

Before Anna can reply, she takes a pen and piece of paper from her pocket and writes something down, then hands it to her.

'This is my address,' she says 'Come round. Maybe Tuesday? If that works?'

'It works,' Anna says, knowing the reply is redundant. What else would she be doing?

'Great,' the woman says. 'I'll see you then.' With that, she walks smartly away, leaving Anna somewhat shellshocked.

She didn't even have a chance to introduce herself, it's all happened so fast. Tucking the piece of paper into her pocket, she piles her used plates on the trolley at the side. When she's finished, she stands at the edge of the room for a moment, looking around her.

It's all so familiar, the smells of roast meat and cabbage, the clank of cutlery against china, the low murmur of conversation. Not so dissimilar to being back at school, really – and perhaps that's why she doesn't mind being told what to do. This volunteer is like the only teacher she got on with, the librarian who was kind enough to give her space to be herself, let her sit in the library whenever she wanted, pick whatever books she chose.

Anna feels warmed by it. Emboldened, too. Pulling her shoulders up straight, she walks over to a group of three women sitting at the end of a table, mugs of tea steaming in front of them. One is telling a story and the others are laughing, too involved to look up at her. She stands for a moment, uncertain, the confidence seeping out of her, before pulling herself together. She's got a job to do. As soon as the anecdote has finished, she puts her hand on an empty chair at the edge of the group.

'OK if I join you? I need help with something.'

They glance from one to the other. The storyteller is clearly the final arbiter as, after a couple of moments, she nods towards the empty chair. 'What?'

'I'm looking for information about someone. A woman called Kelly Green. I know that she spent time in Oxford, and that she stayed here. Do any of you know of her?'

Glances pass between them again, then shrugs. The woman next to the storyteller looks thoughtful.

'It's not a big community. We all know each other, pretty much. The name does ring a bell,' she says. 'Though I'm not sure. Why do you want to know?'

Anna pauses. 'I met her in prison.'

The woman looks at her more closely. The suspicion starts to fade from the faces around Anna. 'How long were you in for?'

'Three years.'

A nod. Anna seems to have passed some test. She's not a tourist – she's been through it, too. 'I'm going to check with someone,' the woman says, picking up her phone.

A few moments later and Anna is in possession of a scrawled phone number. She holds the paper in her hand, reeling at the shock of it. She never thought it would be so easy.

'Kelly's sister. Fern. My mate was at school with her. She was talking about her the other day, how the family haven't seen her in months. Fern asked for her number to be given to anyone who might have information.'

If the sister is Kelly's next of kin, she'll know about the death by now. At least, Anna hopes so. She doesn't want to be the one to break that news. 'Thanks,' she says, 'I can't tell you how grateful I am. I really can't believe this.'

'Don't mention prison if you want her to talk to you.'

It shouldn't have been this easy. The information she needed has simply fallen into her lap, a small miracle in a world bereft of hope. It's not surprising though that she's found her so easily. Once she had the hostel name, the rest was almost bound to follow. It's a small, tight society this, these women brought together by poverty and addiction, falling through the same cracks. They're as hollow-eyed and

229

gaunt as the ones Anna saw in prison, shunted in for a few weeks of custody for something petty, the sentence wildly disproportionate to the devastation caused. Nothing learned, no help given for the outside, only a lesson in cruelty.

All such a fucking waste.

She nods her thanks and leaves the building, the phone number clutched tightly in her hand.

She walks back towards Merton Street, heading down the side of her old college again, looking for a quiet bench on Deadman's Walk overlooking the green expanse of Merton Field, Christ Church Meadows beyond. The juxtaposition of town and gown has never felt so real to her before, and shame at the unthinking privilege of her student years eats away at her insides. But now is not the time for this.

Sitting down, she rummages back in her bag for the miniature phone. She still feels uneasy about switching it back on just in case someone is looking for a signal from it, but she dismisses the fears. She's got no choice, no other way of calling the number she's been given.

As soon as the phone powers up, she dials the number, struggling to hit the right numbers because the keypad is so small. At last she manages to enter it accurately, and taking in a deep breath, she presses the green call button.

It rings three times.

'Yes? Who is this?' The voice is anxious, impatient. Angry. The muscle at Anna's jaw twitches, she's clenching it so tightly.

'Is this Fern? Someone gave me your number.'

'Who is this?'

'My name's Anna. I'm calling about your sister Kelly.'

'Too late for that now,' the woman says flatly.

The family does know, then.

'I know,' Anna says. 'I was there.' *Don't mention prison,* the woman at the shelter had said, but she can't see any other way through it.

'I don't want to hear it.'

'But . . .'

'No. She disappeared on us for months, over a year. Mum at death's door after all she's put us through, and the next thing we heard, she's killed herself inside. I can't talk to you right now.'

There is more than anger in her voice. Sadness, leaking out of her. Anna hunches over on the bench. 'I'm sorry.'

'That doesn't help.'

'I know. My mum died, too.' She pauses. Fern hasn't hung up yet, but any minute she will. 'Look, there is one thing. Who's Louise?'

A harsh noise from the other end of the phone, a bitter laugh. 'Louise is my mum.' Silence for a moment. 'Who is this? Why are you asking these questions?'

Anna opens her mouth, shuts it. This woman can't help. Anna needs someone who's been in contact with Kelly in the last few months.

'Who are you?' Fern growls again. Anna lowers the phone from her ear, looks at it for a second before ending the call and pushing the phone back into her bag.

She sits for a while, staring out across the grass in front of her, Anne-Marie's words echoing in her ears, Kelly's too. She inhales deeply, exhales, looking up at the clouds above scudding across the blue sky. More rowers run past, pulling her back to the moment, and she gets to her feet.

231

Of course it wasn't going to be so easy. She had her lucky break finding Kelly's sister – nothing else was going to be handed to her on a plate. But now she knows less than ever. None of it is making sense. It doesn't mean she won't find the answers, though. She's just going to have to search for them a bit harder. It hasn't put her off the challenge, though. It's fired her up. Starting with those months that Kelly was missing. Her gut is telling her that this is the first thing that she should investigate.

But to do that, she's going to need resources. Shelter, food. The internet. It's time to go back to Tom's house.

There's no point in fighting it anymore.

Only a couple of streets to go, and Anna's steps are picking up. She'll ring the bell, Tom will answer, and once the initial awkwardness is over, he'll welcome her in. Maybe he'll make some more of that lovely coffee, and they can sit together, drink it. They might even share a laugh at her former prickliness. Perhaps later she'll be able to move on from how it feels to hate herself so much, to feel such shame about what happened in the first place, how she ended up inside. Maybe she'll talk about solving this mystery, working some cases for Tom. She'll show she can be indispensable to his firm. She's going to escape her past, build a better future. One in which she can be proud of herself, one day.

She goes round the final corner, looking up to see if there are any lights on at Tom's place.

There's nothing there.

No lights.

No house, either.

She must have it wrong, must be in the wrong street. Taken the wrong turn.

No. She knows Oxford. She knows the street she's on.

And the house isn't missing. Not all of it. Some of it remains, jagged black teeth against the darkening sky. Smoke still drifting up from one corner. Police tape cordoning it off, a patrol car parked across the front.

Her feet are stuck to the ground, heavy as lead. *What the fuck?*

39

Anna can't stop shaking. Her knees have gone, her hands too, the tremors running deep through her. Now she's alert to it, smoke is still acrid in the air around her, a sharper smell than bonfires of autumn leaves, harsh on her tongue.

'You OK?' It's a man walking his dog. He stops next to her. 'Are you ill? You look like you're about to pass out.'

Anna can't speak. She waves her hand in the direction of the smouldering ruin.

'Oh yes, shocking, isn't it? It took hold before anyone could do anything to stop it. Terrible business.'

She doesn't reply, keeps staring up at it while the dog busies itself around her feet, snuffling at her trainers.

'Friend of yours, was he?'

This catches her attention. Was? Does he mean . . .

'Did he get out?' she says.

'Oh no,' the man says, leaning forward and speaking to her in a low, confidential voice. 'No one was going to get out of that one. Once it took hold.' His teeth are pointed and yellow, his tongue darting over them from side to side. There's a hunger in his eyes. 'His dog barking outside, that's what woke me up. Then the smell. I thought someone was having a barbecue.'

Anna turns away from him, repelled. He hangs around for a little longer but eventually, deterred, he wanders off, his dog trailing behind him. She's still staring at the place where the house used to be, but it's not what she's seeing, not anymore. Tom's face is dancing before her, the tentative smile, the lock of hair that kept flopping down across his forehead. He was trying to help her. And now he's dead. At least the dog made it out alive.

But how the fuck has this happened? The whole house is gutted. Could it have been accidental? Her blood runs colder still. Was it her fault? Did she leave something plugged in? She wracks her brains, comes up with nothing. Not even neurosis could make this her fault. If the bedside lamp in her room was switched on, it wasn't by her.

She needs to stop this. It's bad enough already, she doesn't need to make it worse.

As much as she wants to believe that whatever happened here was an accident, the presence of the police shows it's suspicious. It must have been arson, petrol through the letterbox or something.

But that doesn't make sense, either. Why should anyone want Tom dead? He was a nice man, someone willing to go the extra mile for his clients. There's no reason at all that anyone would want to kill him.

Think, Anna. Think.

A screeching of brakes, pain radiating from her shoulder where she landed. She's still carrying the bruises from the car hitting her outside the prison. It really isn't looking like an accident anymore.

Maybe it's not Tom they were after . . .

She looks at the police car again. She should speak to them.

She takes one step forward, another. Then turns around, her head down.

She can't talk to the cops. Her approach, the whole prison record of her, the shambolic jacket, the bag full of sad belongings. They won't listen to a word she has to say. As soon as they clock she's under probation supervision, they'll shut down. Arrest her. Even attempt to pin the blame on her. An easy solve.

It's not right. Tom deserves better. She walks swiftly round the corner, only stopping when she's found an alleyway between two houses where it seems safe to pause for a moment to think. She sinks down on to her bag, head in hands.

Tremors run through her. Was she supposed to be in there when the house went up in flames? She's seen and heard so much, the dead woman in the bunk below her, the whispered words.

She's holding her knees close to her chest, terror clawing at her skin. Someone knows the phone is out there, she's sure of it. The way that it rang and rang so insistently when she turned it on earlier – they must have been sitting there with their finger on redial, pressing it repeatedly until the moment that Anna so recklessly turned it on.

But what are they trying to cover up? The whispered conversation hisses in her ears.

Promise me you'll leave her alone. I won't let you do this. Why won't anyone help me?

Anna's been too focused on herself, her own struggles. She hasn't paid attention to the real threat that's been surrounding her from the moment of her release. The same threat that led to Kelly's death. That killed Tom.

Anna's pad mate might have killed herself, but someone

else was responsible for it – they didn't slit her throat themselves, but they might as well have. Kelly was desperate, she couldn't see another way out. Why? What did that phone call mean? What do they want?

If Anna doesn't find out, she's going to be next. The smell of smoke still lingering in the air around the burned ruins of Tom's house is a grim warning.

She gets to her feet. She can't stay here, close to the scene of the fire, of Tom's death. She needs to get away, find somewhere she can shelter. Collect her thoughts. She pushes her hands into the pockets of her jacket to warm them up and hits a piece of paper. Recollection dawning on her, she pulls it out and reads the folded note with the volunteer's address written on it. The other side of Oxford.

The only person she half-considered trusting is gone. Can she bring herself to involve another innocent person in this madness? There's nothing to suggest she can even trust this stranger. But she's going to have to try. She has no other choice. Once more hauling her bag up to her shoulder, she starts walking, one foot after the other, sounding out a litany to Tom as she goes. Ashes to ashes, dust to dust, a crackling of flames constant in her ears.

Part 5

40

Sunday. The sky is grey and oppressive; not as heavy as the air in the car. Something is sitting on Lucy's chest, slowing her breathing. The radio's on, some kind of easy listening, and every time the word 'love' is sung, she feels her face burn.

Edgar's focused on the road ahead, only turning in her direction when he needs to check the mirror, glancing past rather than at her. Hard to believe that only a few hours ago, he was . . . She woke in the night to find him reading a notebook intently, the brown envelope Victor gave him ripped open, tossed to one side. When he saw she was awake, he put the notebook aside, turned all his attention to her again. The second time she woke, closer to 6, he was gone, but she went back to sleep. He came in at 8, a coffee from Starbucks in his hand, and before she could ask where he'd been he was kissing her again. She digs her fingers into her thigh. Not the time to think about it.

Too late to stop. It crashes in on her. Not like anything she's known before. She doesn't know what happens next between them, though she knows she wants it to happen again. Again and again and again.

He clears his throat. 'About last night,' he says. 'And this morning, come to that.'

Here it comes. The dear John speech. Why it was a bad idea, what he's got to lose, why they should forget it all—

'That was extraordinary,' he continues. Her brain screeches into a handbrake turn. 'This is going to sound insane, but I can't stop thinking about you. Even though you're sitting right here. The way you—'

'Stop,' she says, her cheeks hot. 'Don't. It's so embarrassing.'

'It's not embarrassing at all. You should embrace it. You're a natural.'

A natural what? Lucy slumps in her seat, face sinking into her scarf. She feels about twelve, blushing like this. Exposed.

'I know you'll want to be open about this,' he says. 'And I do, too. It's complicated, though. There's my wife . . . and the college. Maybe we should have waited. But I suppose some rules are made to be broken.'

Flashback to the beginning of term, when Lucy was still contemplating the best way to get Edgar's attention. That's what she had whispered to him in her fantasies. *Some rules are made to be broken.* It sounds different coming out of his mouth, somehow.

'I'm sorry,' she says. 'I should have said no.'

'I'm glad you didn't.'

The miles roll by, a silence between them, but not a distance. She feels very close to him. She's in a state of disbelief – any moment, she'll wake up to discover it was a shitty one-night stand, or worse, that she made a pass at him and was turned down. His hand creeps to her knee.

It's real.

'One thing, though. I was thinking, do you want to talk about my wife?'

There's that word again, *wife*. As far as Lucy's concerned, the less she knows, the better. Keep the shame away. Blood surges up into her neck, blotches forming on her cheeks. 'Is it any of my business?'

'Sorry, sorry. Not my current wife. Gabriela.'

Lucy sits in silence for a moment, watching the brake lights of the car in front of them shine red in the distance. She's not seeing them, though; she's seeing a woman lying dead, blood everywhere.

'You OK?'

She needs to answer. She's not sure what to say. So many questions, she's not sure where to start. 'I am,' she says. 'There's been a lot to take in this weekend, that's all. Let me think about it.'

'I understand,' he says. 'Look, what I'm looking forward to most is sharing my work with you. It's been such a long time since anyone understood me, understood what I was doing. I've got so many projects. So many plans. We're going to be amazing. It will take a while but trust me. We are going to be great.'

This, this is the dream. Everything else is incidental, even the passionate responses he teased from her the night before. Working with Edgar really is everything to which Lucy has aspired.

'I would love that,' she says.

'There's one project I have in mind. Very sensitive. I could use some fresh eyes on it. How would you fancy a trip to the Highlands with me?'

No hesitation. 'I'd love that.'

He reaches over, his hand closing over her thigh more firmly, sliding upwards and squeezing again before he puts it back on the steering wheel and turns his attention to the road.

They're getting close to his home, Lucy realises. He's missed the turning to drop her off. She should tell him – she doesn't want to. She's rolling his words over in her mind, his plans for their future, terrified they'll disappear like smoke the moment she opens the car door.

One final right turn, a crossroads, and they're nearly there. Lucy fights the urge to hide in the footwell of the car, cover herself with her coat. When it comes to his wife, she knows it's better neither to see her nor to be seen. She picks up her bag, ready to make a run for it.

A screech of brakes. She's thrown hard against her seatbelt as he comes to a halt, foot flat on the brake. She looks up, startled. No one in the road in front. But further along, by the gate that she recognises as his, a police car is parked up, its blue lights flashing.

'Christ,' he says under his breath, and flings the steering wheel round to park the car in the nearest gap. He jumps out, leaving the engine still running, the door open. Lucy watches after him for a moment before collecting herself, gathering her stuff quickly and following him.

'Are you all right? Rachel? What's going on?' Edgar is shouting as he runs up to his house, sheer panic in his voice. Lucy's close behind him, but she stops near the garden wall, desperate not to intrude. Two police officers are standing by the doorstep, while a dark-haired woman is just inside the house, a baby in her arms. Edgar rushes to her, pushing the police to one side as he grabs hold of her.

'Rachel! You all right? I thought . . .' he says, his voice breaking.

'I'm all right,' Rachel says.

Lucy hugs her arms tight round herself. *A baby? Seriously?* She should leave; but she's compelled to stay, fixed to the spot. The police.

'Why are you here?' Edgar shouts at the police. He's holding Rachel close to him, hand clamped to her shoulder. Lucy remembers the feel of his hands on her, hunches up even further.

'Do you know a man called Victor Machado?' the police officer says.

Victor. What the hell? Without meaning to, Lucy draws closer to the group by the door.

'Victor? Why?'

The police officer continues. 'There's been a house fire. Two men were inside – one dead, another with very serious injuries. There was a wallet next to him containing ID in the name of Mr Machado, and a note with your address on it. While we wait for information from the Bolivian embassy, we'd like to see if you can help us at all.'

Edgar's face blanches. He staggers forward. Rachel grips hold of him with one arm, clutching the child with the other. Even her lips are pale. Lucy's stomach churns, acid rising in her throat. Whether more from the thought of that nice man, his warm smile, burned to a crisp, or the completely unannounced baby in Edgar's wife's arms, she doesn't know.

'But—' Lucy starts to say, but Edgar interrupts her.

'This doesn't make any sense,' Edgar says. 'He lives in the US.'

'Does he have any connections here?'

'I know he kept in touch with a few people. We emailed from time to time.'

'Have you seen him recently?'

Lucy opens her mouth again, but Edgar continues talking.

'No. I was in Cambridge last night, at a conference. This is one of my masters students, Lucy Morrison,' Edgar says. 'She helped with the preparation for my paper.'

'Right,' Rachel says. Lucy can't look at her. Already stunned by Edgar's lies, the dry tone of Rachel's comment slices through her.

'Look, I think we had all better go inside and find out what the hell is going on,' Rachel continues. 'You too.' She gestures to Lucy as she hovers uncertainly on the doorstep, before ushering the police officers into the house.

'What the fuck?' Lucy mouths at Edgar.

He stares at her intently, before mouthing words back at her – 'Trust me' – before he follows his wife inside. It's not like she's got much choice. Taking a deep breath, she steps across the threshold, pulling the door shut behind her.

41

Sitting opposite Edgar's wife. Edgar's baby. Not what Lucy
had expected, though that's a bit of an understatement. The
news brought by the police has brought them close, physically
if nothing else. She's squeezed on one end of a sofa, Edgar at
the other, Rachel on a chair to the side, the child still clasped
to her. The police take the two chairs opposite them.

Edgar crosses and uncrosses his legs, his impatience evident. Lucy squeezes even further into the corner of the sofa.
She doesn't want him anywhere near her at this second. She
sneaks a glance at him. He looks exhausted, worn in the grey
light of the afternoon.

'It'll be touch and go for the next while,' the police officer
says. 'The next few days will be crucial.'

'What do you need from us?' Rachel says.

'We've been in contact with the Bolivian embassy, but we
urgently need to find out about family or next of kin. There
might not be much time for the individual concerned.'

Edgar nods. His eyes are half shut, as if he's sleeping, but
he straightens himself up to reply. 'I'm sorry, I don't have any
contact details for his family,' he says. 'There's no one in the
UK. Victor used to work with me here ten years ago, but he

returned to Bolivia, and he hasn't been back here until now. We've stayed in touch via email.'

'He came here yesterday,' Rachel says. 'He wanted to see Edgar. I arranged for him to come back for dinner on Monday.'

'Did he say why he wanted to see your husband?' the police officer says.

'Why would he need a reason?'

The female officer looks at her blankly.

'No,' Rachel continues, 'he didn't.'

Edgar shifts around in his seat, his hand starting to drum out a rhythm on the arm of the sofa.

'Whose house was it?' he asks. 'Where was he staying?'

The police officer pauses, as if for effect, then says, 'Tom Wright is the owner. Was the owner, I should say. Although of course we're awaiting formal identification. It may not be him.'

A tremor passes through Edgar; Lucy feels it through the sofa.

'Formal identification?' Rachel parrots. She's pale too.

'As I said at the start, a man was also found dead in the property, his body badly burned.'

More tremors from Edgar. Rachel glances over at him, her face full of concern.

'Do you know the name Tom Wright, professor?' the police officer says, returning to his questions.

'I do,' Edgar replies after a few seconds.

'How do you know him?'

'Professionally. He's a defence solicitor and I work in the field of criminology at the university, so our paths have crossed a few times.'

'And personally?'

Edgar sighs. He gets up and walks to the mantelpiece, leaning his elbow against it as he turns back to face them. 'I presume you know, otherwise you wouldn't be asking the question. On a personal basis, if you can call it that, I know him because he represented the person who was convicted of killing my late wife.'

Lucy jumps. She can't help herself. Rachel turns her head to look at her, and she hunches herself back down, desperate to disappear.

The second police officer joins the conversation again. She's got bright, beady eyes. Lucy has found herself watching her far more than the copper doing the questioning. His face is too smooth, giving nothing away, whereas there's an attentiveness in the female officer's face, a sense that she might be about to raise an eyebrow as if in disbelief. Lucy warms to her, despite herself.

'Your wife. Ten years ago, wasn't it, she died? Around the time you say Mr Machado returned to Bolivia?' the female officer says.

'Correct,' mutters Edgar.

'So you might feel some hostility towards Mr Wright?' she says.

'He was just doing his job. I've always thought highly of him. As did Victor, even though he was also close to Gabriela. They were friends.'

'How very . . . objective of you both,' the female police officer says, writing something down in her notebook.

'He's built a career around it,' Rachel says.

Lucy hunches smaller. She didn't expect her to be so supportive.

'Interesting. Not the usual response.'

'Not the usual kind of case,' Edgar says. 'Look, I don't understand what the relevance of any of that is here. It was a decade ago.'

'True, very true. You'll maybe see why it sparked our interest, though. A man on death's door with your name in his pocket, another man – the man who represented the killer of your wife, no less – dead. Coincidental, maybe. But I don't like coincidences.'

With that, the police officers glance at each other and rise to their feet.

'I don't think we need anything else from you at this stage,' the woman says. 'We'll be in touch.'

'Can I go and see Victor? Make sure he's all right?'

'That won't be possible, I'm afraid.' She sounds anything but sorry.

A couple of minutes later, and they've gone. Lucy is left alone with Edgar and Rachel. He's still standing at the mantelpiece, his face as pale as she's ever seen it, mask-like.

'Edgar,' Rachel says, but he holds up his hand.

'Just give me a minute,' he says.

'Are you—' she starts to say, but is interrupted by wailing, the cries climbing fast in intensity. Rachel rocks the baby in her arms, but the cries don't cease. Lucy peers over, without wanting to look as if she's staring. She can't tell the gender from the clothes, sludgy beiges and cream, topped off with a mop of fine, dark hair.

'Not now, Rachel. Not now. Please. I need to think,' Edgar says.

Rachel nods. She puts the child against her shoulder and

leaves the room. The cries seem to get louder still before there's a sudden calm.

'You didn't tell me about the baby,' Lucy says. 'And why did you lie to the police just now?'

Edgar looks at her, his face still. The face of a stranger. 'I will explain everything. But this is not the time.'

Lucy sits uncomfortably. She can tell the room is normally warm, inviting, its decorations all in the best possible taste, but it feels so cold. Rachel comes back in, without the baby. She switches the light on at the wall as she enters, but instead of rendering it more inviting, the space seems more clinical still, harsh shadows cast now across Edgar's face. He looks old.

'Nap time,' Rachel says.

'Good,' Edgar says. It sounds automatic.

'I don't understand this,' Rachel says. 'I only saw Victor yesterday. I wish I'd asked him to stay last night. This might not have happened.'

'There's no point thinking that,' Edgar says.

Rachel sits down abruptly beside Lucy, covers her face with her hands. Edgar turns his head slowly to look at her. With a start, Lucy jumps up from the sofa so that he can sit next to his wife, comfort her.

He stays motionless, though. Lucy shifts her weight from foot to foot, unsure what to do, whether to stay in the room, walk out, run for the hills and never show her face there again . . .

'I'm going to make myself a coffee,' he says, before he turns and walks out, shutting the door gently behind him, the click of the latch loud as a slam in the silence.

42

Anna knows the way. She went out with someone for a short time in first year who lived in a house up the Woodstock Road, and she'd go up after her lectures were finished to hang out with him. It was a brief relationship, but passionate, and she remembers the joy with which she'd make her way there, the sense of anticipation. Now, it's one of dread.

She knows how thin the ice is where she's walking. Any moment it could crack beneath her feet and swallow her whole. She smelled the acrid smoke from the remains of Tom's house, she heard the screech of the brakes of the car as it tried to hit her after she left prison. She remembers Kelly's muttered words before she died. She doesn't understand how, or why, but danger is stalking her, closer than ever.

She's at the street now, close to the address on the piece of paper. Safety, at least for now. A warm drink, maybe a bed for the night, and she can regroup, work out how the hell she's going to get out of this mess, discover what she can about the dead woman and who was calling her on the hidden phone.

Now she's at the house. It's nice; semi-detached. Spacious. Much bigger than Tom's. Bigger than the student flat she used to visit all that time ago. She glares down at her grubby clothes. Instinctively, she pulls her jacket straight, brushes her fingers through her hair to make it halfway respectable, then gives up. She's not here to impress.

She's here for sanctuary.

She rings the bell. After a moment, a woman opens the door slightly and peers out, full of caution. It's the volunteer from the hostel, the one who gave her address to Anna. Anna nearly collapses with relief – at least she's found the right place.

'I'm sorry,' Anna says, 'I didn't have anywhere else to go.'

'Not another of your waifs and strays,' a man's voice says from further within the house. 'This is not the time.'

'She needs help.' The woman opens the door fully, gestures Anna in. 'Come through here.'

Anna follows her into the kitchen at the back of the house. It's warm, cosy, plants on the windowsills and books on the table. A scent of flowers in the air. So normal that Anna nearly collapses with relief.

'Tea?' the woman says, and Anna nods. The woman has brushed, shiny hair, and as Anna sits down at the wooden table, she feels conscious again of her scrappy clothes, the fact that she hasn't washed since early this morning.

The woman brings a steaming orange mug to Anna and hands it to her before sitting down opposite.

'I'm sorry, I don't even know your name,' Anna says. 'But you were kind earlier, giving me your address. My name is Anna. Anna Flyn.'

The woman nods. 'Of course,' she says. 'I'm Rachel. And as I might have mentioned, I do some work with people who need help to get back on their feet. I think that's what you're looking for.'

Anna hasn't heard it stated so subtly before, so gently. It's easy to say *yes, that's me*, in a way she hadn't anticipated.

'No judgement here,' Rachel says. 'I understand how hard it can all be. Why don't you tell—' She's interrupted by the man, who pushes open the kitchen door.

'Seriously, Rachel, now is not the time. This is more important. Tell her to come back later. Tomorrow.'

Rachel ignores him, returning to the question she was about to ask Anna. 'Why don't you tell me what's going on?'

Anna takes a deep breath, scratches reflexively at her arm. The patch of skin on her arm is itching – her personal weathervane. Too much tension in the air, too much emotion emanating from the man, who has now taken up position leaning against the kitchen counter, the set of his mouth grim. But Rachel is smiling in an encouraging way, so Anna knows she should feel safe, even if she doesn't.

'I was meant to be staying somewhere tonight,' she says. 'But—'

'Where was it you were meant to be staying?' the man says, speaking for the first time.

'A house. Near Cowley Road.'

Another person comes into the room. Much younger, this one, in her early twenties by the look of it. Pretty, too. She stands next to the man, a strained expression on her face.

There are too many people in the room. They're too close to her, looking at her with an intensity that wrinkles her skin.

'I've just got out of prison.' The words burst out of Anna's mouth. She's suddenly angry with this audience gawping at her, like she's an alien that's landed unexpectedly in their kitchen.

'It's not like it's tattooed on your head,' the man says, his voice surprisingly mild, considering how worked up he was only moments before. 'But yes, I was wondering.'

His honesty disarms Anna, the defensiveness she's surrounded herself with lowering a touch. 'Sorry,' she says.

'I understand,' he says. 'It can take time to adjust. But you're in the right place. We're good people here. My name's Edgar, and this is Lucy, one of my students.' He points at the young woman. 'Look, we'll sit down. Stop standing over you.'

They join her at the table. Anna looks over at all three of them, assessing each in turn, prodding at them in her mind. Each of them smiling reassuringly, even though there's an undefined tension in the air, some sense of conflict. It's not directed at her, though. She can tell them what's happening. Or some of it, at least.

'I got out on Friday. There was an ... incident in the prison, which meant that I had to be interviewed about something before I was released. This solicitor represented me in the interview. I got out very late and he ended up putting me up in his house here on Friday night. He was going to give me some work, too. Starting on Monday, like I told you,' she says, looking at Rachel. 'I stayed in the hostel last night, but I was going to go back and stay with him tonight. So I went to his street.'

'What happened?' Rachel says.

'I didn't get very close. But I could see it. It was one of those terraces, you know, off Cowley Road.' The smell's in her nostrils again, heavy at the back of her throat. 'There were police nearby. I didn't talk to them. Only an old man who was passing. He said that someone had died. So I panicked. That's why I came here.'

'Why were the police at the house, Anna?' Rachel says. She's speaking very quietly.

'It had burned down.'

The tension in the air shifts, a chain of electrical reactions, a spark lighting another and another. Anna looks at each of them, seeing strain, alarm cross each of their faces.

'What was your solicitor's name?' Rachel again. Quieter still.

'Tom Wright.'

The words land like stones.

43

Silence. Lucy has no idea what to do. By the look of them, neither Edgar nor Rachel do either. They're motionless.

'Why are you all staring at me like that?' Anna's shifting from side to side in her seat, her hands tucked into the sleeves of her black Puffa jacket. There's a slight smell coming off her, an undertone of bonfire. But of course, it's not bonfire, nothing as benign as that. Lucy shivers at the thought of flames engulfing the house, the charred ruins this woman must have seen.

'Tom Wright? You knew him?' Rachel says. She sounds totally shaken.

'I said so. He was my solicitor. Why are you all looking so shocked?'

'The thing is,' Rachel says, 'that we've just been told that a longstanding colleague of my husband's has been seriously injured in a house fire. He was staying with Tom Wright.'

'Victor's my friend,' Edgar says. 'Not just my colleague.' Anguish comes off him in waves; his fists are clenched tight by his side. Lucy has to exercise every ounce of self-control she has not to move closer and put her arms around him.

'I can't get my head round this,' Rachel says. 'How come you didn't stay with him last night?'

'I slept in the hostel. The one where I met you,' Anna says. She's speaking quietly, her face averted. 'I was trying to be independent – Tom had already done a lot for me. I'd already stayed with him for one night, and he was giving me work. I didn't want to be too much of a burden.'

'What time did you leave his house?' Rachel says.

'In the afternoon,' Anna says. She pauses, then: 'Look, what are you getting at here? Are you trying to suggest I had something to do with this? Why would I want to hurt Tom? I thought you were going to help me, not make accusations against me. I don't have any idea what happened.'

'Did you go and talk to the police when you got to the house?' Rachel says.

'No. I was too scared.'

'What is the point of all these questions, Rachel?' Edgar says. 'Do you really think this woman has anything to do with it? Stop playing Miss Marple.' He's been sitting, shaking his head, but now he leaps to his feet, jumping up with such force that he pushes his chair to the floor behind him. Lucy jumps, pushes her hands tight between her thighs to hide their tremors.

'Edgar,' Rachel says, reproachfully. 'Calm down. I'm just talking to Anna.'

'Don't fucking tell me to calm down,' he says.

'You need to sit down. We need to work out what's going on.'

'Like some pound shop Agatha Christie? Tell you what, it was Miss Scarlett over there in the doorway with a tin of petrol. This is a complete waste of time.' He points straight at Anna whose cheeks flush as red as the colour he's named her.

'Don't be ridiculous, Edgar,' Rachel says. 'Sit down and be reasonable.'

He doesn't sit down, leans against the kitchen counter. Lucy can almost feel a pulse coming from him, matching hers.

'You said there was an incident that meant you got out of prison later than was planned, Anna,' Rachel says. 'What did you mean?'

Anna looks around from one to the other of them, as if weighing up how much she can trust them. Lucy can't work out how old she is; she could be anything from twenty-five to forty, lines in her face that tell of sleepless nights and hard living. She'd said she was in prison – how long for, Lucy wonders. And for what? Despite all her left-leaning credentials, her usual caution about rushing to judgement on anyone, Lucy doesn't trust Anna. It's all too weird, the coincidences that are building up.

Anna evidently feels similarly cautious. It takes her a long time to speak, and even then, the words come out slowly.

'There was trouble on another wing. They needed to move someone into my cell, so I was put on the First Nights Unit for my last night. A woman was brought into the cell I was in halfway through the night, and by the morning, she'd killed herself. She cut her own throat. I was checking her and as I was standing there, the guards came into the cell. They thought I must have killed her, so the police interviewed me. Eventually they realised they were wrong, so they let me out.' She pauses, as if choosing what to say, then continues. 'Tom represented me, ended up giving me a bed for the night. That's it.'

Silence. The tension is back in the room, so solid Lucy could lean her head against it. She'd love to. She'd love to shut her eyes, go to sleep, and for all this weirdness to be over. But she knows she can't.

There's something else, too. Anna has left something out, she's sure of it. She was going to say something after *they let me out*, but she didn't. Lucy wants to know what it was.

'Do you know who she was?' Rachel says. 'The woman who died?'

'They said her name was Kelly Green,' Anna says. 'The woman who I was asking about earlier.'

Lucy doesn't recognise the name. Edgar and Rachel are looking at each other now, interest in Anna gone.

'This is going to sound crazy,' Rachel says. 'But Victor appearing, and now Tom being killed? It's all too much of a coincidence. Edgar, it has to be her. Marie.'

Her voice is so scared the hairs rise on the back of Lucy's neck.

44

Who the fuck is Marie? Who are these people, staring so intently at one another? Who is that young woman sitting on the other side of Rachel, her face fraught with anxiety? Edgar had said she was one of his students – what is she doing in his house on a Sunday afternoon? None of this is making any sense. Anna is more confused than ever – and considering the last three days she's had, that's hard to believe.

Edgar and Rachel both seem to be waiting for the other to speak, but neither is willing to start. In the end, it's the girl who leans forward and breaks the silence.

'Is Marie the . . .?' she says, not finishing the question before Edgar nods once, abruptly. The girl continues. 'Marie was the woman who killed Edgar's first wife Gabriela, ten years ago. She was represented by Tom in the trial, she knew Victor.'

Anna's walked into the middle of a shitshow. 'I should go.'

Edgar nods at the same time as Rachel shakes her head. Rachel glares at him. 'No. Please don't,' she says to Anna. 'You're not in the way.'

'It's nothing to do with Marie,' Edgar says.

'How can you be so sure?' Rachel says. 'She might have been released. Have you been keeping tabs on her?'

'I just know,' he says. 'It has nothing to do with Marie.'

'How can you be so sure?'

'Because it's not possible.'

'She killed your wife, Edgar,' Rachel says, though there's nothing triumphant in her words. Only a deep sadness.

Edgar looks down at his hands on the table in front of him as he twists his wedding ring round and round his finger. 'I'm going to do some work.'

He leaves the room.

'Hiding behind his work. What he always does,' Rachel says, her voice emotionless. Flat. 'The only thing that matters to him.'

Lucy makes a strangled noise, deep from her throat. Anna looks over at her to see she's flushed completely; even the tips of her ears are bright red.

'I'm sorry,' the girl says, the words bursting out of her. 'I didn't know you had a baby.'

'It's not bad enough that he's married?' Rachel says, more gently than Anna would have expected under the circumstances.

'I don't . . .' Lucy says. 'I mean . . .'

'He can't help it, you know. It's how he's put together. None of it means anything to him, not really. It's a curse, being so handsome. People just throw themselves at him. And he's very bad at saying no.'

Lucy makes another strangled sound. Anna looks from her to Rachel, back to Lucy again, realisation dawning on her. The girl can't possibly go any redder than she already is – Anna half wonders if steam might start coming out of her ears. The tension Anna sensed from the start builds so high that she is about to stand up, run out of the room to get away from it, but after a moment, Rachel laughs, as if she's decided that she's tormented Lucy enough.

'Look, I'm not blaming you for it – but I do think maybe you should protect yourself a bit more. It will only end in tears. The only thing he takes seriously is his work. Ever since Gabriela died . . .' She stands up. 'OK. Rowan's going to be asleep for a while yet – there's time. Will you come with me? I want to show you something.'

Before Anna can quite clock what's going on, they're sitting in Rachel's car, a Mini, driving up Banbury Road out of Oxford. Anna is sitting in the front beside Rachel, Lucy in the back. The girl is so crumpled, so shrunken, that Anna reckons they could have stuck her in the boot and she wouldn't have complained. The afternoon has darkened to evening, a couple of stars beginning to shine in the dark blue of the sky, all lit up by a huge moon. The worm moon. Sometimes known as the death moon. Anna remembers the lunar names, learned long ago at school. A chill runs across her skin.

They drive for a while. Every traffic light is red against them. *Stop. Don't go.* Anna wants them to take the hint, turn round. She can't stand the increasing pressure. The indicator is ticking, a relentless noise that's getting inside her head, buzzing under her skin.

'For God's sake,' she starts to say, but at that moment they take a left turn off the main road. Anna catches a glimpse of a sign, only able to read the word 'Cemetery' before they drive past it, slowing near a series of low buildings. Rachel pulls the car over into a parking space and gets out, Lucy following. Anna sits for a moment, reluctant to go anywhere further with these women, to be caught up anymore in the madness of it.

She could walk away now, disappear quietly into the night. It's not her problem; not her side of the road to clean. These people have nothing to do with Kelly. It's not like she has anywhere else to go, though, and her bag is back at the house, all her worldly goods. She's got too little to be able to leave that behind. No choice. Not really. She gets out of the car and joins them.

Rachel leads them forward. It's nearly dark, but still light enough to be able to see the path, the gravestones laid out neatly in a row. Far tidier than an old Victorian graveyard, the stones are straight here, not tumbled over by tree roots and subsidence. Rachel is ahead of Anna, Lucy by her side, and they stop walking after a couple of minutes. Anna catches up with them.

They're standing by a white marble headstone, engraved in gold. Rachel shines the torch from her phone on to it.

GABRIELA RODRIGUES PEREZ
1985–2014
MUCH LOVED, MUCH MISSED

'What are we doing here?' Lucy says. She's clearly as confused as Anna.

'She haunts Edgar,' Rachel says. 'Or rather, her death does.' She kneels and pulls a couple of weeds up from next to the headstone, rearranges a wreath that's leaning up against it. 'We didn't bring this wreath, you know. I came up to visit at the beginning of this week. That's when I knew something might be up,' she says, her voice slightly sing-song, far away, as if she's already halfway through a conversation that Anna and Lucy haven't been able to hear until now.

'It could've been Edgar?' Lucy says.

Anna is saying nothing. She doesn't want to know.

'He hardly ever comes up here; never, really. I sometimes visit, just to pay my respects, let her know how he's getting on. It feels like the least I can do. No one else visits, though. Her family are all in Bolivia, what's left of them. I was really confused when I found the wreath here.'

Anna draws closer, a wave of sadness passing over her. This poor woman, dead in a strange land, no one to visit her other than the new wife of her bereaved husband. She looks more intently at the wreath. It's withered now, the colour faded, the petals pale in the gloaming. But it was clearly expensive, an impressive arrangement of roses and lilies, ornate in its presentation.

'Who do you think left it?' Lucy says.

'I wasn't sure,' Rachel says. 'But when Victor turned up at the house yesterday, I knew. He was a friend of Gabriela's. Knew her family back in La Paz.'

'Why are you showing us this?' Lucy says.

'Because something's up. There are things here that should be left buried.'

45

It's so dark that even though the path is smooth, Lucy nearly stumbles as they walk back to the car. No one is speaking. It must be a beautiful place in many ways, trees all around, beds of roses, but all Lucy can see are the bones under the grass, skulls grinning out at her from every headstone.

Lucy sits in the front on the way back, watching Rachel as she drives, staring intently through the windscreen as she negotiates the dark streets on the way back to the house in Woodstock Road. It's busy, but not overly so – it feels like no time until they've arrived, Rachel pulling into the drive with a crunch of gravel.

Lucy is exhausted. She's kept clear of cemeteries and the like ever since her mother's funeral, a short, fraught event, the details of which she's mostly managed to erase from her mind. There weren't any flowers, that much she does remember – her father told the few mourners to give the money to charity instead, and the coffin went into the crematorium oven unadorned.

Enough of that. She's involved in someone else's tragedy now. She follows Rachel as she leads them straight through the house. She opens the back door and ushers them outside again. The garden isn't lit, but there's sufficient light from the back of the house for Lucy to see how long it is – and how overgrown.

'Neither of us have green fingers,' Rachel says. 'It's Gabriela who was the gardener.'

Lucy's blood runs cold at the idea that Rachel lives in the house in which Gabriela was killed.

'You live in the same house?'

'Edgar didn't want to move,' Rachel says.

Lucy squints into the darkness as they walk down the garden; there's a shrub covered in yellow flowers in the middle of a flower bed struggling to hold its own in the mass of weeds and overgrown grass, piles of dead leaves banked up everywhere.

'I did try when I first moved in,' Rachel says, half-laughing, 'but it was far beyond my skills.'

They're at the end of the garden now. There's a wooden fence with holes in it here and there, through which Lucy can see nothing but darkness.

'What are we looking at, exactly?' Anna says. She sounds out of breath, grumpy. Scratch that – tired.

'This,' Rachel says, gesturing at a large shed. It must once have been a smart structure, more like an outdoor office than merely storage for garden tools, but its timbers are stained and cracked, its windows filthy, draped in spiders' webs. Rachel switches the torch on her phone back on and waves it round – Lucy sees flashes of foliage, green paint, before the light is switched back off.

'What?' Anna says.

'This was Gabriela's. She loved gardening, kept all her tools in here.'

Another crash of exhaustion. Lucy could quite easily curl up in the sheltered corner, wrap her scarf around her head, sleep for a week. She knows she's about to hear something she doesn't want to know, doesn't want to be told, doesn't want to be made her responsibility in any way. It's unstoppable, though, the tide of revelation that's overwhelming her. Anna looks overwhelmed, too, her brows furrowed in concentration.

'No one has been in since she was killed,' Rachel says. 'Edgar locked it up – too painful for him. He couldn't bring himself to demolish it, though that might have been better.'

Edgar. So much pain swirling around him, thick in his wake. At the mention of his name, guilt grips Lucy's stomach, the heat of shame burning up again in her cheeks. A flash of his face above her, bearing down on her . . . Not now.

'Victor's come up with a theory that it's where Marie was hiding.'

Lucy looks again at the shed. It's practically derelict, the space full of nettles. There's a chill in the air; a chill in Rachel's voice. Lucy shivers, wrapping her arms closely around herself.

'Hiding? What does that have to do with now?' Anna says. 'I mean, it's awful. But why do you think it's relevant?'

'She hid out here. Watching the house before she killed Gabriela,' Rachel says. She's speaking so quietly now that both Lucy and Anna have had to stand very close to her, a small huddle, though one from which Lucy derives no warmth. They stand in silence for a while before Rachel speaks again. 'I don't know. But when he turned up at the house, Victor seemed incensed. He was desperate to talk to Edgar about something. He always used to talk about how she must have planned it all out, how he thought she must have been camping out somewhere, spying on them.'

'I don't understand what difference it makes, though,' Anna says. 'I mean, she was convicted of the murder. What does it matter if she was spying on the house or not?'

'Because of how Edgar reacted,' Rachel said. 'These criminologists – they're desperate to forgive, to see the best in people. Victor wanted Edgar to understand that what Marie did wasn't on the spur of the moment. It was *planned*. She watched the house. She thought it all out. And that makes all the difference in the world. Victor wanted to make sure the parole board knew, too. Marie's release on licence will be coming up for consideration soon. Rehabilitated or not, Victor didn't want her getting out. He wanted to make everyone understand that it was premeditated. Even Edgar wouldn't be able to forgive that. He'll take a lot, but when he turns on someone . . . I saw him lose his temper once – it was terrifying. He intervened when a man was hitting his wife but put it this way, he didn't hold back at all. He was lucky the other guy didn't want to press charges.'

46

They go back inside the house. Anna glances at Lucy – the girl looks as if she's freezing. Anna is cold too, though not sure if it's the temperature or the fact that exhaustion is now threatening to shut her down completely.

Once they're in the kitchen, Rachel tells them to sit down before excusing herself and leaving the room. Anna hears her tread as she walks upstairs, the sound of water running from a tap. Then a cry. Anna and Lucy both run out of the room immediately to find Rachel halfway down the stairs, her face panicked.

'Edgar's gone. He's taken Rowan, too.'

'Gone where?'

'I don't know.'

They join Rachel on the upper floor. The doors along the landing are all flung open – except for one, which is secured with a padlock. Anna peers over Rachel's shoulder to see an empty cot in the corner of a small bedroom, an empty baby sleeping bag cast on the floor.

'Edgar never does this. He's terrified of being left in charge,' Rachel says. 'This makes no sense.'

Anna moves past Rachel into the room. There's a piece of

paper on the windowsill. She picks it up. Rachel's name is scrawled on the outside. She hands it over and stands back while Rachel reads it, before wordlessly handing it back to Anna.

Sorry sweetheart, but Rowan wouldn't stop crying, wouldn't take a bottle, nothing. I've gone for a drive to see if that helps. Might stop in at my sister's. See you in a bit.

'That's OK, surely?'

The panicked expression is leaving Rachel's face. 'I suppose. I guess he didn't know how long I'd be. He hates the sound of babies crying.'

'Why don't you call him?' Lucy says, but Rachel is already holding her phone to her ear.

'No reply. He might be driving,' she says.

Anna looks again at the padlocked door, questions running around her mind. Before she can ask about it, Rachel directs them back downstairs and into the kitchen, where she gestures at them to sit, puts the kettle on.

'I'm calling his sister,' she says, leaving the room again.

Anna looks around the room, all its charm faded now. 'I should go,' Anna says. 'I'm just in the way.'

'Please stay,' Lucy says. Her jaw is set. 'I don't want to be on my own with them.'

'But—'

'I don't know what to do,' Lucy says.

'What do you mean?'

Lucy shifts around, pushing her hands up the opposite sleeves, holding her arms on the table. 'Edgar told me to trust

271

him. But then he lied to the police. We saw Victor in Cambridge yesterday. Why isn't Edgar telling them about that?'

She looks terrified. Anna stretches out a hand to her and Lucy takes it.

'You should tell Rachel.'

'I don't want to make things worse,' Lucy says.

'I think they're about as fucked up as they can be, right now,' Anna says. 'Hard to see how it could get any worse.'

47

They sit in the kitchen for a while. Lucy makes tea for them both, unnerved to be carrying out such a mundane task in Edgar's kitchen. There was a time when it would have been her dream to be so close to him. Now it feels like a nightmare.

After they've finished the drinks, Lucy washes up the mugs, along with a couple of dirty glasses that were by the sink. She's exhausted, but she doesn't want to stay still, either. *Trust me*, Edgar had said. On what basis, though? He's a liar and a cheat, she knows that for certain. What else might he be hiding? Her eyes catch on the highchair on the other side of the table, some colourful plastic bowls sitting on its tray. It looks wholesome, innocent – shame claws at her craw.

Nothing left to clean, she sits back down. As she does so, there's a shout. Rachel.

'Come up here,' she says, her voice carrying down faintly from the top of the house.

The women shoot to their feet and run up the stairs to find the padlocked door opened, revealing a ladder up to the loft. They climb up to find Rachel.

'What the fuck?' The exclamation comes out before Lucy

can stop it, but the other two ignore her. They're transfixed by what's in front of them.

Screens. At least six of them, rigged up to the wall in front of a desk, on which a big computer sits. There's more computer equipment on the floor, big white boxes, wired to the screens. They're all dark, and one of them is cracked, as if someone has thrown something at it very hard. The computer screen is lit up, open to emails. Despite the evening chill, this space is overheated, warmth pumped out from all the computers. It's stuffy, a plastic smell in the air. Lucy's already starting to overheat, sweat prickling on her neck. She pulls at her T-shirt to loosen its hold.

'I never come up here,' Rachel says. 'It's Edgar's place, when he needs to concentrate. He doesn't like anyone else even tidying it. But given everything that's happened, I thought I should check . . . Look at these emails.'

Lucy and Anna stand at the computer and start to read. It's an email chain between Victor and Edgar, the first email sent earlier in the year.

Victor to Edgar: *Gabriela's parents understood what this might mean as soon as they found it in that box of her belongings. They're kicking themselves for not looking at it all sooner, but it was too upsetting. They don't even speak English, but they know from just the sight of it what it means. So there's no excuse for you. You* know *what this means. You owe me an explanation. And you've got to accept that there was more to Marie's motivation. She was stalking Gabriela. You as well. It's clear as could be. Look at it, practically burned into the writing. She didn't just lose control the night of the killing – she'd wanted Gabriela dead for months. She'd been watching you, waiting for the moment to strike. If you won't tell the parole board about it, then I will.*

Edgar to Victor: *I owe you nothing. There's nothing to be gained from that. It won't bring Gabriela back.*

Victor to Edgar: *At the very least, it would mean Marie wouldn't be entitled to an early release. Some justice is better than none.*

Edgar to Victor: *It's under control. There's nothing else to discuss. You should destroy it and get on with your life.*

Victor to Edgar: *Let me be clear, if you won't tell them, I will. I'd prefer it if we were in agreement, but I'm giving it to them regardless.*

Something clicks in Lucy's head. *Burned into the writing. You should destroy it.* The notebook. They're talking about the notebook. It hovers on the tip of her tongue.

'There's more,' Rachel says.

She hands a sheaf of A4-sized papers over to them. The pages show images, stills from a CCTV camera. Two women, one old, one young, inside a bare stone house, and outside in a landscape that looks barren, remote. One shows a sheep staring straight into a camera. Another shows the old woman collapsed on the floor, what looks like vomit around her. In another, the old woman is standing very close to the young woman, a broken bottle in one hand.

'What's this?'

Rachel doesn't reply. She hands Anna another piece of paper, this one a list of items.

Gairloch order:
Usual food
Almond milk
Chocolate
Whisky x4
Lilies

Lucy looks at the paper blankly, then back at the photographs. She thinks about the email chain, Edgar shutting down discussion. Her eyes return to the list.

'Where's Gairloch?' she says, keeping her voice steady.

'Somewhere up north. In the Highlands, I think,' Rachel says. 'Why?'

A top-secret project in the Highlands, that's what Edgar said in the car earlier. *I've got too close to it.* Is this what he was talking about? Lucy doesn't answer Rachel's question, asks one of her own. 'Do you know who these women are?'

Rachel nods, once. Her lips are folded tightly. 'That one,' she says, pointing to the young woman.

'Who is she?' Lucy asks, though she has a good idea.

'It's Marie,' Rachel says. 'I don't recognise the other woman.'

'I think I can answer that,' Anna says. She points up at the wall opposite, where there's a collage of newspaper stories pinned to the wall.

KILLER MUM GIVEN WHOLE LIFE SENTENCE
TRAGEDY OF CHILDREN STARVED, BEATEN,

BURNED BY THE ONE PERSON MEANT TO LOVE THEM

A mugshot stares out, dark roots, blank eyes; younger, but unmistakeably the woman in the CCTV printouts.

'Do you know when these were taken?'

'There are dates on the printouts,' Rachel says. 'This one was taken a few weeks ago.'

Anna's eyes are shifting between Rachel, Lucy, the computer screens, the printouts. She looks as unsettled as Lucy feels. 'Does that mean she's been released?'

Lucy is joining the dots. The secret project. The Highlands. 'My God,' she says. 'This place.' She points at the printouts. 'It's a secret prison.'

'It doesn't look much like a prison, though,' Anna says. 'Look at this shopping list: whisky, flowers. It sounds more like a holiday camp than punishment.'

'No wonder he didn't want Victor poking around in Marie's case,' Lucy says.

'How far would Edgar go to stop him?' Rachel says. Then she seems to gather herself. 'No, I'm being ridiculous. He can't have had anything to do with what happened to Victor last night. He didn't even know he was in the country.'

'Lucy, you'd better . . .' Anna says. Lucy knows exactly what she wants to say.

It's now or never. Lucy's choice. Trust Edgar and keep his secret. Or . . .

A deep breath, then: 'Edgar was lying. We saw Victor in Cambridge yesterday.'

'What the hell?' Rachel says. 'What happened? Why didn't Edgar tell the police?'

'I don't know. He told me to trust him, but I don't know what to think anymore.'

Rachel's shaking her head. 'Edgar has always felt like he was above the law.'

Some rules are made to be broken. That's what he'd said to her. But this is beyond anything she'd ever imagined.

'You said Edgar can be terrifying when he loses his temper. How far would he go to stop Victor interfering with Marie's case?' Anna says.

'Not as far as trying to kill him,' Rachel says. 'I'm sure of it. Anyway, he stayed in Cambridge last night. It can't have been him.'

But Lucy's stammering now, stuttering to get something out, her face bright red. 'Um, I'm sorry, this is hard . . . but maybe he could have come back. I woke up in the middle of the night and he wasn't there. Then, when I woke up in the morning, he was back. He said he'd gone for a walk, bought a coffee.' Even her ears have turned pink.

Rachel nods curtly.

'He could have done it,' Lucy says. 'He could have driven back to Oxford and come back to the hotel. There was time.'

No one speaks. Anna tucks her hands into her pockets, shivering slightly, though the roof space is as warm as ever.

'Anything else you want to tell me?' Rachel asks.

Lucy twitches at the question. But before she can respond, some more papers on the desk catch her eye. She picks them up, leafing through them, flicking random sheets out of the way. She's not sure exactly what she's looking for, but after a couple of moments, she finds something, her fingertips jolting at the discovery as if it's electrified. She holds it out to the others.

'Look at this.'

Incoherent ramblings, crazed capital letters in black ink scrawled across the page.

I KNEW YOU LOVED ME AND NOW YOU'VE SHOWN ME. THE MOST AMAZING CON-VERSATION OF MY LIFE. WE'RE GOING TO WORK TOGETHER, EVERYTHING. I KNOW WHAT TO DO – YOU'VE TOLD ME. IT WON'T BE LONG NOW TILL YOU'RE MINE

'What the fuck?' Rachel says. Anna is standing beside her, her face equally startled at the sight of the demented scribblings.

'The notebook,' replies Lucy. 'Marie's notebook. These must be the scans of it. Edgar said Victor had sent them, but Edgar wouldn't take them seriously.'

'What notebook?' Rachel asks.

'Marie kept a notebook – a handwritten diary. Victor found it in a box of Gabriela's belongings that her parents had kept. It's why he's so insistent she can't be set free. What was it his email said? "She'd been watching you, waiting for the moment to strike." '

Rachel's white to her lips. 'Proving Victor's theory that Marie planned to kill Gabriela from the start. Edgar never believed that could be true.'

Lucy nods. 'And now Victor's almost been burned alive.' What the hell was Edgar so desperate to hide?

'It's impossible to know what all this means. Without the actual notebook, there's no way of giving this context. These pages could be anything,' Rachel says. She's leaning over the desk beside Lucy, looking intently at the papers.

'Edgar's got the notebook,' Lucy says. 'Victor gave it to him yesterday. He has all the evidence. We have no idea what else could be hiding in those pages.'

Rachel rifles through the desk herself, papers flying.

There's a long pause, before she takes in a deep breath, exhales shakily. 'Dear God, Edgar. What have you done?'

48

Anna is relieved to get back down into the kitchen, so homely in comparison to the claustrophobia of the loft. Maybe they've let their imaginations run away with them. None of it's possible. Remotely plausible.

Lucy's head is dropping with tiredness. Anna's exhausted, too. Rachel is pacing from side to side, seeming unable to settle no matter how many times she sits down at the table. Anna wants to tell her it's all right, it's going to be fine, but she doesn't have the words.

'You should lie down,' Rachel says at last to Lucy. 'You're falling asleep in your chair.'

'I should wait up, though.'

'There's nothing to be done until Edgar gets back home. We don't know anything until we've spoken to him.'

'But what if—'

'We don't have any idea what he's been doing with this secret prison. It could be legit. He's very senior, he's got all these connections at the Ministry of Justice.'

'But—'

'You're exhausted, Lucy. It's not going to help anyone if

you collapse on us. Come on, let's all try and get some rest. While we still can.'

There's no arguing with her. Even if Anna wanted to.

Anna's trying not to think about the fact that the last time she shared a room with another woman, she ended up staring a corpse in the face. Lucy is only too alive, though. Young, too, falling asleep almost the moment her head hits the pillow of one of the twin beds to which Rachel has shown them.

Anna can't sleep, despite how knackered she is. There's an unreal quality to everything now, the air wobbly, askew, as if she's stepped through some fissure in time. She clutches hold of the bedspread, hoping its woven texture will help to ground her, but it doesn't work. She's there but she's not, floating above her own head in observation.

It's running on fumes, that's what's done it. Nothing has been real since the nightmare began with Kelly's death. In the space of three days, Anna's gone from being in prison to becoming what feels like a fugitive. Though she still doesn't know what she's trying to escape. Or who.

Without interruption at last, away from the catastrophe of this household, Anna's thoughts come back to her own predicament. She'd thought that the fire at Tom's house had been intended to hurt her, but perhaps she was wrong. Edgar could have been involved; there's an explanation for it, implausible as it may seem. After all, he did have a reason to get rid of Victor.

But then, someone might be after her – the screech of the tyres as the car tried to hit her outside prison rings in her ears still. Anna rolls over, clutches the bedspread more closely. The terror she's fended off all day is closing in. She can't give way to it, though, can't give in. It might have been an accident. Pure coincidence that the moment she stepped out of jail, a car went momentarily out of control.

Should she share everything with them, these two women she's never met before, has no reason to trust? Of course not. *Trust no one*, that's been her rule for all these years, and she sees no reason to change it now. She's not going to tell them about the phone, the way it rang and rang yesterday. It's got nothing to do with all this – they have enough to think about already.

She shivers, despite the duvet, the bedspread in which she's cocooned. Maybe she'll never be warm again, never free her mind of all these sounds and smells that linger, haunting her.

Then fear grips her by the throat, bringing her straight back into the here and now. Perhaps Victor wasn't the intended target of the fire. Maybe someone was trying to kill her, not him. She's never going to be able to sleep. The hold tightens, her heart rate rising to an unbearable level. It was her; someone wanted to shut her down. They knew somehow that Anna was meant to be staying at Tom's house last night.

But how the hell would they know that? The only person who knew apart from Tom and Anna was the probation officer she spoke to, who agreed to vary the address on Anna's licence so that she was lawfully permitted to sleep there. Mentally, she steps back, pours cold water over the hand of fear clutching at her. It lessens its grip.

Tightens again. Anna curls up as small as she can, trying to hide from the thoughts that are besieging her. There is someone who might know. Someone who is closely involved with the criminal justice system. If Edgar has the power to set up a secret safehouse for murderers . . .

She's being ridiculous. There is no link between Edgar and Kelly. Kelly has nothing to do with this. The situation is bad enough without Anna coming up with far-fetched theories.

She closes her eyes. She's so tired – if only she could sleep.

It feels like no time has passed when she's woken by a hand shaking her shoulder. Anna opens her eyes to find Rachel leaning over the bed.

'I need your help,' she says. 'I'm sorry to wake you, but you seem less out of it than Lucy.'

Anna looks over at the girl, whose mouth is open, her head thrown back. She's snoring.

'What is it?' She follows Rachel out of the bedroom and downstairs.

'Edgar's sister called. She's just realised that Edgar didn't put any nappies in the bag for Rowan. Would you mind taking this?' Rachel says, gesturing to a full carrier bag.

'Taking it where?'

'She lives in a village outside Oxford. There are no shops nearby. You can take my car.'

Why can't you do it? Anna puts the question out of her head. 'I don't have a licence,' she says instead. 'I'm not meant to be driving. It's not that I don't want to help.'

'It's an emergency,' Rachel says. 'We can't leave a baby in a dirty nappy.'

'Are you sure it's safe for me to leave you here?'

'I can deal with Edgar. I'm sure there's a proper explan- ation.' Rachel doesn't look convinced.

'We should tell the police what we've found. It's not safe.'

'I don't want to tell them anything until I've given him a

chance to explain. That's why I'm waiting for him to get home. Please, Anna. I can't bear the idea of poor Rowan . . .'

Just then, there's a crash at the front door.

Edgar comes crashing into the room, veering from one side of the doorway to the other. He's hammered, stinking of alcohol.

'What are you doing?' he says.

Rachel wheels around to face him. 'How have you got in this state? How could you take Rowan off like that?'

'I went to my sister's, left the baby. She's perfectly capable of looking after babies. You shouldn't have left me on my own to deal with it.'

'Why the hell have you drunk so much?'

'I'm upset, all right? Victor is my friend.'

Lucy sticks her head round the kitchen door, her face tightening when she sees Edgar. She comes in slowly, stands behind Anna.

Rachel's not letting him off the hook. 'What have you done with Marie? I know everything.'

Edgar roars. He lunges at Rachel, his arms flailing, but he's too drunk. She manages to side-step him and he falls to the ground. Anna is poised, ready to leap to Rachel's defence, but instead of raising himself up, Kraken-like, Edgar slumps his head between his knees and starts to sob, a low, guttural sound that rips right through Anna. Through Rachel, too, by the look on her face, and Lucy.

After a moment, Rachel kneels beside him, puts her hand on his shoulder. He turns to her and leans his head against her, wiping his nose on the back of his sleeve. They stay in that position for a few minutes, while the sobs gradually decrease in intensity.

There's a connection between them. However aggressive it seems, the way that they hold on to each other looks solid to Anna, unbreakable. She steals a glance at Lucy. By the stricken look on the girl's face, she can see it too.

At last, the sobs subside. He gets up, clutching Rachel for support, and sits at the table. The burst of emotion seems to have sobered him somewhat – he seems steadier than before. Rachel gives him a pint of water and stands over him as he drinks it, then sits down opposite him.

49

Lucy's emotions are in complete flux. She's been obsessed with Edgar for years. She knows he needs her, but when she looks at him now, he seems shrunken, pathetic. In comparison to him, Rachel is vibrant, beautiful. It's not just that she's so much younger than him. It's her whole demeanour. She's so much more alive. Lucy feels a wave of shame for ever going near him.

Rachel is looking at him with an expression of pity. Love. Edgar's staring back at her intently, too, as if he's trying to read her face, memorise it. If Lucy didn't know better, she'd say it looked like a long farewell. She bows her head. She's been messing with something she can't understand, she sees that now. He's all withered, hunched – bleached, as if someone has washed all the colour out of him.

'I thought I was doing the right thing,' he says.

'What have you done, Edgar?'

It feels like a purposefully vague question. Lucy's breath catches in her throat at the thought of how he might answer it.

'I got funding for a research project,' Edgar says. 'It was about prisoners on life sentences. Whether there was a way for them to be reintegrated safely into the community, whether living off the land would work for their rehabilitation.' He has sobered up a lot, but he's still slurring his words as he speaks and Lucy needs to concentrate hard on what he's saying. 'There was this woman I'd talked to a lot through my work. She killed her kids – the lowest of the low in terms of public opinion. She was due to be let out, but there was nowhere for her to go. She was going to be hounded wherever she went – you know what people are like about killer mothers.'

'What does this have to do with Marie?' Rachel says, her voice measured.

'I'm getting to it,' he says, the anger of earlier resurfacing. He pauses, drinks some more water. 'Let me just finish. I thought this could be a way of looking after that woman. Seeing if it might have broader applicability for other lifers. Much cheaper overall than keeping them inside. If I could get it to work. I put together a research project, putting her in a house that was effectively a prison, but without any of the restrictions you'd expect.'

'What was it?' Lucy says. She can't help bursting in.

'A home,' Edgar says. 'A quiet place that she could live almost normally, without the intrusion she'd get anywhere else. She wasn't eligible for an anonymity order, though her solicitor tried. Tom, actually. You know, there are very few anonymity orders granted. They only go to people like Maxine Carr and Shannon Matthews' mother. The Bulger killers, too, of course—' He's veering off course, describing the minutiae of the scheme. Lucy can see it's annoying Rachel, though she would love to hear more about it.

'Please, stick to the point, Edgar. You can explain the details later. Where was this house?' Rachel says impatiently.

'In the far north of Scotland,' Edgar says. 'Really remote.

Wilderness. I got funding from the Ministry of Justice. Told them it was a research experiment. We sent a regular supply of food. The basics. Essentially off-grid living, so she could live in peace.'

'You've always loved killers more than anything else. You're obsessed with them.' Rachel takes a deep breath. 'You still haven't explained how Marie fits into this.'

'I thought she'd be able to help. Plus I felt responsible for her.'

'She murdered your wife,' Rachel says, her lips almost white with tension.

'We know about the notebook,' Lucy adds.

Edgar doesn't react to either of them. 'I shouldn't have encouraged her. I knew she had feelings for me. I didn't have the heart to tell her to leave me alone. It was my fault. I didn't think about the consequences.'

'Nothing's changed there, then,' Rachel says, as if she can't help herself.

Lucy feels the words like a whip crack across her face, so strong she nearly flinches. She takes a deep breath. 'I told them about the notebook, Edgar. Rachel knows.'

'Just leave it tonight, will you?' Edgar says. He sounds so weary now, tiredness seeping out of his voice. He slumps again. The brief spark of life he'd showed when he was describing the house has disappeared. He turns back to Rachel. 'I got Marie out early, so that she could look after the woman.'

'You did *what?*' Rachel spits out the words. She stands, pushing her chair over, slamming her hands on the table, full now of furious energy. 'Why, Edgar?'

'You heard me. I got Marie out to look after the woman.

She's elderly. And it had been so long since she'd lived in the outside world. She'd never have coped on her own.'

'But why Marie? There are hundreds of other women who could have done the job just as well.'

'This will sound mad, but I felt sorry for her. She lost control that night. And yet, at the same time, I wanted to keep her away from us. I didn't want you to be at risk.' He reaches out his hand to Rachel and after a moment, she takes it. 'I thought it would be a way of helping her while keeping her away. I thought it was the right thing to do.'

Thought. Past tense. Lucy can't help but pick up on the word. Does he still think so? Surely not, looking at the mess around them.

'I don't think you were thinking at all,' Rachel says. 'I can't believe you'd be so stupid. Did anyone know about it?'

'I couldn't tell anyone what I was doing. I can't now,' Edgar says, and his voice is so full of pain. 'I'll lose everything.'

'What do you mean?'

'I stretched the truth to get the funding. I created the impression that this was a fully staffed project. I couldn't tell anyone the whole point was that I was letting these women out without direct supervision. I overrode probation, filed false reports with them for years about what the women were doing. If it comes out that I was gaming the system to favour two murderers . . . You know how much criticism I get as it is. The university is full of people who want to destroy me.'

Confirming what Soraya said to her at that Formal Hall. It feels like a lifetime ago. Lucy isn't surprised to hear he's made enemies. Anyone that prominent would be bound to have antagonised people. But she can't begin to get her head round the idea that he'd have manufactured a research project in order to benefit a child-killer and the woman who murdered his wife.

Rachel seems to think the same.

'You are the most arrogant bastard I've ever met,' she says. 'This is fucking unbelievable.'

'I was trying to do the right thing,' he said, piteously. 'I was trying to keep you safe.'

'Don't even start,' Rachel says. 'You wouldn't know the right thing if it bit you in the arse. You weren't trying to look after me. You were trying to show how superior you are to everyone else. How above them you are. *Ooh, look at my superior ability to forgive and rationalise evil, ooh.*'

Lucy almost laughs, the mockery so skewering of the academic ego. But the savagery behind it takes any humour out of it. Rachel is glaring at Edgar like she wants to kill him.

'Also, how is treating people like that "doing the right thing"? Forcing them to go and live off-grid goodness knows where, totally dependent on you? That's just playing God.'

'It wasn't like that,' Edgar says.

'It was exactly like that. What did Victor have to say about it?'

There's a very long silence. Edgar looks fixedly in front of him.

'Edgar, did you talk to Victor about it?' Rachel says. 'Is that what you and he were arguing about in Cambridge? Lucy said that you were arguing.'

Edgar goes brick red. He gets up and strides over to where Lucy is sitting. She's nearly knocked out by the reek of alcohol that comes from him.

'Did you try and kill Victor, Edgar?' Lucy says, her voice steady.

'Of course I fucking didn't. Keep your nose out of my business,' he says to her with a snarl. 'You know nothing about me and Victor. Nothing at all.'

She's never seen him like this. It's given her a completely different view of him, the wolf emerging from the academic, left-leaning sheep she thought he was. It's a thought that makes her blood run cold.

Edgar keeps ranting. 'He couldn't just leave it to me. He wouldn't trust me when I told him to leave it alone. He thought that Marie needed to be kept in prison for longer, to be punished more. Like I didn't know that already. What does he think I was doing?'

Rachel explodes at this point. 'What the fuck *were* you doing, Edgar? I saw the fucking list. Flowers, whisky. Chocolate. That doesn't look like you were spoiling her. That looks like you were putting her up in a fucking hotel.'

Edgar looks astonished for a moment, before he starts to laugh, peals of cackling that ring through Lucy's head. Any minute, it's going to explode. Then he stops, stands with his hands outstretched in front of them. 'You want to know what I was doing? I'll show you what I was doing. Wait here.'

The women freeze. Edgar stamps out of the room, up the stairs, up the metal ladder to the loft. A few moments later, the stamps happen in reverse.

'Had a good look around in there, did you?' he says.

'What did you expect me to do?' Rachel says.

'It's exactly what I'd expect you to do. You missed these, though.'

Lucy looks down at the handwritten notes, squinting to read them spread out on the kitchen table where Edgar's thrown them.

Effects of starvation. In order to explore this, no food was delivered for a period of three weeks...

Scylla is distressed by drunkenness - plan to deliver alcohol to Charybdis to see what effect this has...

Lights on and off all night, extreme discomfort observed...

Charybdis in a state of deterioration due to excess alcohol. Further supplies to be delivered to see what effect this has.

Lucy looks up again, blinking. Confused. 'What the fuck? Who the fuck are Scylla and Charybdis?'

Edgar's mouth twists. 'Homer's mythical monsters. Don't you think they're good names for two real-life monsters?'

'A classical allusion,' Rachel says, her voice withering. 'How cute.'

'Give that here,' Anna says, taking the papers from Lucy. She skims through them, disgust showing on her face. 'What is this, the Stanford Prison Experiment?'

Lucy breaks in. 'You weren't *looking after* those women. You were fucking with them. Those notes are observations.' She frowns. 'All those screens upstairs. You were watching them. The whole place must be wired up with CCTV.'

Edgar starts to clap his hands. 'Now you're catching on,' he says. 'This was no holiday camp.'

'That's appalling,' Lucy says. 'You've betrayed everything you said you believed in.'

He starts to laugh again, stops, the sound breaking into a sob. 'If it's any consolation, the idea was pure to begin with. There was something about the power of it, though. After my mother died . . . I told you it changed everything. I said that to you in the car. I don't know. The idea of what she meant to me, how good a mother she was – I couldn't stop thinking about it, comparing. Marie killed an expectant mother. Janice killed all three of her own children. You talk about betrayal, but what about what they betrayed?'

'So you took it on yourself to punish them?' Lucy says.

He reaches into his inside pocket and pulls out a notebook, its black cover mottled and torn. He waves it at the women. 'Yes, and I'd do it again,' he says. 'Look at this. I've read it now, cover to cover.' His voice has a strange emphasis to it, though Anna can't work out why. 'Cover to cover. An eye for an eye, a tooth for a tooth. You read this, then tell me what you think.' He pauses. 'She's going to come for me,' he says. 'For all of us. It's only a matter of time.'

'What do you mean?' Rachel says. 'How is she going to do that? Don't you have cameras trained on them, watching every move they make?'

'All the cameras are down. I've no idea what's happening. Or where Marie is.'

'Are you serious?'

'Deadly serious. The experiment has collapsed. I've got no way of finding out now what's going on. For all I know, she's on her way here right now. She might even have arrived already. I have no idea where she is.'

With that, he leaves the room, slamming the door behind him.

50

Lucy looks from Rachel to Anna, back to Rachel. Shock moves swiftly to decision – the women don't discuss it for long.

'You can back out now,' Rachel says to Anna. 'This isn't your problem. It might be dangerous.'

'I know I could,' Anna says. 'But Tom was kind to me. I feel as if I'm involved. I'm not running away. Marie needs to be found. It's too far for Lucy to go on her own.'

It's true, it's imperative that they track Marie down, and fast. There's no alternative, extreme as it is. Telling the police that the convicted killer may be on the loose is out of the question. They'll only dismiss it out of hand. The story is so outlandish, it'll be met with derision. Edgar has made sure of that, the levels of secrecy around his project impenetrable. She should be up north – there's no easy way she could have escaped, but something dark is afoot in Oxford. The house fire is evidence enough of that. Either they wait here for her, sitting ducks, or they take the fight out to her.

Lucy knows what she'd prefer, every time. And by the mulish set in Anna's jaw, Rachel's too, they feel the same.

Of course, however much suspicion attaches to Marie, Edgar himself isn't entirely off the hook for the fire. There's still some reason to suspect him – he did have a motive to keep Victor from meddling. To keep evidence of his continued dealings with Marie quiet, too. Sure, he could have taken the notebook and destroyed it but soon enough, Victor would have noticed the lack of activity, started to ask questions. Edgar's been psychologically mistreating these women for years – how far would he go to keep his reputation clean? It's no wonder he didn't want anyone to see that notebook.

So they can't leave Edgar on his own. He needs to be contained until they can find out what's going on. The only argument is whether it's safe to leave Rachel alone with him. She's adamant that she can handle it.

'It's only for a couple of days. I can manage. He's going to be completely wiped out with a hangover all tomorrow – not in any fit state to kill me.' She smiles wryly. 'Marie's the convicted killer here. You're the ones who will need to watch out.'

Her tone is almost jovial, but no one laughs.

Now Lucy is sitting behind the wheel of Rachel's car, Talking Heads on the radio. How did she get here? Rachel tried persuading Anna to drive, but she refused point blank, pale as paper as she said no, not immediately. She'd have to get used to the idea first.

'It'll be a lot for Lucy,' Rachel said, not letting up the pressure. Lucy took one look at the fear on Anna's face and told Rachel to lay off.

'They do these distances in their sleep in the States,' she'd said, taking the keys from Rachel's hand.

They're on the M6, heading north, the address of a shop in Gairloch written on a piece of paper. Rachel has found emails between Edgar and the Scottish grocery store, lists of provisions to be delivered to the safe house every week. The level of detail is staggering. Lucy can't get her head round how devious he's been; faking research grant applications, writing up findings, faking records of probation officers and employees who don't even exist, moving funds over to his own account incrementally so as not to arouse suspicion that what he's actually done with these two serving prisoners is stick them without supervision or infrastructure into the middle of nowhere, watched by numerous cameras for his private entertainment.

The corruption of power here has been absolute.

And to think that such a short time ago, Lucy was lying in a bed in Cambridge with this man, feeling as if all her Saturdays had come at once. So stupid. Exactly the kind of idiot she's always despised, falling for her teacher like that.

Anna is dozing, her head flopped against the window of the passenger door as the miles roll by. The sky slowly lightens to grey. No sunrise to be seen today, no scattering of pink clouds, a glorious rising of orange into blue. It's overcast, the colours dulled, muted, although the changing leaves on the trees along the verge offer some respite, a forest fire of amber and rust tones.

There's been no time to make a proper plan. They're going to have to rely on their wits. At least Anna's years in prison have sharpened her instincts, given her experience of looking after herself, something Lucy knows she herself lacks, at least to the same extent. Between them, though, she hopes they'll work it out.

And hope is all she's got to go on. Hope that the journey will go smoothly, hope that they can locate the mysterious safe house. Hope that Marie is still there, not down in Oxford, wreaking havoc, as they fear she may be.

Right now, her most fervent hope is that the car is up to the trip. The engine's been making banging noises for a while, and there's a smell of hot metal leaking into the interior, almost like something is burning.

Not that she wants to think about it, but Lucy has a lurking sense of unease about whether she's even legally driving the car. Rachel had assured her that she was covered by her insurance, and Lucy chose not to enquire too deeply. If they break down, it could be awkward.

The traffic is building up, rush hour nearing as they approach Manchester. Lorry after lorry, banks of them, the wheels as big as the Mini they're driving. The smell of burning rubber is growing. Lucy's nervous. She's in the middle lane, no gap to either side of her, when she feels the power of the engine start to die. Her foot's flat on the accelerator. Nothing.

She flicks the hazard lights on, hoping to God she'll be able to steer the car on to the hard shoulder.

'What's going on?' Anna startles awake.

'The car's dying,' Lucy says, her heart pounding hard, hands icy cold as she clutches the steering wheel. The car behind is honking and she's got about thirty seconds max before she loses all momentum and the car comes to a halt in the middle of the motorway.

She's about to brace, ready for impact, when a truck driver in the lane next to them finally notices there's an issue and brakes so that she has space to steer through a gap and on to the hard shoulder, where the car judders to a halt, smoke emerging from the bonnet.

It's not a hard shoulder, though. It's a smart motorway, the lane sometimes operational. And it could become operational now – at any moment.

'Get your door open, get out now,' Lucy screams at Anna, who blinks, still dopey from her sleep. '*Now!*'

At last, Anna clocks what's happening and flings her door open, jumping out of the car with her holdall, just about managing to jump over the barrier to safety on the other side. Lucy is about to follow her, her hands shaking so much it takes her what feels like hours to undo her seatbelt. She sits waiting for a momentary break in the traffic so she can get out more safely, but the stream of cars is relentless. At last she climbs over to the passenger side and as she exits the car, there's a screech of tyres, and—

51

Anna scrambles up the bank. She's looking down the motor-way at the oncoming traffic when a red car catches her eye, weaving its way between the lanes in true boy-racer style. Instinctively, she throws a hand up, urging him silently to slow down, stop, but of course he can't see her, can't read her mind.

She looks round for Lucy, to share her fears with her, but Lucy's not with her. Not behind her. She looks at the abandoned car in horror to see that Lucy is still getting out.

Almost in slow motion, she watches the red car undertake a lorry and move into the inside lane, the so-called smart lane, the so-called hard shoulder, and she's willing him to see the Mini, and she's screaming at Lucy to get out before it's too late, but the lorry is there to his right and she can almost feel the desperate calculations his brain must be making, before it's too late and he's crashed straight into the back of the stationary car.

Anna ducks, recoiling from the bang, the crash of broken glass, the roaring noise of cars around them. Lucy. Where is Lucy? She scrambles back down the slope.

Lucy is just beyond the barrier, lying on the ground in a crumpled heap, buried in the long grass. Anna rushes to her, putting her hand on her neck to see if there's any pulse. It's there. Faint, but there.

Lucy's eyes flicker open at Anna's touch. 'What happened?' she says.

'You're lucky to be alive,' Anna says. 'A car smashed into ours. You must have been thrown clear. Can you move everything?'

Lucy shakes her head. 'I've done something to my shoulder,' she says. 'I can't move it. And it really fucking hurts.'

Anna exclaims in sympathy. Her hands are shaking now as the adrenaline spike starts to wear off. Horror is surging in to replace it, a visceral terror that's griping at her guts, tearing into her brain, nothing there but a silent scream. Lucy is shaking too, great tremors rolling through her.

Despite Anna's shock, though, her brain's running crystal clear. *Concentrate, damn it.* She needs to focus. Then it comes to her, cold certainty. They need to get the hell out of here. Right now. No waiting to find out what's happened, no telling the police about the engine stalling. No checking the driver of the other car. They don't have the time.

They. Lucy is grey with pain, beads of sweat breaking out on her forehead. There's no way she's in a fit state to make a run for it.

'We need to get up the hill before anyone sees us,' Anna says. 'Let's just get a bit further out of here, and then we'll call Rachel.'

'I don't think I can walk,' Lucy says.

'I'll help you.' Anna puts her arm under Lucy's shoulders, avoiding the injury, and urges her to her feet.

'But what about . . .?' Lucy says, waving her hand at the wrecked car on the motorway.

'We've got somewhere to be. This is done. We'll talk to the police later.' They don't have time to argue.

Anna half drags, half carries Lucy up the slope to the top, where it opens into a field. They're very near the slip road off the motorway, and Anna reckons that there must be a service station somewhere close by where she can leave Lucy safely.

'I'm calling Rachel,' she says. 'Then I'm going to hitch. It's the only way.'

'Hitch?' Lucy says. She's going into shock. They'll need to find some sugar for her, a hot drink, get her to sit down and try and process what's happened. Deal with her injury.

'We don't have a car anymore, and we can't exactly nick one. Not unless we want to find ourselves picked up immediately.'

'We're going to get arrested whatever we do,' Lucy says. 'We've just abandoned a crashed car.'

Time to get assertive. 'We're in this now. It's Macbeth, right? Too far through the blood bath to turn back. That's my view. But if you think there's a better way, go back down there now, wait for the police. They'll be here any minute.'

They face each other for a moment, the sound of sirens growing ever louder in the air. Anna is desperate to get moving, but she can't leave Lucy.

Lucy reaches a decision. 'OK. We'll try and get this sorted. But after it's all done, we're going to go to the police and tell them what happened with the car.'

'Sure,' Anna says, happy to promise whatever it takes. She'll deal with it later. By then, it'll be the least of her problems; the breaches in her parole licence are enough on their own to send her straight back inside.

This is a moment when she could disappear. She's out of

302

Oxford, away from London and the strictures of probation. She could hitch a ride and go far, far away from all this mess. It's not like she's any closer to solving the mystery around Kelly. All she's done is throw herself headlong into a pile of someone else's mess.

She knows she can't escape, though. And more to the point, now Tom is added to the list, too. He was kind to her. She owes him answers, if there are any to be found. *That's tough*, the words of compassion he spoke to her when she told him why she was in prison in the first place.

She stops walking. Now it hits her like a truck, what she's running away from. The smell of burned oil, overheated metal, scorched rubber, the noise of the crash itself – it's thrown her into the past. Not to when she was hit outside prison. Not then. Earlier. Much earlier. Another deafening impact. Another mangled car.

'I need to sit down for a moment,' she says to Lucy. 'I'm sorry. I just need . . .'

The shock is hitting her in waves now. Her head's empty of everything other than the accident that ended her life as she knew it, the sounds of the different cars crashing intermingling in her mind, the screeching of brakes.

Lucy is looking at her, worry written on her face.

'I was in prison for drink-driving,' Anna says. 'I got involved in an accident. My nephew was in the car.' She stops, takes a deep breath. 'They said he might never walk again.'

Lucy reaches her uninjured hand out towards Anna, puts it on her shoulder. Pulls her in for a hug. Anna is rigid at first, full defence mode, expecting any moment for the warmth to disappear, for the impact of her words to hit and for Lucy to reject her. But she doesn't. The girl stands there, holding her close in a one-armed embrace, and the last of Anna's defences melt. She collapses on the younger woman's shoulder, sobbing.

It's not long, though, before she pulls herself together. 'OK. Let's call Rachel.'

Lucy nods. 'Can you speak to her? My head is killing me.' She hands her phone to Anna, along with a scrap of paper Rachel had given them with her number. Anna makes the call.

'There's been an accident. You need to collect Lucy – she's hurt.'

At last they get to the Travelodge by the services. Every part of her aches from supporting Lucy there. She doesn't want to think about how much pain Lucy is in.

She gets to reception and requests a room, using Lucy's credit card. Once secured, she collects Lucy, smuggling her past the receptionist so he won't see the state of her, although the man couldn't be less interested.

'It's not actually broken,' Lucy says. 'The pain is all right. I'm coming with you.'

Anna looks at her, at the tense set of her jaw, the sweat and dirt smeared across her face. 'Rachel is on the way,' she says. 'It's all sorted. You've got her number. You call her, you tell her where you are. She'll be with you by tomorrow. You know I need to get up north fast, find out what the hell is happening with Marie.'

Lucy nods. She's sitting on the bed now, her back propped against the headboard. Anna fusses round her arm, propping a pillow up underneath it.

'Is that better?'

'Yes. Thank you.'

'Write your number down for me – I've got a phone. I'll take Rachel's number too.'

She throws pen and paper to Lucy, who scrawls the digits down for her. It's not ideal using Kelly's phone, but Anna doesn't have any choice. At least it's still there, buried in her bag.

'Now go,' Lucy says. 'I'll be fine.'

Anna isn't convinced, but there's no choice. She looks back once at Lucy, grits her teeth, and leaves.

52

It's easier to find a ride than she'd anticipated. She persuades a lorry driver for Rannoch Fisheries with an Inverness address on the side of his truck that there's nothing he'd like more than to drive her back up to Scotland with him, re-assured by his Aran jumper and avuncular face. He looks a safe bet, though she reminds herself again about appear-ances. It's only when they're safely sitting in the cab of the truck, breathing in the fumes of smoked fish, his usual cargo, that she stops to think about the confession she's made to Lucy.

Forgiveness. Learning to forgive yourself and others. The core lesson of successful rehabilitation, the aspect of society that's most lacking. Why should society take it easy on her, though? She'll never allow herself to forget what she did, the damage that she's caused.

'You're lucky you didn't get caught up behind that crash,' the lorry driver says. He's been silent until now, but he's obvi-ously feeling more comfortable with his passenger.

'What crash?'

'Apparently there's been a smash on the section leading up the exit by the services. Stationary car on the hard shoulder, hit by another. Lucky only two cars were involved, but it's caused a hold-up.'

'Christ.'

'Yep. Not great. Those smart motorways have got a lot to answer for.'

'Awful. How do you know about it? Is it on the radio?' She glances over at the stereo, which has been burbling out pop at a low volume.

'Mate of mine stuck in the jam behind it.'

'Any idea why the car would have stopped?'

'Who knows? All sorts can cause an engine to cut out.'

'I don't know anything about cars really,' she says with a giggle, trying not to despise herself too much. 'What kind of thing do you think would be most likely? A tyre bursting?'

'Well, yeah, that's one thing. Or an issue with the gearbox. Spark plugs. Electrical failure. Sometimes even something as simple as the wrong oil.'

'The wrong oil?'

'Yeah, if you put oil in that's the wrong gauge, it can make the engine seize up.'

'How would you know if that was happening?' Anna says, her voice as casual as she can make it. Idle chitchat, that's all.

'Burning smell as the engine overheats, banging. That kind of shit. Before it grinds to a halt. I mean, it wouldn't stop immediately – it would be like being in neutral. The car would still have forward momentum, at least for a little. Depend how fast it was going in the first place!' He guffaws at the end, clearly enjoying the vision he's conjured up of a speeding car suddenly losing its power.

Anna isn't laughing, though. The hairs on the back of her head tingle.

She shakes it off. She's being paranoid. It's no wonder, either. So much has happened in such a short time. It was an accident, and it's down to this stupid motorway system that she can't even begin to understand.

The miles pass slowly. Anna shifts from side to side in her seat, desperate now to get to her destination. The situation is out of control. There's a trail of destruction behind her, from the dead woman in the cell onwards: the fire, the crash, that strange attic full of screens. None of it makes sense. The only solid fact she can grasp on to is that of death, pain, the grave of a woman unvisited by anyone from one year to the next. The scent of lilies dying in the night air.

The driver turns up the radio, talked out for the time being. Anna will achieve nothing by staying awake. She shuts her eyes and lets sleep in.

Anna wakes with a start as they pass a turn-off to Glasgow. It's early afternoon now, the truck trundling along in the slow lane as it eats up the miles. The crash is far behind them, the pain of her confession, too. She feels better for having aired it, lighter. She knows there's no easy remedy to the situation, but perhaps when this is all over, when she's navigated her way out of this mad situation in which she's found herself, she might contact her family, even if just to be rebuffed by them once more.

Anna's glad she's slept – she's going to need to stay alert for the latter part of the journey. From Inverness to Gairloch is still a fair distance, and she's already had all the luck she could hope for in finding this lorry that's taken her so much of the way.

'Is there a bus that goes to Gairloch? From Inverness, I mean?' she says.

'Aye, yes, there is one. Is that where you're off to, then?'

'Yes. I'm visiting a friend. All a bit last minute,' Anna says, suddenly aware that an explanation might be required. He's not interested, though.

'I'll drop you at the coach station,' he says. 'Not far from my work. You should be able to find something all right. Public transport system's shit, right enough, but I think you'll be able to get there.'

'Great. Thanks.'

There's no more conversation for the rest of the journey. Anna's desperate to go to the loo, but she doesn't want to ask the driver to stop. It's more important she gets there – the sooner she arrives, the sooner she can return south, get back on with her life.

She watches the cars passing in the opposite direction, the rhythm of it hypnotic. The further north they go, the more beautiful the countryside becomes. The height of the lorry's cab gives her a perspective she doesn't normally have, an opening up of vistas that would be closed to her from the vantage point of a car. Not all bad then, this turn of events. She shakes away the thought. Not the time nor the place to be looking for silver linings.

They pull in at the coach station in Inverness. Anna thanks the driver and clambers out into air colder by far than it was in Oxford. She pulls her scrappy jacket tight round her.

She's in luck with the coach; there's one leaving in only an hour. Only four a week. Anna offers up thanks to the ether. Someone is taking care of her today, that's for sure, smoothing her passage like this.

She wanders round the vicinity, locating first the loo, basic but clean, and then a sandwich shop, which is about to close.

She persuades the owner to make her some food with what he's about to throw out. The lettuce especially has seen better days.

Anna's seen better days, too. It's been four days since she left prison. To her surprise, a part of her is missing the routine, the warmth. She may never have got that close to anyone, but there was still a feeling of companionship from the other women, a sense that they were all in it together.

She'd felt that companionship with Lucy, too, but that poor girl is out for the count now. The impact of the crash must still be reverberating through her. Anna hopes she's not in too much pain, that Rachel has been able to get to her and bring her home.

It's time to get on the coach. Anna finds a seat and leans back against the grubby upholstery, exhausted. She can't sleep, though, her mind too full of what might happen next.

The countryside rolls past the window, the purple heather blurring dark as the light falls. Despite everything, Anna wouldn't swap places with anyone right now, looking out at the long view after all those years of concrete walls and shortened vistas. She gazes out until the light fails entirely, and only then does she sleep.

It's dark by the time she arrives in Gairloch. She walks straight from the bus station to the shop address that Rachel had written down for her, a small, independent supermarket, but it's already closed for the night. She'll need to find somewhere to sleep. Before they left, Rachel had pressed some money into her hand, which with the cash she has left from leaving prison means Anna still has enough for a bed and breakfast.

She paces around the town for a while, discounting one for

looking too flash, another for being too rundown. Goldilocks. She knows she needs not to be so damn picky. At last she spots one that's just right, a bungalow on the outskirts of town with a sign for vacancies.

Within a short time, she's tucked up in a comfortable room, pink counterpanes and flowery cushions abounding. The proprietor even rustles her up a round of sandwiches, much nicer than the one she had earlier. The woman asks her no questions other than how long she's planning to stay, happy with the cash payment she's proffered.

Peace. For the first time in years. In the eye of the storm, a moment of calm. She's grabbing the opportunity with both hands.

Pouring a large slug of bath oil into the bath in the en-suite bathroom, she perches on the edge and inhales the vapour, fragrant with lavender. Maybe the nicest scent she's smelled in years, not a million miles from the bath oil she used to use, before. Stripping off her travel-stained clothes, she slips under the bubbles, holding her head in the water, her hair streaming around her. With her eyes shut, the steam and the soothing scent playing round her face, she could almost be back in her old bath, in her old life, cleansed of it all.

She's about to drop off, relaxed like she hasn't been for such a long time. She moves her foot to turn on the hot tap and catches the bottle of bath oil which falls on to the floor with a thud, making her jump. Her drowsiness disappears with a jolt, also her calm. She should be relaxed, but now she can't hush the thoughts in her head: what's to come tomorrow, the mission that she needs to see through.

She hasn't planned this properly.

She hasn't planned this at all.

But she doesn't want anyone else to die. With that thought, she hauls herself out of the water and washes her hair. Time for sleep.

First sitting for breakfast is at 7am, and she's ready and dressed on the bell, starving now despite the sandwiches of the evening before. As soon as she's scraped her plate clean of the fry-up, she picks up her belongings and makes her way back to the shop, ready to sit outside until it opens.

At 8.30am, a middle-aged man approaches the shop and unlocks the door. He looks over at her, but doesn't seem overly interested in who she is, barely reacting as she approaches.

'This is going to sound a bit strange,' she begins. 'But I'm here to ask about one of your customers. One you deliver to.'

'I can't give out any addresses,' he says, half-heartedly.

'You've been making a regular delivery to this isolated place. You're emailed with instructions, and it's paid for remotely. Groceries, most likely, enough for two people.'

He inclines his head, just a fraction, but enough so it could be interpreted as a nod.

'Please can you tell me where it is?'

The man's face twists. He doesn't look confused, though. He knows what she's talking about.

'Who are you?' he says.

'My name is Anna. I've been sent to find someone. But I'm not sure where to look. Not unless you help me.'

'Why do you want to find them?'

'I don't mean them any harm.'

He looks her up and down. 'You don't look harmful.'

'Please,' she says. 'I've come a long way.'

He thinks, gives one firm nod, the movement very definite.

'I'll take you there,' he says. 'Or at least to where I deliver the boxes. The rest is up to you.'

Locking the shop door again, he leads her to the four-by-four in which he drove up. They get in the car and he starts to drive.

'I'm Robert, by the way.'

Anna smiles politely.

'For years I've been getting those emails,' he says, his eyes focused on the road. 'The woman – I've never actually spoken to her – she leaves a list in the box, what she needs for the next week. Sometimes they let her have it.' He laughs to himself. 'The fresh chillies, that was a pain. I had to make a trip to the big supermarket to get hold of them. It's bizarre, what I'm asked to deliver. There's no sense to it.'

'In what way?'

'Sometimes bottles of whisky, sometimes not. The amount of food fluctuates. Mostly alcohol, the last few weeks. The last emails I received, they asked for a bunch of white lilies to be delivered. That was the first time there'd been anything like that. And a magazine, a true crime one. Another time there was an envelope posted to me, and they asked me to put it in the box.'

'Did you do it?'

'I did. Then last week, the payment didn't come. I tried calling the number I've got but the phone was switched off. It went straight through to voicemail. If it wasn't for that, I wouldn't be taking you now.'

Anna believes him. She thanks him for the information and settles back against the headrest for the remainder of the journey. The road is narrow, the hills rising above it steep and magnificent. She's read somewhere that the area is known as the Great Wilderness, and she can see why. It's empty of people, of other cars, even. Solitary, silent – the perfect place to hide people, if that's what someone wanted to do.

Eventually, the truck pulls up in a lay-by beside a loch. They walk down wooden steps to a small jetty where a motorboat is moored.

'You all right on the water?'

She nods.

'You can swim?'

Nods again.

'It's over the other side.' He points to the opposite side of the loch. It looks miles away. Remote, though. The setting becomes more and more logical. No one would come looking for a child-killer here.

The boat chugs across the smooth surface of the loch. It should be soothing, it should remind Anna of being on holiday, of lazy days spent messing about on the water, but she's wiped happiness like that from her mind.

She looks out at the water. It's clear, inviting. She wouldn't want to fall in, though. The sun is shining, but the air is biting cold and the temperature of the water must be fridge-like. Even a strong swimmer wouldn't be able to survive in it for long. No one could have swum across. No way out.

53

By the time they reach the middle of the loch, Anna is experiencing a kind of sensory overload. She's finally hit her limit, the contrast between inside prison and outside overwhelming. The loch is unbearably beautiful, mountains reflected in its depths, the water mirror-like, the space around them almost endless.

They are growing closer to the far side of the loch – and maybe closer now to some answers, though Anna doubts it. Maybe she'll be on this quest forever, dodging death by a whisker day after day, just as she has since Friday, when she woke up to find the woman in the bunk below her dead.

She should have thought more of Kelly. As soon as she gets back home – but no, there is no home – as soon as she's back in Oxford, she'll find out what's happening to Kelly's remains, pay her last respects. Maybe, after all this, Anna will have to accept that she was just not meant to find out the answer to what happened to the woman. But at least she can say goodbye.

She needs to say goodbye to Tom, too.

Death's stalking her. She's the Jonah. She shivers at the

thought, floating over deep water. She's escaped death by car, by fire, by car again – at some point, her luck will run out.

Before her ruminations can get too bleak, though, the boat bumps its way into a jetty on the other side, considerably less polished than the one from which they departed: no neat steps leading away, just a rough slope up to a path that Anna can see snaking into the distance.

'This is where I leave the box of supplies,' Robert says. 'Every Monday morning. They'd leave the empty box here too, with a note in it each time giving their requests. Last week, though, no one had collected the box from the previous week. That's never happened before.'

Anna sits in the boat a moment longer, not sure what she's meant to do, before getting up suddenly, rocking the vessel from side to side as she jumps out on to the jetty. She's glad to have solid land back under her feet, though it feels like she's still moving. There's an unsteadiness to her.

Robert sits still in the boat.

'Where do we go?' she says.

'I don't know,' he says. 'I've never come further than this jetty. That's not in my job description. Not my business. If I'm not being paid to do it, I don't want to know. But if you follow the path, you might find them. I'll wait here for you.'

Jobsworth, thinks Anna. She suppresses the thought. No point seeing him as the enemy. It's harsh terrain – maybe it breeds harshness in those who live here. Or the ability to get on with the business of survival, no questions asked about anything not directly concerning them.

She starts up the path, hands deep in the pockets of her coat. It's a rough path, but clear enough in the ground, the earth beaten hard beneath her feet. It must be difficult in winter, ice and snow likely to make any ascent treacherous. But for now, she follows steadily where it leads, up and round the undulating slopes. It's not long before the jetty is out of sight, only a view of a stretch of blue water beyond to show where they've come from.

She's in trouble if Robert doesn't wait for her. She'll never get round the loch. He wouldn't leave, though. She hopes.

Now she's out of breath. Prison-cell workouts are fine as far as they go, but they haven't prepared her for this slow, inexorable climb, the air cold and clear as she draws it into her burning lungs. She stops for a moment, looks around from the top of the hillock she's reached.

Then she spots it: a building in the distance, the angles clearly manmade rather than naturally formed, standing out from the rest of the landscape. Truly isolated. Privation or just private – she can't decide. Some people are so notorious, though, it could be the only way to have anything approaching a normal life. It would be a long way for a mob with pitchforks to trek.

She could see herself living here. It's so beautiful. So clean. Fighting with the elements, but not other people. If her family reject her final attempt at reconciliation, then perhaps—

But it's too late for that. Edgar's experiment is over.

She keeps walking, energy growing the closer she gets to the house, curiosity driving her now, adrenaline too. The uncertainty of what she'll find.

It's close now, close enough that Anna can see the roof, the chimney. There's daylight shining in places through the holes in the roof and—

She comes to a halt.

317

A grim replay. She's been here before. Bile rises in the back of her throat.

It's not a house anymore. Blackened bones, tumbled rubble. All burned down.

No one alive to be seen.

She wants to turn and run, but she can't. She needs to keep going. Incomprehensible as it seems, this must be the place. Perhaps she's too late.

She's nearly upon it, and over the tang of heather, the whiff of sheep droppings, Anna is picking up another scent. Like that of Tom's house, though fainter, less biting. It's there, though, traces of an earlier fire, only recently extinguished.

Another fire; Tom's house, now this. Her nerves are tingling, a pricking in her thumbs. Something wicked . . .

She's at the house now. The ruin. The first floor and roof are extensively damaged, the ground floor less so, the door still in one piece. She'd better check the rooms to see what else she can discover, but every instinct is telling her to keep out, to stay away. But she's faced worse things than this. She takes a deep breath and puts her hand up to the blue painted door, the paint cracked and blistered, pushing it open. For a moment, she hangs in that liminal place, before taking one step, then another, moving forward into the remains of the house.

Much of the inside has been destroyed. No one could be living here. Only the external walls are still standing, their solid stone sturdy enough to withstand what must have been intense heat, the insides scorched. She looks overhead to see skeleton beams, all that remains of the first floor. What's left of them are stumps, flamed to uneven points. There are great gaps in the devastated roof through which she can see straight up to the sky.

The stairs are partly intact. It's too dangerous – she should get straight out of there. But she needs to see. Staying close to the wall she creeps up one step at a time, high enough that she can see the total devastation in the floor above. If anyone were up here, there's no way they could have survived.

The smell of smoke is overwhelming in here. And another smell, though maybe it's her imagination. Barbecue. As from the wreck of Tom's house. Whether it's real or not, she needs to get away from it. She retreats down the stairs as fast as possible, running out of the ruins, gulping in deep breaths of the fresh air. There's no sign of anyone in the vicinity. Once she's recovered her breath, Anna walks around the building, alert to any signs of habitation. But there's nothing.

She's too late.

54

The beauty of the view's been tarnished. Its isolation has been abused, the remote austerity a prison for these poor women. It might beat any prison that Anna's been inside, but she imagines trying to find her way out of here on her own, without any reliable supplies, and her heart quails at the thought.

She's nearly at the jetty now, and to her relief the boat is still in place, Robert smoking a cigarette and looking out to the water. He doesn't even raise his head as she approaches, not until she's upon him, getting into the boat.

'We need to get back.'

He nods, starting the engine. *Don't rock the boat*, Anna tells herself. *Don't rock the boat. Leave it.* She bites her lip.

But why the fuck didn't this man question what was happening more? How has he let this situation continue, delivering box after box of food, taking in the money, never stopping to ask why or what he was doing?

He won't make eye contact, staring resolutely away from her. He's not going to help them beyond this, Anna's sure of it. She needs to ask, though. 'When I get back to Gairloch, I need to borrow a car. For at least a week, if not longer. Is there any way you can help?'

He doesn't reply.

She pushes on. 'You told me you were curious.'

He still doesn't reply.

'There are going to be a lot of questions to be asked soon about what the hell has been happening over there. I'll be informing the police about what I've seen. How much do you want me to tell them about your role in all of this?'

A long silence. An unspoken negotiation: threat meets fear. At the mention of the police, the man twitches. 'I'll help as much as I can,' he says. 'As I've always done. My wife has a wee car that she doesn't use much – we can sort you out with that.'

Anna mutters her thanks. No more argument. She just wants out of this place. The beauty's worn off now. It's sinister, a crow cawing on the side of the road, the clouds looming over them, grey and threatening. It's going to rain any minute. At least they're off the hills now, off the loch, safe under the cover of a hulking four-by-four.

They don't talk for the rest of the drive. Anna welcomes the silence, trying to displace the fear that's growing in her. Maybe both women died in the fire. She'd think that, were it not for the fire at Tom's house. There's a pattern emerging, a flickering of flames in the front of her mind.

She's going to have to call Rachel to tell her what she's found. The burned wreckage of the house, in which the devastated bodies of both Janice and Marie might be lying. There's no certainty for this, though. Marie could be on the loose. She could have torched this house in the wilderness.

She could have torched Tom's house, too.

Anna's not sure if her fear is misplaced, but she knows that if she'd been treated in the way that these women have been, she'd be out for revenge. She needs to warn Rachel. But the tiny phone is dead, its battery finally exhausted.

They pull up outside a bungalow on the outskirts of the town, very similar to the bed and breakfast in which she stayed the night before. There's a small silver car parked in front of it, its windscreen covered in bird droppings. The man wasn't lying when he said that it wasn't used much. He hurries into the house while Anna gets out of the four-by-four. Her legs have seized up despite the short journey. She bends forward and touches her toes, stretches from side to side as she tries to loosen her limbs, stiff not only from all the travelling but also some residual pain from the accident on Friday.

The man returns from the house and thrusts a car key into her hand.

'You've got forty-eight hours, then I'm reporting this vehicle stolen. I don't care about what you do with it. I never want to see you again.'

With that, he turns round and strides into the house, slamming the door behind him. Anna shrugs, then unlocks the car. She's not going to think about her terror of driving, or the fact she swore she'd never do it again. She's not going to think about the fact that she doesn't have a licence, either. She's just going to do it. There's no time for anything else. She'll worry about it all later.

The tank's half full at least, so she'll be able to get some distance in before she needs to stop. She'll buy a charger then, call Rachel and Lucy. For now, she needs to get on with it. She puts her hands on the steering wheel, taking in a deep breath. Only six hundred miles to go.

55

Lucy knows she's got the easy part of the job, sitting in a hotel room until she's picked up, but her anxiety is going through the roof, her imaginings darker and darker. She's desperate to leave, but it's impossible. She's got to wait. She reads through Rachel's phone number again and again until the number is fixed in her brain, but there's no point calling it. Realistically, she knows she's going to have to spend the night here, but as the light fades, her mood plummets, and her sleep is restless and full of nightmares.

She's so relieved to see Rachel the following day that she bursts into tears as soon as she hears the knock on the door, only just resisting the temptation to throw herself on to Rachel's neck and hug her half to death.

'I'm sorry it's taken so long, but I had to pick up Edgar's car from town, then drop stuff with Edgar's sister for Rowan. The poor baby wouldn't settle for hours, and I ended up falling asleep too. You all right?' Rachel says, looking at Lucy's bad arm.

Lucy's fashioned a sling from a pillowcase. 'It's not as bad as it was yesterday,' she says. 'I don't think it's broken.'

'Thank God for that. The last thing we need right now is a

visit to A and E,' Rachel says. She looks around the room. 'Luxurious as this is, I think we'd better make a move back.'

Lucy's ready to go. She follows Rachel out to the car park.

'My neighbours are very worried about car thieves in our street now,' Rachel says, unlocking the car.

Lucy gets in. 'Why?'

'I had to report my Mini as stolen after the crash. The police came round this morning. They'd traced the vehicle back to me and wanted to see if I knew who was driving.'

'I'm so sorry,' Lucy says. 'I did my best.'

'It's not your fault,' Rachel says, reversing the SUV smartly out of its tight space and manoeuvring round the car park to the exit. 'You were lucky it was no worse.'

Lucy is picking at the skin around her nails. 'Are the police after us? Anna and me?'

'I don't think so,' Rachel says. They emerge on to the motorway opposite the site of the accident. Lucy peers over, trying to see if there's any trace of the crash. Nothing she can see from here, although there must still be debris, bits of broken glass scattered along the tarmac.

'No one died?'

'No one injured, even. Other than you.'

'Have you heard anything from Anna yet?'

'Not yet, no.'

'I feel terrible for leaving her on her own to deal with it,' Lucy says.

'It wasn't your fault,' Rachel says again. 'Accidents happen. You'd have gone with her if you could.'

'Where's Edgar?' Lucy says, suddenly realising she hasn't asked. 'Is he still at your house?'

Rachel nods. 'I locked him in our room. Just in case.'

They fall into silence. Lucy is falling asleep and though she tries to keep her eyes open, she can't. She's just so tired.

'Wake up,' Rachel says. 'Wake up. We're here.'

She must have slept for hours. They're parked outside the house in Oxford, Rachel's hand on her arm shaking her awake.

'I'm sorry, I didn't mean to be out cold the whole way,' Lucy says.

'You must have needed it.'

They go into the house together. It's dark, the curtains closed in the front. Rachel takes her through to the kitchen and puts the kettle on, gesturing at the chairs round the table. Lucy takes the cue, sits down. Despite her long sleep, she's still exhausted. Rachel goes out of the room and Lucy hears muffled shouts from upstairs, thumping. *Edgar.* She stiffens, wondering if she should go to help, but then Rachel comes back into the kitchen, her face drawn. Without mentioning the noise that's coming from the room above, she makes two cups of tea and brings them over to the table, sits down beside Lucy. She's looking tired. The last couple of days have been tough on her, too. From the moment Lucy and Edgar arrived at the house on Sunday to find the police there, it's been relentless.

'How is he?' she says.

'Furious,' Rachel says. 'He thinks I'm being paranoid, controlling him. He's forgotten what he told us about Marie last night – that's one benefit of whisky, I suppose.' She sounds very clinical as she says this. Lucy tries to keep her expression neutral, but she doesn't quite manage it. 'I know it sounds harsh,' Rachel says. 'Unfeeling. I'm just trying to keep it together, salvage what we can. He'll stop being so aggressive, soon. It's in his best interests.'

Lucy's ashamed of herself. Rachel's dealing with a horrific situation far more calmly than she could ever hope to herself. 'At least he can't get out,' she says.

'Let's hope not,' Rachel says.

They're talking about him normally, Lucy realises, as if Edgar and his wife have had a row about something run of the mill. Not about murder, revenge. Killing. She takes a deep breath. 'You're not scared he might . . .'

Rachel holds her hand out in front of her. It's steady, almost, but there's a faint tremor running through it. She lets it hover there for a moment before drawing it back. 'Scared?' she says. 'I'm fucking terrified. It's not just Edgar. It's Marie – she killed Gabriela when she was six months pregnant. I mean, imagine it. What would she do to me? To Rowan?'

There's nothing Lucy can say.

They sit in silence for a while before Rachel makes another pot of tea, chucking a couple of packs of biscuits on to the table: chocolate-chip cookies and rich tea biscuits. Lucy looks at them for a while before reaching out for the rich teas. Chocolate is too decadent for an occasion like this. Rachel evidently feels the same, taking one from the pack of plain biscuits as she sits down, though she doesn't eat it, just snaps it in half, then quarters, piling the pieces up haphazardly by the side of her mug.

Anna should have called by now – that's the only thought going through Lucy's head. It's late. Surely she's had time to get to the place where Marie is living, found out what the hell is going on, be on her way back by now? She should have called.

Even though Lucy has only known Anna for such a short period of time, she really wants her to be all right. She feels so sorry for her, the wariness in her eyes and the watchfulness with which she takes every step. It must be unbelievably hard for her, the terrible shock of Kelly's death and everything that's happened since.

Not to mention the revelations that Anna made to her after the crash. Lucy knows she was reacting to the shock, the words pouring out of her, beyond her control, but she hopes that Anna isn't regretting telling her. She wants to help. Or at the very least, be a friend to her.

Rachel pours some red wine, makes some food – pasta and a tomato sauce. Lucy pushes it round her plate, her appetite gone even though she's barely eaten all day. Rachel doesn't eat much, either. She puts a plate of food together for Edgar.

Once they've finished eating, Rachel washes up.

'Let me help.'

'I'm fine,' Rachel says. 'You should get some sleep. Why don't you go upstairs? I'll wake you the minute there's any news.'

At the mention of the word 'sleep', Lucy is already yawning. 'If you're sure I can't do anything?'

'I'm sure. Go on, get to bed.'

Lucy's so tired she's practically asleep before her head hits the pillow.

56

A hundred and fifty miles to go. Anna has driven as far as she can, but tiredness is beating her. She's not used to driving, overwhelmed by traffic and nerves. The thought of the terrible car crash that injured Toby is never far from her mind, though she fights hard to stop it from taking over. She pulls into a service station north of Manchester and grabs a burger, locating a charger for the mini phone at the same time. She sits in the car with the engine on, listening to the radio while it charges.

As soon as there's enough battery, she calls Lucy's number. It rings, but there's no answer, so she leaves a message. Then she calls Rachel's number – her phone is switched off. Anna can't make them pick up, she can't get there any faster than she is already going, and she needs to rest. She lowers the seat and sleeps.

She's back in prison, in a long corridor lined with identical doors. It's endless, stretching out further than the eye can see. She's kneeling, a toothbrush in her hand, and her task is to scrub the corridor floor inch by inch, every part of it, before she'll be allowed to speak to her sister again.

Someone keeps ringing a bell to force her to keep moving.

It rings every time she stops for breath, puts down the tooth-brush that's becoming so heavy. If only they'd stop ringing that fucking bell . . .

She wakes with a jolt. The little phone is ringing, over and over again. Her first instinct is to ignore it, but then she remembers. She takes the call.

'Oh my God, Jesus fucking Christ.'

The words are so jumbled up Anna can barely understand them. 'Who's that?'

'Me. Lucy. Anna, quick, you've got to come quick.'

'What's happened?'

'He's dead.'

'Who?' shouts Anna.

'Edgar!'

'Jesus, seriously?'

Lucy coughs. 'I'm looking at his body right now.'

'Fucking hell,' she manages to reply.

'Marie got here first, Anna. We didn't find her in time. Let alone stop her. You've got to come.'

'I'll drive as fast as I can.'

'I don't know where Rachel is. I can't find her. Jesus, fuck, there's blood everywhere.'

'I'm on my way.'

Every traffic light turns red against Anna. Every bus stops in front of her. Every turn she wants to make is blocked by cyclists, slow and wobbly, or impeded by aggressive cour-ier riders, streamlined as sharks. Anna is tempted to get out and run.

This nightmare needs to end.

At last she's arrived. She sharply pulls the car into the

drive, nearly cutting up a cyclist as she does so. He pedals off, screaming obscenities.

The curtains are still drawn, the house shut off from scrutiny, its eyes closed. Anna carelessly parks the car at a diagonal angle and jumps out, not even stopping to slam the car doors shut. She rings the front doorbell, yelling Lucy's name as she thumps on it repeatedly. There's no answer. No sound from within. She runs round the side of the house to the back. Every curtain is closed, the house as inscrutable at its rear as at its front.

She peers through the patio doors at the kitchen within. It's empty, dark, wine glasses still half full on the table. The bottle is tipped on its side – the wine leaking from it looks like blood on the white table. Anna shivers.

She tries the patio door handle but it doesn't budge, locked tight. The windows are all closed, too. She picks up a loose piece of paving stone from the nearest flower bed, and wrapping her hand and arm in her top, she smashes the rock into the glass panel, hitting it again and again to clear the shattered glass out of the way. When she's finished, she drops the rock and carefully reaches inside, feeling for the latch. Finally, the door opens.

There's that familiar feeling. The one she had when she woke in the cell just a few nights ago, crushed with terror. It's like a cold stream oozing from the house, a freezing lava of dread that will destroy everything in its flow. More than anything in the world, she wants to turn and run.

She's got no choice.

She paces round the ground floor but sees no one, only smears of blood on the kitchen floor.

One step, the next. She's up the stairs now, on the landing, facing a series of closed doors. Anna pushes open the first door she comes to, rushes in.

The room is dark, the curtains still shut. The air is thick and warm, a stale smell, unpleasant. A metallic undertone with which she's only too familiar. Anna covers her nose with her hand instinctively, taking in shallow breaths through her mouth. She pulls open the curtains, flinging the window open too in order to get some air in.

Then she slowly turns round, knowing before she even looks what she's going to find. Edgar is lying motionless on the bed, his head covered in blood.

Anna puts her fingers to his throat to see if there's a pulse. Nothing.

He's gone. No one could survive that bad a head wound.

Nausea grips her by the throat, but she swallows it down. No time for that now. Where the hell is Lucy? She searches the other bedrooms, the loft, but the girl is nowhere to be found.

Back in the kitchen, there's cold air blowing in through the broken pane of glass in the patio door, shards smashed all over the floor. The wine stain is drying on the table. Anna reaches over and sets the bottle upright. Birds are singing outside, a smell of woodsmoke. If it weren't for all this, she could be in the country, on holiday somewhere green.

Woodsmoke.

Not again.

Anna rushes to the patio door to see a plume of grey smoke coming from the shed. There's a crackling sound; it's faint, but growing louder the more intently she listens.

She runs down to the bottom of the garden. Lucy is lying prone in front of the shed, blood coming from her head, but there's no time to check on her. Anna grabs hold of the door handle. It's hot, but she tightens her grasp, twists it. The door won't budge. She takes a few steps back, braces herself and runs at it. It doesn't give. She does it again, running at it with full force. This time, some of the flimsy wood shatters. Pulling at the broken panels, Anna makes a space big enough for her to push herself through.

The air is thick, hot, smoke stinging her eyes and sticking in her throat. She pulls her top up over her mouth and pushes further into the shed, blinking through the murk. It's full of tools, rubbish, flames flickering out from the far corner.

And in front of her, slumped on the floor, Rachel. Anna gets to her, pulls her up to her feet, drags her out of the shed as fast as she can, pulling her back towards the house. When they're a safe distance away, she lets go of Rachel, placing her gently on the ground. She's barely conscious, her hands tied in front of her, her ankles too. Then she returns to the burning shed, pulls Lucy away too, scared that she's going to aggravate her injuries. Terrified that if she doesn't move her, she'll be caught by the flames.

A siren in the distance, getting closer by the second. Voices, a thundering of footsteps past her.

Rachel and Lucy are safe. But where the hell is Marie?

Part 6

57

A month later. Lucy doesn't want to be back in a crematorium with its stench of lilies. Death flowers. The smell is crawling up her nostrils. But she had to come, had to support Rachel. Anna can't. She's been recalled to prison for breach of her licence. The bond holds between them all, the three of them united through the horror of the last weeks.

The chapel is full. Colleagues of Edgar, friends of the family. They come up and quietly say hello to Rachel, kiss her cheek or touch her on the shoulder, patting baby Rowan on the head. No one looks with any curiosity at the young woman sitting on her own.

Lucy owes Rachel. She knows this. She touches her forehead, the skin pink, nearly healed. She knows what happened now. They told her everything when she came round after the attack. As she had ten years before, Marie was lying in wait outside, and took her chance to strike while Rachel was upstairs and Lucy was in the garden. She attacked Lucy by hitting her over the head with a blunt object, possibly an empty bottle, and once she was out cold, she went for Edgar and Rachel.

She didn't get far. The police found her in a field just outside the ring road. She's been held in custody ever since. Anna hasn't seen her yet, though she has told Lucy she looks out for her in the echoing corridors of the prison.

They sing hymns, sit, stand at the right moments. Lucy's thoughts are stuck on their roller coaster. Edgar did good work; he wasn't a good man. His ego, his infidelities – all of it brought them to this point. It's hard to feel too much sympathy for him. At least this way, his reputation has been mostly preserved. The Ministry of Justice has tamped down any suggestion of impropriety – it's their reputation at stake, too. Same with the university.

Such a waste. This room's packed with mourners, fellow academics from all round the world, all the researchers with whom he'd collaborated on such important work. A women's prison has just been opened in the north of England based on his principles. The speaker is giving the eulogy, laying out Edgar's professional achievements. A lot of plaudits.

No mention of his misuse of Ministry of Justice funds to set up his secret experiment. No mention of how the power of it went to his head. The closest it comes to uncovering his misdeeds is when he's described as a *maverick, who marched to the beat of his own drum.* The room ripples with knowing laughter.

One brief reference to him as a family man. No one can labour that description of him, even in a eulogy.

Lucy still has so many questions. There's so much she'll never know; how Marie escaped, why the house in the Highlands was burned down, whether it was Edgar or Marie who was responsible for the attack on Tom and Victor. However friendly Rachel might be to Lucy, she's still on the outside, shut out from the endless meetings Rachel's had with the police, visit after visit to the house by teams of forensics.

'I'd like to invite you now to take part in a moment of quiet reflection, while we play a piece of music from one of Edgar's favourite recordings, Barber's *Adagio for Strings*.'

A shuffling, rustling, as the congregation settles itself down. The music begins. Despite herself, Lucy feels her eyes welling up, unable to resist the emotions of the occasion anymore. Her feelings are still all over the place – love for Edgar, the memories of how his work inspired her through the years after her mother's death. The guidance he gave her when there was none to be found from her father.

He wasn't who she thought he was, though. Pull back his mask, and there was darkness inside.

58

It's strange to go back to normal after the drama of the last few weeks. Lucy struggles to concentrate much of the time. With Edgar gone, so has the point of her studies here. Her feelings are still so confused, so full of conflict, that she's finding it hard to move on. The image of his dead body haunts her dreams.

A couple of weeks after the funeral, Rachel messages, asking Lucy if she'd like to come for supper. It's a Friday, the night of another Formal Hall, and Lucy accepts Rachel offer with enthusiasm, relieved that she won't have to get through a night of insinuation from the likes of Alexandra and Jessica. They've been friendly since Edgar's death, but not in a way that seems genuine, questioning her about the scurrilous details like vultures picking through carrion.

Lucy picks up a bottle of wine en route and makes her way to the house. It's a balmy evening, the sky clear, a light breeze tossing around the last of the blossom from the trees. Hard to believe the situation she found herself in just a few weeks ago. The headaches have stopped now, the wound fully healed.

She's missing Edgar less than she was. With him gone, the spell of the obsession has been broken. She can see now how

338

much she had latched on to the idea of him, looking for any source of support. It's good that Rachel has been able to forgive her for her affair with Edgar. Lucy is not proud of what she did.

Rachel hugs her when she arrives. She's lost weight, her shoulders bony under Lucy's hands. It must be tough. The hall is lined with cardboard boxes full of paperwork, the screens from the loft piled up in the study at the front of the house. Rowan's asleep in a pushchair in the hall.

'It's going to take months to sort through it all,' Rachel says. 'I've asked college if there's anyone who could help me. Presumably they'll want to archive some of his earlier research material – his life's work is here. It might be useful one day – parts of it, anyway.' She stops, hitting herself gently on the head with the heel of her hand. 'I'm being so stupid. Would you help me?'

'Are you sure?'

'You're the perfect person. You worked so closely with him at the end. I'll let college know I've found someone – if that's all right with you?'

'I'd love to help.'

They go through to the kitchen. It's still homely, but the warmth has gone, dust on surfaces, brown leaves on some of the plants. There's a fragrant smell coming from a pot on the stove, though.

Rachel pours a glass of wine for Lucy, one for herself too, and they sit at the kitchen table.

'How are you?' Lucy says.

Rachel shrugs. 'It's hard. I keep thinking he'll walk through the door. He'd be so sad to see all his work dismantled like this.'

'I remember what it was like when my mum died,' Lucy says. 'It took me ages to realise fully that she wasn't coming back.'

They sit together in silence for a moment before Rachel pushes herself up to her feet.

'Would you like something to eat?'

Lucy nods. Rachel dishes up, a chicken tagine. It's hot, savoury; the more Lucy eats, the more she wants to eat. Food's tasted like cardboard the last while, but this is cutting through. It's not the meal, though; it's sitting with someone who understands what's happened, what they've been through.

'You look tired,' Rachel says. 'Aren't you sleeping?'

'Not that much. I'm finding it hard to settle. Waking up early.'

'Me too.'

Lucy keeps eating. Whenever she comes close to the end of her glass of wine, Rachel tops it up, and she dishes a second portion on to Lucy's plate as soon as she's finished eating.

'Thank you,' Lucy says. 'It's so kind of you to be looking after me like this.'

'Good to have something else to think about.'

By the end of the meal, Lucy is replete, full as she hasn't been for some time. Perhaps it's that fullness, or the wine, but she's beginning to feel drowsy. It must be because she's starting to relax. It's hard to keep her eyes open.

'Looks like all those sleepless nights are catching up with you,' Rachel says. 'Do you want to go and lie down?'

Lucy wants to say no; she wants to make a start on Edgar's papers right now, help Rachel out. Rachel is the one who has suffered the real loss, after all. But she's losing her battle with sleep. The suggestion of stretching out on the sofa, lying herself down, sleeping for just an hour or two, is too tempting to resist.

'Would you mind?' she says, hardly able to articulate the words.

'Of course I don't mind,' Rachel says. 'Go and lie down.' She points to the sofa that runs the width of the kitchen. With an effort, Lucy gets up and lies down on it.

'I'll just get you a blanket,' Rachel says. 'Won't be a minute.'

Lucy's too tired to reply. She tucks her head more comfortably into a cushion, asleep as soon as she shuts her eyes.

Someone's clawing at her wrist, shaking her. Hissing in her ear.

Wake up wake up WAKE UP NOW.

Lucy doesn't want to wake up. She can't. Her eyes won't let her. She wants the noise to stop. It's not stopping, though, it's carrying on, intensifying, and now someone has pulled her to her feet.

'Keep her moving,' a male voice says. 'She needs to wake up.' It sounds familiar, though she can't place it.

Lucy wants to tell him to leave her alone, let her sleep. She can't say the words. She's slumping on to the hands that are supporting her, barely able to put one foot in front of the other. Someone's screaming in the distance, and there's a smash of glass breaking.

Footsteps are coming closer now, a heavy tread. She's been picked up, the weight of her taken into someone else's hands, and she's lying down again, if they would just leave her alone—

59

Words are rusty for Marie, her tongue slow to form them. She had the old story down pat, but now she's having to learn a new one. She thought she knew her skeletons, but she was wrong. They've been put together backwards – now she needs to re-form them, revise.

It's time to talk. She leans forward to the hospital bed, takes the girl's hands in hers.

Where to start, though? At what beginning? The point where she fell in love with her teacher, like all the best stories? The point where he fell in love with her, too? Or so she'd thought. It *felt* true, though. Right and true and everything she could want. Everything he could want, too.

'You and Edgar?' Lucy says.

'Yes.' Marie bows her head.

But he already had everything he could want. With a baby on the way. That's when she'd got drunk, gone round to his house. Met his wife. They'd sat together, talked, but then – according to the old narrative – something in Marie must have snapped. She's never been able to remember what happened next. The last memory she has is of passing out, hammered, before coming round and going to find Gabriela upstairs in her bedroom – in *their* bedroom, the room she shared with Edgar, whom Marie loved – and standing with her hand upon the doorknob, before blackness descended.

A dark, blood-red mist. That's what the prosecution said in their opening speech. She couldn't argue with it. She was found passed out drunk next to Gabriela's body, knife in hand. She'd drugged the poor woman, they said, waited for her to sleep, slashed at her. Watched her bleed out. It must have happened. It must have gone the way they said. As they spoke, a red fury glowed in Victor's eyes while he watched her like a viper from across the court. If he could have killed her right then on the spot, she knows that he would have.

A pause, then: 'That's what they said I did,' Marie says. 'I believed them, too. I mean, I was so jealous of Gabriela sometimes. There were some moments I wanted her to be dead. Not to kill her. But I accepted I could have done it, so I went with it. Pleaded guilty, accepted the punishment I was given – a life sentence, with a minimum term of twenty-three years. I served five years in prison. When Edgar contacted me to tell me about his proposed scheme, that I could be released but that I'd be totally isolated, looking after a child-killer . . . well, of course I said yes. I didn't think I deserved such kindness.'

She describes the years in the wilderness, the hunger when the food didn't arrive. The elation when there was something extra in the delivery. How vulnerable it felt to be completely in Edgar's power.

Lucy is scowling with concentration. Marie knows that the girl's confused, that she only regained consciousness a couple of hours ago. It might be too soon to be laying all this information on her, but in her shoes, Marie would want to know.

Footsteps at the end of the bed. Lucy looks up, blinking in surprise. Victor has arrived. He smiles at her, his face unscarred although he's got bandages round his neck, his hands. Lucy smiles back, a warmth creeping up inside her to see him so comparatively unscathed. He takes a seat next to Marie, touching her shoulder as he does so.

'You're OK?' Lucy says.

'Later,' he says. 'Keep going.'

Marie resumes her story. 'Sometimes, it would calm down. For a long time, things had been normal – regular deliveries, nothing strange. But over the last months of it, it's like we went back to the bad old days, when it was so unpredictable. Strange items in the deliveries. A true crime magazine with a child-killer on the front. That had Janice in pieces. A bunch of lilies, too.'

'Why lilies?' Lucy says.

'They were the flowers at Gabriela's funeral. Hundreds of the things. The stench was awful. They arrested me as I walked out of the crematorium. I've never forgotten the smell.'

Lucy pulls a face. 'I can't bear them, either. Not since my mum's death. People kept sending them even though my dad said not to.' Her grasp tightens for a moment on Marie's.

Marie takes in a deep breath. 'That wasn't the worst, not by far. The worst was the booze. They kept sending it – *he* kept sending it. Janice drank herself to death. I don't think he cared about her, not so much – he did it to torture me.'

Victor interrupts. 'I thought Edgar wasn't paying attention when I emailed him about the notebook. Turns out I was wrong. Not that he could tell me – he knew I'd go straight to the authorities if it came out that he was running psyops on his own little prison experiment – psychological operations.

Basically, he was trying to mess with their brains. He didn't want anyone to interfere. That's why he was so dismissive.'

'That notebook,' Marie says. 'It turned everything on its head.' She stops and roots through her bag, then pulls out a letter, the envelope already open.

'The notebook. Buried for so long in a box of Gabriela's belongings that were sent back to her parents. They could finally bring themselves to go through it – told me about it the moment they found it. I tried so hard to get Edgar to pay attention, but he had his own agenda,' Victor says. He pauses for a moment, his face contemplative. 'At least he listened in the end. Edgar dropped a letter to me in hospital. It was when he took the baby to his sister's. There's a note addressed to you inside – we opened it, I'm afraid.'

'What is it?'

'Just read it.'

Marie knows what it says. She's read it so often she knows it by heart.

Dear Lucy,

You won't believe me, but that was wonderful. I wish I'd met you sooner. But it's too late. I won't bore you with platitudes about meeting someone better – obviously you will. But I hope you'll remember me with a little kindness.

I don't have much time. I've given the notebook to Victor. I recognised the handwriting immediately. The only place where it wasn't properly disguised. Where she's discovered that Gabriela is pregnant, she thinks that I've been lying about it being a marriage in name only. It's the last entry she wrote – she was clearly too upset to remember to be discreet.

I was wrong. We were all wrong. Marie didn't stalk Gabriela, or kill her. I've done a monstrous thing.

It wasn't Marie. It was Rachel. I've been blind all along.

She's going to kill me now, but I hope she leaves enough evidence that she can be brought to justice at last. Victor's right – some people don't deserve forgiveness. I'm one of them. This is all I deserve, too.

Thank you for last night. It was amazing.
Edgar

Lucy looks up from the page, meeting Marie's gaze.

'Rachel was obsessed with Edgar from the moment she set eyes on him,' Victor says. 'We never knew. She was a student here ten years ago, that's when she met him. She fixated on him right then, hiding in the shed, spying on Gabriela, writing these horrific notes. She could pretend to herself they had an unhappy marriage, but when she found out Gabriela was pregnant . . . that's when she lost it. Marie turning up off her face when Rachel was about to attack Gabriela was a gift to her.'

'She set me up,' Marie says. 'I felt so guilty about everything, I just took it. And she waited in the wings, made herself useful to Edgar. I loved him, but he was a weak man. Always had to have a partner.'

Victor picks up the story again. 'She thought she'd got away with it, but the moment I told her that the notebook had been found, her time was up. That's why she tried to kill me. She didn't know I was going to come to Cambridge to find him.'

'She might have got away with it, too,' says Marie. 'So many factors at play. Victor coming to Cambridge, Edgar reading through to the end and finding those pages in Rachel's handwriting. My escape.'

'Did she want us to find you? When she sent Anna and me north?' Lucy says.

Marie shakes her head. 'It was only when she listened to Anna's message saying I'd escaped that it gave her one last desperate chance to try and get away with it. When she sent you guys off in the car, she was in full destruct mode. Scorched earth.'

A pause. 'She was trying to kill me. And Anna,' Lucy says. It's not a question. 'She did something to the car. She knew it was going to crash.'

Victor nods. 'You tried to take Edgar away from her. Anna was just collateral damage. She wanted you to die, she was going to kill Edgar. She was totally reckless, even locking herself in the burning shed in a desperate attempt to make it look as if Marie had tried to kill her after murdering Edgar. But she didn't get away with it this time.' He doesn't need to say any more.

60

'Marie,' Lucy says. 'Why did you leave?'

Marie looks over the ward, but she's seeing the hills instead, Janice's face in death. 'Two things. Firstly, Edgar sent photocopies of some of the notebook pages – he'd printed off the scans Victor emailed before he came over, put them in the food box. *I know exactly what you did*, that's what he said. He meant it to be threatening, to show why he was punishing me. But as soon as I saw them, I knew it wasn't me. I knew I hadn't written them, and that meant I wasn't the one who had killed Gabriela. It was such a release, to discover that. It sounds ridiculous that I accepted that I had, but the evidence seemed so strong. I'd blanked so much out of my mind.'

She's silent for a while, still far away. With an effort, she brings herself back. 'I couldn't leave Janice, though. She wouldn't have survived without me. But it's thanks to Edgar's lack of care that she didn't last longer. That's what I can't forgive. He knew the effect that alcohol had on her. He watched it enough times on the CCTV, how messed up she got. How difficult it was for me to deal with. But he was trying to torture me, any way he could. Janice drank herself to death. I set the house on fire, said my goodbyes, and I left. Hitched my

348

way south. It took days. I wish I'd got here sooner . . . If I'd been faster, Edgar would still be alive . . .' She bows her head, unable to suppress her sadness anymore. 'I know he was a shit, but I loved him. He loved me. Then he thought I'd murdered his wife. He was furious with himself as much as me. That's why he was so appalling to me afterwards.'

Victor looks at Marie, holds out his hands. 'He did love you. Look, he might have been married, but it was only on paper. Gabriela was with me. She was carrying my child. We met at university; she came with me to the UK. Edgar married her for me, for us, so she could stay in the country when her visa ran out. We were so stupid; we didn't think about what the repercussions could be.'

'I'm so sorry,' Lucy says. 'You lost them both. That's terrible.'

'I don't understand,' Marie says. Her brain has suspended itself above her head. She's hearing his words, but they have no meaning.

'He didn't know he was going to fall in love with you,' Victor says. 'It was before you were on the scene. If he'd known, I don't think he would have done it. It was an act of friendship to me, nothing more. He loved her too, but only as my wife. He could never forgive himself for the fact that his actions put her in the way of such terrible harm, ruined my life too.'

Marie can't quite take in what Victor is saying.

'I'm sorry, I should have told you before,' Victor says. 'It never seemed the right time, though. There's been a lot going on.'

Despite herself, Marie laughs. It's the biggest understatement. 'In the notebooks, Rachel talks about Gabriela cheating on Edgar. Did she just see the two of you together?'

'Yes,' Victor says. 'We were careless. But we had no idea what danger she was in.'

Marie nods. 'Edgar must have been so angry – he was trying to do something good and it led to carnage. The loss of your wife. The loss of your child.' She reaches out to Victor, squeezes his hand.

'There isn't a day goes past I don't think of them, how it should have been.' There's a long silence.

'Do you think he ever had good intentions for me and Janice? I mean, when he set up the scheme?' Marie says.

Lucy has a reply to this. 'I've been thinking a lot about that. I think he did, to begin with. I think it was genuinely intended to be a way of dealing with lifers that was more humane than just locking people up and throwing away the key. But he said something to me about the death of his mother, how it changed everything.'

'They were always very close,' Marie says.

'So that will have fucked with his head, to put it bluntly. Plus the power of it. No one individual should have that much control over another's life – it can only ever go wrong,' Victor says.

Now for the more immediate past. Victor's escape from the fire, for one thing.

He'd become friends with Tom, bonding through work, he explained, despite Tom's original representation of Marie. He'd gone to Tom's place that Saturday when he got back from Cambridge, went to sleep in the spare room, exhausted, woken only by chance by the smoke alarm when the fire started. He got downstairs to find that Tom was already overwhelmed by smoke, dead on the ground, a strong smell of petrol in the air as the front door burned in flames. It wasn't long before the smoke got Victor, too. He was lucky that the fire brigade made it in time.

'Rachel again?' Lucy says.

'Yes. She wanted that notebook destroyed. She thought I had it. Didn't care who else was hurt.'

'Why didn't they arrest Rachel sooner?'

'Not quite enough evidence, although they knew it was her after I showed them the proof. They just needed this one final part. I'm afraid that's why you had to suffer what you did,' Victor says. He's looking anywhere but at Lucy.

'You mean . . .'

'We had a feeling that she might do something to harm you. That's why we were watching from the back.'

'You were in the burned down shed?' Lucy says.

He nods. 'With a police officer. Many other police officers stationed along the back, in cars at the front. There's been a lot happening in the last few weeks. Marie was back in prison, briefly, though we managed to get her released on bail pending appeal given the circumstances. Turns out the wheels of justice can turn fast when they want to. And when the Ministry of Justice takes an interest. Anyway, three eye-witnesses to Rachel's attempt to poison you. Your glass has been taken off for analysis. We've got her now.'

Marie knows what Rachel will be going through now, adjusting to being in custody for the first time in her life. She shakes her head. 'I guess she'll get what she deserves.'

Lucy says, 'What's happened to the baby?'

Marie swallows. 'That's the other thing. With Edgar's sister right now. But the police are pretty sure the baby wasn't theirs.'

61

Just one more night. Then it finishes. The time Anna's had to serve on recall of her licence will be over. She was worried she might end up in the same jail as Rachel, but so far they haven't crossed paths. Maybe there's a note somewhere in the system warning that they should be kept apart.

This time, it's going to be different. When she gets out in the morning, there'll be people waiting for her. Her new family, Lucy and Marie, the women who've visited her throughout this stretch, who've found accommodation for her, a volunteer position in the same law centre where Marie is employed now that her murder conviction has been quashed. It's a start.

She talks to Kelly's sister sometimes, too. Fern is less aggressive the more Anna explains. She'll visit the grave when she gets out, even if she's no closer to understanding what happened to Kelly. The inquest's due to take place in a couple of months – they're hoping it might give them some answers. Even though she didn't find out what Kelly wanted her to discover, she did her best. At least she helped to resolve the awful situation with Rachel, Marie and Lucy. She's started to prove she may have some worth.

And best of all, she has her old family. Lucy made contact with Marc, talked him round; she even managed to get hold of Sally, persuaded her to start speaking to her sister. It helps that Toby is recovering. He came off life support eventually, and with time and effort, he is learning to walk again on his own.

Her sister and Marc haven't forgiven her yet, not fully. But they know how sorry she is. They haven't visited her in prison, but they've asked her round to lunch, in the house that they're now sharing again. She'll see Toby. Her heart bursts at the thought.

One day, she'll learn how to forgive herself.

The shouts, the smells: it's all so familiar. But this is it. The last time.

When she steps out of the gate tomorrow morning, she's never setting foot back inside again. This part of her life is over. Even the patch of eczema on her arm has healed. It's time for a new chapter to begin.

And there they are, Marie and Lucy, standing outside the gate. This time, no one tries to run her down. It turned out it had just been a random joyrider, nothing to do with who Anna was or what she might know. The driver was nicked the next time he tried it, targeting another woman as she waited at the bus shelter on her release.

The two women take the bus with her, the train. They take her to the flat she's going to share with Marie. They make her tea, sit her down and tell her everything, all the details it's been so hard to describe in the noise of prison visits.

She tells them everything, too, all the details she kept quiet before. No more secrets.

'Let me see the phone,' Lucy says. 'I can't believe that poor woman smuggled it in inside herself.'

'Don't be so squeamish,' Marie says. 'You'd be amazed what you can pack in a prison pocket.'

Anna pulls a face of mock-disgust, goes to her bag to find the phone that's been stashed there since she was put back inside. It still has some charge. She switches it on, hands it to Lucy.

'You could fit that up you,' she says. 'No problem.'

'Charming,' Lucy says. She flicks through the buttons on the phone. 'That's odd,' she murmurs. 'Why are there so many calls from Rachel?' She flicks through more. 'In fact, why is Rachel's the only number in the call log?'

'There aren't any calls from Rachel. I called her once, that last night. That's it, though. She never called this phone.'

'She clearly did,' Lucy says. 'This is her number. And there are loads of calls. They go back months. It's definitely hers – I'm sure of it. I memorised it that awful night while I was waiting for her to collect me. Why?'

Anna stares at her. 'I have no idea. But we're going to tell the police. And we're bloody well going to find out.'

EPILOGUE

There's nothing left for Kelly. She's fucked everything up. But it's not all her fault – she knows that now. She's been stitched up completely. She should never have trusted that woman, never should have believed her when she said she was Kelly's friend. Her baby's been stolen from her, simple as that.

Who's going to believe her, though? It's between a smack-addict shoplifter and a professor's wife. No one's going to take her side. If she reports it to the authorities, the baby will be taken straight into care. Who'd let Kelly be a mum?

Louise. Her little Louise. Her biggest hope. She was going to make her family proud, show them how she was worth a second chance. She had the flat, she had the job, the support from the charity. She was going to show them what she could do, why they should let her back in. *Mum, meet your name-sake, your granddaughter. I named her for you.*

That'll never happen now. Her mum'll die before Kelly gets out of here. She'll never get to meet Kelly's baby. Her sister will never know she's an aunt, that her kid's got a cousin.

Kelly should never have accepted help from that woman at the hostel, let her look after Louise for her. Nothing ever comes for free. The pack of heroin Kelly found in her pocket – she knows it wasn't hers. Rachel must have put it there to tempt her back into addiction. But Kelly didn't need to take it. Or the rest, hurtling back out of control, the way she always has. That woman knew what she was doing, all right. She knew how impossible it would be for Kelly to keep clean.

Kelly can't go on. Louise has gone. Everyone's gone. She'll never break free. Rachel's made that clear. She'll do anything to keep Kelly's baby.

It ends now. Kelly's got the blade. At last the pain will stop.

But before she does, she's going to leave the phone with this sleeping stranger. She tried to wake her, but she can't. There's no way to explain. But maybe, just maybe, there's a chance. She can't let Rachel get away with this, setting her up, stealing her baby like this. Kelly's own flesh and blood.

If she thought she could destroy Rachel, she'd stay alive for that. She'd do everything in her power. But there's no chance, not now she's inside. No one's going to listen to her. Social services would never let her keep Louise.

Please, she urges the stranger. *Please turn on the phone, see the number. Track her down.*

It's a long shot, but it's all she's got.

The only way to get Louise home.

Acknowledgements

Jack Butler said, '*Shawshank Redemption*, but women,' and Alex Michaelides encouraged me to go back in a legal direction with a love triangle thrown in. Femi Kayode read a thousand words a day of the draft as it slowly emerged, persuading me to keep going. Without all this, this book would never have been started, let alone finished, and I am very grateful to all three of them.

Jack had the further, deeply unenviable task of wresting my first draft into some kind of order and I am in awe of his editorial skills and patience – thank you. This book really wouldn't exist without him. My agent Veronique Baxter has borne the brunt of panics and calmed my nerves brilliantly – I am very grateful for this too. None of this would be happening without her.

I am so lucky to be published by the fantastic teams at Wildfire and Headline – my thanks in particular to Rosie Margesson, Joe Yule and Jessica Tackie for their superb PR and marketing skills. I know how much work goes into publication and sales and I'm very grateful to everyone who plays a part in this. Booksellers and bloggers are core to a book's success and I appreciate so much the support that my books receive.

A writer is nothing without their readers – I am very grateful to every single one.

Thanks for all the chats, Sarah Pinborough. We got this! And to Sophie Hannah, my gratitude for the encouragement. Dream Author Coaching has been an invaluable support.

To Kathryn, my thanks. It's been transformational.

Jaynee San Juan makes my family life so much easier and looks after us so well – we appreciate everything you do and are very grateful indeed.

My friends have had to cope with me sobering up and disappearing down multiple editing rabbit holes this last year – thank you for putting up with me. I love you all. My thanks in particular to Katie for fighting through that first, mad draft and seeing something in it, and to Georgina, Justin, Isla and Ruairidh for their kindness and hospitality in the very final stages of my editing – the best writing retreat in the Alps.

Nat, Freddy and Eloise – none of it would be possible without you. I love you all so much.

My last book was dedicated to my dear friend Sarah Hughes, gone too soon. Sadly, this book is dedicated to another dear friend, Agnes Frimston, whose life has ended far too early. I miss them both more than I can say.

AUTHOR'S NOTE

Michael Howard was wrong – prison doesn't work, at least not the way that we do it in this country. I am indebted to a number of books written on the subject by authors far more experienced and knowledgeable than me. I would like to recommend the following as being particularly helpful and well worth reading in their own right: *Criminal* by Angela Kirwan and *The Life Inside* by Andy West. *The Secret Prison Governor* by Anonymous was the source of inspiration for my secret prison, and *Breakfast at Bronzefield* by Sophie Campbell gave an unvarnished account of life inside a women's prison. And of course, *Crime and Punishment* by Fyodor Dostoevsky and *Resurrection* by Leo Tolstoy.

Podcasts were also a great research resource, especially *Banged Up*, *Life After Prison* and *The Forensic Psychology Podcast*.

Finally, my thanks and apologies to the great criminologist Alison Liebling, Professor of Criminology and Criminal Justice at the University of Cambridge and Director of the Institute of Criminology's Prison Research Centre. I plundered her brilliant interviews and published papers, putting to them to my own use – hers is the quote I give to Edgar about Sonia and Raskolnikov. At least I gave her a keynote speech in my fictional Cambridge conference – the audience would have been far better off listening to her than fawning over Edgar. I have found her work to be deeply inspirational.

ABOUT THE AUTHOR

Harriet Tyce grew up in Edinburgh and studied English at Oxford University before doing a law conversion course at City University. She practised as a criminal barrister in London for nearly a decade, and subsequently completed an MA in Creative Writing – Crime Fiction at the University of East Anglia.

Blood Orange, her debut novel, was a Richard and Judy Book Club pick and a *Sunday Times* bestseller. *The Lies You Told* and *It Ends At Midnight* were also *Sunday Times* bestsellers. *A Lesson in Cruelty* is her fourth novel.